By Piper Bee

This is a work of fiction. Names, characters, places, and incidents either are the product of the author's imagination or are used fictitiously. Any resemblance to actual persons, living or dead, events, or locales is entirely coincidental. Disclaimer: Chapter ("Track") titles are actual song titles and the artists are represented in the back of this book.

Copyright © 2020 by Piper Bee

All rights reserved. No part of this book may be reproduced or used in any manner without written permission of the copyright owner except for the use of quotations in a book review. For more information, address: piper@piperbeeauthor.com

First paperback edition June 2020

Book cover art by Amelia Buff

ISBN 978-1-7349492-0-9 (paperback)
ISBN 978-1-7349492-1-6 (ebook)

piperbeeauthor.com

Sensitive content warning:
Brief, non-graphic descriptions of sexual assault are contained in this book.
Seek help from a trusted source if needed.

Playlist

This one is for my biggest supporter and the love of my life,

Jimmy <3

Track 01 - Can't Blame A Girl For Trying

Before I hit thirteen, my arms were perpetually sticky with watermelon juice for the month of July. That subtle sweetness dripping from firm, pink flesh was like a bite of summer. I always kind of wanted to be like a watermelon: shiny and tough on the outside, but mostly soft and sweet in substance. It's funny how freely we dream when we're kids.

That childlike freedom eludes me now that I'm an 18-year-old glorified mascot for my big brother's baseball schedule. And since there is no replacement for the "lucky" baseball tee he gifted to me (which must be worn at *every* game), sticky watermelon-juice arms are a no-go. Any remnant of a stain somehow makes it "unlucky."

I'd say my brother's sports superstition is strong, but he's actually just controlling.

"Shoot!" I thumb the brown patch of mud that materialized on my shirt. I don't know why I decided to put it on two hours before his game.

"What?" Lena asks, perching herself up on her elbows. We're sitting on this fallen tree that's in a secluded clearing near my suburban neighborhood. Her raven hair tickles the bark. No one at school would guess that cheer captain Lena Garcia would drape herself over a log to get a tan.

No one but me, I guess.

"I have to go home and wash this before the game," I tell her. "Carson will flip if it's dirty."

She scoffs. "My dad says you're never supposed to wash a lucky shirt."

Explaining this quirk has gotten a bit old. "Yeah, well, even Carson's superstitions are particular, I guess."

"Screw your brother, Joy!" She rolls her pear-colored eyes. "It's just a stupid shirt."

I'm glad Lena seems immune to Carson. He's a dangerous kind of handsome, but she always brushes him off. Given that she's dated like eight guys since I moved here last year—due in no small part to her supermodel Greek/Latin genes—it's basically a miracle they never happened.

I swing my leg over so both my feet dangle off one side of the tree. *Deep breath.* There's a sparkle of fuzz dancing in the air, glowing from the sun. Sometimes I wish I could float away like that, drifting in the summer breeze. But even once I've graduated from the demands of high school, it won't be that way. I'll be glued to a stadium seat all summer.

Impromptu log-lounging with Lena is as free as I'm gonna get.

I brush the spot with my knuckle. "I can probably spot clean it."

"Wait, isn't it glee's karaoke night? I saw Cale put like ten posters on your locker."

"I told him I wasn't going."

Lena sits up and gapes at me. "But you *want* to go, right?"

I don't answer. Of course I want to, I just can't.

She flops back and continues her unnecessary tan. Her even, medium skin is beautiful enough without sun. My freckles get darker, but that's it.

"You break your back for your brother, Joy," she sighs. "The world doesn't freaking revolve around him."

But mine does. It has to. Otherwise he might break again.

Lena doesn't know that. We've only been friends since the start of senior year, but I still worry every day she'll figure out what happened in our old town last year. No one has yet, thank God.

I hop off the tree, my Converse squishing in the soft ground.

Lena shades her eyes. "Don't go yet! I want to soak this up a little longer."

"You know the sun is supposed to age you."

"Oh my god, I had no idea," she says monotone, then she closes her eyes to bask in it.

This is her favorite spot. When she found out that I lived in the neighborhood across the street, she freaked out in a good way. Her mansion is up in the hills, with an incredible view of the countryside, yet she brings me to this decaying log time and time again.

There's a gleam in her eyes whenever she talks about the guy that brought her here.

"Jin's coming home soon," she says. "Finally."

Jin Park is Lena's neighbor and childhood bestie. She's kept her love for him a secret for years, I guess. All her other friends knew him when he went to our high school, but I've yet to lay eyes on this Korean God of Handsome.

"Do I get to meet him this time?" I ask, hoisting myself up on the log again.

"Only if you promise not to fall in love with him like everyone else does."

"I've kinda sworn off boys for the time being." It's easy to say, but kinda hard to face.

She props herself up to squint at me. "Why *is* that? Are you sure you swing that way?"

"Oh yeah, I like guys." There's no doubt about that, it's just... they've gotten me in trouble. Hence the reason we got the hell out of Salem a year ago. But I can't tell Lena that. "I'm just busy. Carson's baseball schedule is super demanding, and it was brutal catching up to Willow Haven's grad requirements. I don't anticipate my first year of college will be easier."

"I know mine will be," she says, closing her eyes under sunbeams again.

I laugh. "How could you know that?"

"Because Jin will be there." Her soft, full lips roll out a pleased smile.

God help this Jin guy.

♫

Lena and I cross the field heading back to my house, jaywalking across the street and passing the very suburban sign that reads "Oak Meadows" in chipped navy paint. Each house in my neighborhood has one of seven faces and one of nine neutral paint jobs. Mine is the color of oatmeal. The only thing that makes it distinct is Dad's random Seahawks gnome.

And sometimes, Carson's red Dodge Dakota parked out front.

I walk into the entryway and peel my mud-covered shoes off my feet with my toes. Guess I'll have to wash those, too. Lena closes the front door after me, shutting out the crisp summer afternoon. I see straight into the galley kitchen, the beige ceramic tile reflecting the sunlight onto my brother making himself a sandwich.

Shirtless.

Ugh. Why couldn't he just wear a shirt?

Wet, copper curls dangle over his sharp jaw, dripping onto his baseball muscles. He glances over at me, his mouth half full. He frowns when he sees my tee. "You're gonna wash that, right?"

I walk up to him. "When you put a shirt on, you can complain about mine."

His eyes focus past me and onto Lena. He swallows and stretches his lips into one of his charming smiles, as if I'm not right in front of him. "Hey, Lena."

"Hi, Carson." Lena cocks her head with a sardonic smile, giving Carson the eyes she reserves for all the boys that have no chance with her.

She folds her arms. "Joy can't go to your game, 'kay?"

I whip my head around, my chest pounding. "Lena!"

"What? He knows you have the glee thing, right?"

Deep breath. I turn to Carson, ready to diffuse. "I never said I was going to that."

His brow tenses. "What, you don't want to come to my game?"

"I'm coming to the game," I assure him.

"That's not what I asked. Do you *want* to?" There's a subtle sparkle of sadness in his honey eyes when I don't answer right away.

"I mean… I wanted to do karaoke, too," I finally say.

A muscle in his jaw pops, but he nods. "Yeah. I get it." Then he softens. "It's a lot of games."

The calm way he takes a bite of his sandwich unsettles me. What… happened to my brother?

I pinch my shirt. "I'm gonna go put this in the wash," I say, my wide eyes watching him. There's no way he'd re-

11

lease me just like that. I'm at every game. We nod at each other before his first pitch every game. I wear this stupid shirt to *every game.*

"No, you should do the singing thing," he says. "Do what you really want."

I shift toward the hall, but look back at him. I'm so confused. But if he's okay with it, maybe I should. "I'll go get changed then. Be right back."

Carson sets the plate on the counter. "I actually gotta get dressed too. Later, Lena." He winks at her. *Barf.*

She rolls her eyes with no hint of a smile. Pretty sure there's no danger of them getting romantic.

In the hall, Carson leans over my shoulder and whispers, "She's into me."

"No, but it's cute you think so," I whisper back.

We pass the gallery wall of mixed childhood photos and kid-mindscapes scrawled in crayon. Coordinated Halloween costumes, Carson's first Little League portrait, my over-painted face grinning post-dance recital, and various sibling side hugs and missing tooth grins. It's evidence that we're attached, but it's also a bit of a facade. Something broke before our teen years, and none of us really know what.

Carson stops at his open bedroom door. His room is shades of blue with clothes scattered like paint splatters.

I put my hand on my door frame, looking over at him. We end up here a lot, on opposite sides of the hall, glancing at each other before we enter our own spaces. He'll always be my barely older brother.

"I'll miss you at the game," he says, almost wistful, but not quite. He's never been good at emotions outside of thrill and anger.

"I'll miss you, too."

I head into my room, the sound of his door closing offset from mine.

The truth is, I'm a little lost without Carson. We take care of each other. That's why I'm going to his school, Frederick University. That's why I show up at all of his games. I traded my life in Salem so he could have a real future. Even if he's not the most thoughtful brother on the planet, I'm loyal to him.

But I'll be damned if I'm not excited for some actual fun.

I pull my phone from my back pocket and text my only other friend, fellow glee member and textbook class clown, Cale Thomas.

>*JB: Guess what?? I can make it tonight! Pick me up?*

It takes two seconds for him to reply.

>*CT: YASSSSS!!!!! I'm sobbing Becker*
>*CT: SOBBING*

>*CT: Gonna be LIT with you there!*
>*CT: See you at 7 sharp Almond Joy*

I giggle at the rapid succession of quips. Typical Cale.

>*JB: Sure thing Cale Salad :)*

I'm buzzing with good nerves now. Cale's like an energy drink that hits you right up front and keeps you going as long as he's around.

I grin looking at my closet. No matter what I wear, I'll feel on top of the world tonight.

♫

"Wait, you're not coming?" I bolt upright on my mom's floral couch, abandoning Instagram.

Lena sits criss-crossed next to me, scrolling through whatever feed is on her phone. "I'm not even in glee."

True. But I'm not really friends with anyone except Cale, who's friends with *everyone*. They'll all be vying for his attention, no doubt. I want to argue with her, but I'm terrible at conflict.

Guess I'll just suck it up and let the singing be enough. It usually is.

"I still have to pack for next week, anyway," she says.

"It only takes like a couple hours to pack for a weeklong vacation."

She eyes me. "Maybe for *you*."

Lena's an odd mix of careless and high-maintenance. She constantly curates her outfits and perfects her makeup, but when she whines about wrinkles or chipped nails, she's completely joking. I'm the only one who gets her humor, I guess.

But maybe we're all an odd mix of careless and high-maintenance, for different things.

I have a well-organized closet with a few vintage pieces, my brother's sports-related hand-me-downs, and yoga leggings galore. When I try to look cute, I pick one piece to center my outfit around. Tonight, my favorite gold peplum top.

It's a special occasion, after all. The first night I've had to myself in forever.

My phone chimes on the coffee table. I grab it.

CT: 5 *mins*

14

It's 6:55 PM. I thought "sharp" meant basically nothing these days, but I should never underestimate Cale. I've learned this.

When I pass the entryway mirror, I tug strands of my dirty blond hair to adjust my black and gold bow before going outside to wait for Cale.

"You're cute, okay? Stop being so fidgety!" Lena slaps my arms. I obey her and we walk out the door.

Cale's beige, unwashed Ford Escort that he affectionately calls "the beater" rolls up at the edge of my fresh-cut lawn. Seven *sharp*. The engine rattles in a concerning way. He turns it off and the sputtering sound makes it seem like the car is struggling to decide if it should shut off or not. It does.

Cale pops out of the car with both arms in the air. "The chariot arrives!" His dark brown skin gleams in the sunshine, but his open-mouth smile is brighter.

"I see I'm the only one who decided to dress up," I say, looking him up and down with fake smugness. He's in his usual pretends-he's-a-baller uniform: a crimson t-shirt that's two sizes too big, shiny grey basketball shorts, and pristine Nike high tops.

"Um, THANKS FOR NOTICING MY HAIRCUT," he chimes, rubbing his head. I crack up because there's no way his already close-cropped hair is more than a centimeter shorter.

"What's wrong with your car?" Lena asks, adopting a judgmental lilt.

He rubs the hood. "I think what you mean, Miss Garcia, is how did my lovely beast get such a unique purr?" Cale points his forehead at her and waggles his eyebrows.

Lena bursts out laughing. "Okay, *Mr. Thomas*."

"At least he *has* a car!" I'm a bit sore about the fact that Carson's 12-month seniority over me is the lone factor in his vehicular inheritance.

"You should really change that," Lena says.

I swing my mini backpack over my shoulder. "How? I have no money to get my own car."

"You could take the dog-sitting gig."

"Lena," I sigh. "Your house is way up in the hills. I have to use *a car* to get there. The need is cyclical." I draw a circle with my finger. She already offered to pay in advance, but the money wouldn't buy me a car with a working engine. The circle motion also represents the number of times we've gone around this conversation.

She shrugs and starts fishing her own car keys out of her fringe purse.

I head for Cale's passenger door. "Enjoy packing."

"Don't have too much fun," she says with a wicked grin. *As if.*

I try the handle but it doesn't open, so I look to Cale. "It's locked."

Cale reaches by me. "Nope. Nope. Just persnickety!" He pulls the handle up with both hands and lifts the door up just enough that it cracks open. "But I love her!"

I get in the car and Cale shuts the door for me. He rounds around the front and crashes into the driver's seat. Then he looks out the window and winks at Lena. She laughs at him.

It's significant how different her reaction to Cale's wink is. Cale's just goofy and genuine, giving the wink like it's a gift of comedy. Carson only winks when he thinks he'll get something.

Notable difference.

Cale starts up his crap car, grinning at me with his thick lips while it rumbles.

"And we are off, milady!" He puts the car in gear and the jolt forward sends my heart racing.

But it's not just the fact that I'm startled. I'm bubbling like a can of shaken up soda, ready to burst.

♫

I was not expecting Garth of all people to pick such a cool place for karaoke. I mean, cracked wood bar with old-school stereo karaoke machines, sure, but this... it's modern, angsty, and refined. Really, the opposite of Garth. But I gotta be honest, that country boy is a lot more than he looks. He's a baritone with a taste for jazz *and* Selena Gomez, wrapped in a plaid button-down and blue jeans.

The Boxal has anime graffiti on the walls, ultra-sleek purple velvet furniture, and a chandelier made of silver tubes. And that's just the entry.

Cale grabs Garth on the back of his thick neck and shakes him like a maraca. "Ooooh! This place is BANGIN', G!"

I can't help but notice Cale's Nikes glow purple in the blacklight as he bounces between everyone like a pinball lighting up a machine. I tend to trail behind because, despite having impressed this group with my voice this past year, I only connected with one. The one who shook me out of my shell the first day of glee and continued chip away at what was left the rest of the year.

Cale hangs back and sticks to my side. Almost literally.

He elbows me over and over. "You ready? You ready? YOU READYYY?"

I squeeze my eyes shut and scream, "I'M READY!" My giggle dwindling, I add, "Thanks for picking me up."

A black-clad staff member with a myriad of carnival-themed tattoos ushers the front of our eight-person group down the hall, so we follow.

Cale shrugs. "I aim to please, Almond Joy. I aim to please."

"I owe you."

In response, he rushes ahead and turns to face me, walking backward. "Careful, Becker. You say that, you *might* just have to make good on it." He cocks his head and swivels around.

As he jogs ahead, I'm really, *really* curious if he means something by that.

Our private party room boasts a slick tangerine couch that curves in a U-shape around a giant screen flipping through ads. Cale weaves through the others and immediately grabs the tablet, fiddling with the karaoke program. On the table is a mirrored tray covered in sodas with various fruits decorating the glasses.

I'm eyeing the one with the watermelon wedge.

"Ooooh!" Cale laughs like a maniac with his face lit up by the tablet. "They got it! Semi-finals showstopper!"

Okay, now I'm excited. We killed it with that number last April.

Everyone squeezes themselves between the couch and the table to find a spot. Cale jumps over the back of the couch and plops right next to me.

"Duet?" he says, holding out a mic to me.

"DO IT!" Emma shouts, sort of echoing the word. She's our blonde, bubbly cheerleader. Not, like, an actual cheerleader, but the one who is pumping everyone up. Second only to Cale.

I grin, holding eye contact with Cale as I snatch the mic from him.

Cale starts "Somebody to Love" by Queen with his lone voice, and everyone else joins right after with the choir vocals as the karaoke machine pumps out the piano.

And Garth comes in with his deep command of the word "love."

Then it's me. I stand up where I am and grip the mic as my singing voice vibrates into the limited airspace, behaving beautifully through each up-and-down note. Then Cale stands up and takes the other part, rivaling Freddie Mercury with his smooth delivery. The rest of the group hits each verse with their choral expertise, sounding like an energetic church choir.

Pulling this song out is even better without judges or Mr. Allen Jr. constantly tweaking our form. It's fun and vibrant, like the room widens when we come into the song together. Me and Cale harmonize like it's instinct, and Cale's expressions as he sings are over-the-top and authentic at once.

I get this sense of belonging when I cry out to the sky with my voice. I honestly don't feel separate from the song, the message, or the emotion of it. When I sing, it's in my veins. My hips and head and arms respond in rhythm. Everyone else claps or stomps to the beat, all moving as one.

We might've lost semi-finals, but being in-sync like this is its own victory.

Emma takes the final high note, channeling power like Aretha Franklin. Cale yelps when she hits it just right.

We're all a bit out of breath when it's over and the high lingers for a few seconds. I love this part, floating atop the finish as if it's still going. The camaraderie of crushing a performance is kinda unrivaled. I reach for the watermelon drink, giddy and so glad I came.

But what sucks about highs like this: they end.

I notice my phone buzzing on the table with my mom's picture. It turns a fraction with each vibration. If Mom's calling me now, it can't be good.

♫

Mom's voice is always frantic. Always. But I can't tell if it's normal frantic or seriously-wrong frantic. I step outside into the neon pink twilight to find out which.

Seriously-wrong frantic, for sure.

Carson threw out his shoulder.

I lean against the uneven bricks on the wall of The Box-al. *Of course* he would injure himself when I wasn't there. Maybe even *because* I wasn't there.

I should've gone to the game.

Every self-deprecating thought I'm thinking about myself is echoed by Mom's cracked voice on the other end of the phone. It's like throwing hot sand that gets blown back into your face. *I'm a terrible sister.* I shouldn't have skipped the second tournament game. Baseball is his career, singing is my hobby. Carson really needs my support.

"The medic said his season is most likely over!" she yells at me. She's definitely been sobbing.

"Mom..."

"What's he going to do now?" she questions, though it's less a question for me than for the universe.

Will he have another outburst? And at who? That's my question. Last time it was the mayor's kid.

The swell of the karaoke joint's music flows out when the door opens. Someone just walked out, but I don't bother to see who it was. I'm swimming in a thousand what-ifs. No. More like drowning.

"You ok, Joy?" It's Cale. I suddenly realize I'm crying. Ugh. How embarrassing.

I pull the phone away from my ear and muffle Mom's cries on my shoulder. "My brother got hurt during his game."

"That sucks," he says. I just nod, afraid I'll cry more and turn into my mother if I keep talking.

Cale offers to give me a ride back home on the spot.

I plop my sad self into Cale's car. My gaze lands on the tape deck and I wonder for a second how many of those I've seen in real life. The old-school green numbers show the time. 8:09. I was out for a hair more than an hour.

Once we're on the road, Cale turns up the staticky radio and ukulele strums blare. He belts out the song, which is particularly ridiculous because it's Sabrina Carpenter's high and sweet voice singing about being a stupid girl in love. *Singing* about crying ironically pulls me out of my wallowing.

I'm actually shocked at how well Cale makes the song his own. He gets the high note like it's nothing. This song is definitely going on my summer playlist.

I'm in better spirits when the next track hits the speakers. I get a thrill of recognition.

"I love The Crux Constellation! I can't believe they're on the radio!"

They balance the synth, beat, and acoustic guitar so harmoniously. The singer croons about love as far off as another galaxy.

"Whoa, she sounds *just* like you," Cale says.

"Really?"

"Yeah, it's crazy close!"

I pay closer attention. He has a point. It's hard to unhear.

The incandescent street lights flicker on. Once the song is over, I'm hoping Carson's season actually is over.

"Sorry about your brother," Cale says, almost like he's reading my mind.

"It's okay." I backtrack. "I mean, it's not, but if he can't play, that actually means my summer frees up. I'm so used to his games that I didn't even make plans. Well, that and I don't have a car so..." I trail off.

"Speaking of that, I got an idea to run past ya." There's a sly smile on his plump lips.

"Go on."

"Ok, so you know Lena?" he starts. My eyes narrow.

"She was at my house, Cale. She's literally my only other friend."

He nods knowingly. Like a mental *duh!*

"Well, I don't think she really knows *me*," he says. He bites his thick lower lip.

I blink. Not Cale, too. Poor guy.

He stutters a bit. "I-I, just, I don't think she thinks of me *romantically*."

"Yeah, I got that. You know there's a support group, right?"

Cale throws his head back in a single laugh and then snaps back to the point. "Seriously, though. I'm hoping to maybe persuade her with a crazy plan. And it involves *you*, Almond Joy."

I point at myself and mouth "me?" He nods profusely.

"So if I wanna hang out with Lena... the best way is through you, right?"

"Right..."

"But if I hang around too much, she'll be kinda weirded out. So I thought you and me could *pretend* to date for part of the summer..."

I laugh like he's joking. He is joking, right?

"Why would that work on her?" I finally ask.

"You kidding? Lena's jealous of you, Becker!"

Of me? This petite, freckled, wears-her-brother's-old-clothes girl makes *Lena* jealous?

"No, she's not," I say with resolve.

"She definitely is. You're smart and got wicked pipes, girl!"

"But *Lena*—"

"Yes, she's fine as hell! She knows it. Obviously I know it. But you've got the girl next door thing working for you."

"Really? Is that why you picked me to be your fake girl-friend?"

Cale laughs generously. "I'm just sayin'... maybe she'll look my way if she can't have me. Don't underestimate the power of being off-limits." He flashes me a grin.

I nod, but only because I'm following. Not agreeing.

"So? It's good?" he asks, excitement registering on his shiny cheeks. My nodding abruptly changes to shaking my head.

"No." He silently pleads, I hesitate, and he's not looking at the road and I'm getting nervous and OKAY, I amend it! "I mean! I don't know! I'd have to think about it."

He grips the steering wheel, tensing his shoulders, then sighs. "What if I sweeten the deal?"

I size him up. "How so?"

"If you agree, you can be the proud new owner of this here vehicle." He gestures to the inside of his car. "I'm get-ting a Hyundai, manufactured this century, as a graduation gift, so gotta do something with the beater." He winks at me.

Despite that the night has turned to black, I know my wide eyes light up the interior of this piece of junk.

A piece of junk that could be mine.

Track 02 - The Middle

G raduation. The first day of the summer in between high school and college. Stepping out on the courtyard to meet my family after the ceremony, I squeeze my diploma.

Sweet, seedless summer, here I come!

I should think it's a shame that Carson can't play the season. I *should*. But my fantasies about what this summer is going to be like flood my brain. Lena's poolside, soaking up the direct sun with a sparkling strawberry lemonade and chill house playing. Binge-watching Netflix well into the A.M. Staying past dark at the state fair. Hitting outdoor concerts in the middle of the day. Day trips to the beach for a picnic. Never once worrying that watermelon juice or barbecue sauce won't come out of the lucky baseball tee, because my brother won't make me wear it.

At the moment, though, I still need him to drive me everywhere. So, in that way, I'm not free. But, there is Cale's little deal. I haven't accepted it yet because...

Fake boyfriend? I've never even had a *real* one. Does that make it better or worse?

It's not like I wasn't going to invite Cale to hang out with me and Lena, but I see his point about freaking her out. His plan is convoluted, but no other guy has tried it on her, so who's to say it wouldn't actually work?

And I'm getting sick of Carson bargaining rides for my small amount of freedom. He can never just drop me off or pick me up because he's a good brother. Also, since he threw out his shoulder, he took a job doing administrative and odd jobs at a Victoria Lake Resort, taking his sweet, sputtering truck with him.

When it comes to me, Carson always wins.

I scan the sea of navy robes and caps for my brother's capless curly halo. It's weird to think we were switched last year when he graduated.

It's a bobbing, apparently-recently-cut-his-hair head that I see first.

"Almond Joy!" Cale chants through the crowd. He scratches his neck with his cap in hand.

"Cale Salad!" I say.

His abrupt clap startles me. His face is all business. "Snag a seat next to me on the party bus. We gotta talk."

"Sure thing!" I say, despite my nervousness. He doesn't seem to notice. He's off greeting some of his many friends with high-beam energy.

I know I *need* a car. And a summer with a fake boyfriend who also happens to be a good friend should not be a bad trade-off.

But my insides twist around. I'm really not the best liar. Mostly because I don't want to lie.

Lena's visible through the crowd, all legs even in flappy navy graduation robes. I suddenly recall we were supposed to sit together on the party bus. I'd feel guilty if I didn't know without a doubt that there'd be twelve cheerleaders in line to take my spot.

Where is Carson? Crowds are a bit disorienting for me, even in the open-air courtyard. Unless I'm performing for them, I'm not really a crowd-person. Usually it's the other way around, but I embrace it.

A body barrels into me and nearly knocks me down, carrying the scent of rose-and-sugar perfume. Lena. I'm immediately at ease. I remember when she was voted homecoming queen, I thought we'd never be friends. But I tutored her when we did physics homework, and later she told me that it was nice to have a friend who didn't think she would stay dumb. I didn't know what she meant until I witnessed her reputation for myself.

"I'm so glad that stupid ceremony is over! I thought people exaggerated when they said you could die of boredom." Her overly-disgusted face makes me grin. She's extra bouncy for a person in five-inch heels who hates dull social rituals. Her manicured hands grip my shoulders and square me to her.

"Five-thousand names," she says. "Five. Thousand."

"More like five hundred. Which really isn't that many," I tell her, and she raises a perfectly preened eyebrow at me. "But it felt like an eternity," I add.

"At least we have Grad Night!"

My heart leaps a bit even thinking about getting on the party bus and finding my seat next to Cale.

Am I really going to say "fake yes" to fake dating?

Lena's olive skin looks airbrushed. Her raven hair catches the wind perfectly, like a shampoo ad.

Then there's me, still pale after an hour of tanning, and covered in freckles, like a grainy image in comparison to Lena. No matter how many amazing photographers capture sad, freckled subjects, I'll never feel glamorous.

Cale's comment about me having a "girl next door" thing wasn't unwelcome, though. Still, it's easy to see why he'd go for Lena. I'm thinking he might need all the help he can get.

"Oh, by the way, any word on dog-sitting?" she says. I forgot they leave for Italy in a few days.

"Still no car," I say.

She rolls her eyes. "That's so unfair! Diamond loves you. I don't want to take him to the kennel. Can't you borrow Carson's truck?"

Speaking of Carson...

"She's here!" I hear him say. He and my parents have finally located me. Carson's field tan stands out in the harsh sun and navy-clad figures. My brother is the kind of handsome that makes him stand out like he's an actor slipping through curtains. Of course, I can only see my big brother.

"Congrats, you two!" he says with that charming grin that never works on Lena.

"Yeah, thanks. Why can't Joy have your truck?" She says it flat and like it's all one word.

I know he's catching ears with that charismatic laugh of his. Once people get a look at him, they're stuck like flies in honey.

"I need it for my job at Victoria Lake and all my physical therapy sessions. She's outta luck."

Ah, yes. Victoria Lake Resort. The big, fancy natural recreation community with giant grounds that attracts enthusiasts of Pacific Northwest nature. Willow Haven, my current unremarkable town, is only about an hour southeast, but technically that's from the resort entrance. It's enough to justify Carson staying on resort grounds while he tackles odd jobs and heals his shoulder.

He tries that cocked-head grin on Lena and she rolls her eyes.

Lena turns to me. "I'll be on bus four. Later!"

I wave as she walks back into the crowd.

I spot Mom's salon highlights and Dad's coke-bottle glasses. Mom hugs me. Her small-boned German arms have a lot of strength in them when I make her proud. Hugs like these are only offered on holidays or when we accomplish the Saturday cleaning.

"I'm so proud of you," she says. "It's too bad you weren't valedictorian, though."

There it is. Where I still lack full achievement.

My always-silent Dad offers me a side hug, and a forehead kiss since it's a special occasion, which makes my underachievement melt away.

Then, I face Carson. We might butt heads, but I still expect him to show me he's proud that I graduated and survived a hard year. He smiles. It's not big, not silly, not dreamy like a lot of his other smiles. It's the most genuine one in his repertoire.

"Congratulations, Joy Bear," he tells me.

I honestly couldn't be happier if I heard the jingling sound of the truck keys. "Thanks, Racecar."

♫

Heavy bass and purple track lights deliver me from the high school's concrete courtyard and into the buzzing party bus. The atmosphere jolts me awake for the school-funded party like an espresso shot.

I see Cale's frantic waving above the seats. "Joy!"

Great. I've got to squeeze past over-excited teenagers to get to the back. I hold my breath, trying to maintain composure as I pass the rows of maroon and teal upholstered seats. This bus looks like it's from the '90s, but I can't tell if it's clean and old or ironic and new.

Lena's barricaded in the front by guys ready to change their relationship status, should the need arise, which is presumably why Cale chose to sit in the back. Doesn't seem like she even noticed that my seat is left open.

"Sit, sit!" Cale says as I get near.

As soon as my butt hits the seat, the bus shifts forward. The driver doesn't seem to care that half the students are still standing. People shout goodbyes and wave out of the windows, but I focus on Cale. He does a quick "coast is clear" check of the perimeter.

"So? What'd you decide?" he asks.

"It's just… what if I don't want to be off the market for a fake relationship?" My voice is a bit of a whisper on the last part.

"Wait wait wait. You eyeing someone, Becker?"

"Pfft! No, I just… you know, might… at some point," I say sheepishly.

He fake-wipes his brow. "You had me for a second there!"

Cale's comedy puts me at ease, but he still seems nervous. His knee bounces up and down. He bites his plump bottom lip and glances at the front of the bus.

Damn. I guess he really does like Lena.

And I *know* I really like the sound of a beat-up old car to call my own.

"Ok, fine!" I give in. "I'll be your girlfriend!" *Only for the summer*, I repeat in my head. My rapid heartbeat still doesn't seem to register this as a business deal.

Cale lights up, even though I was certain it wasn't possible for him to be… brighter.

"Girl!" he says, and suddenly his arms wrap around me, squeezing my shoulders. Just as quickly, Cale lets me go and stands up. Then he pounds the roof of the bus with his floppy hand.

"This girl," he starts loudly, and it's like I feel the flood of mortification before it hits me. Because the last thing I want is the attention of 50 seniors on me right now. "...has just agreed to be my girlfriend, y'all!"

When the entire party bus whoops, Lena's howl pierces the crowd. She grins wide and I cover my blushing face. Guess we'll see how good of a performer I really am.

♫

June 11th

My throat is sore and dry from endless karaoke at the family fun park, but it was worth it. My first night as a fake girlfriend was actually pretty fun.

And pretty not different from just being friends. So that's nice.

I snagged a few hours of sleep after getting home from the all-nighter. I'm bleary-eyed when I get a text from Lena.

LG: Jin is back from university and HOTTER THAN EVER

That's right. *Jin*. The ridiculously gorgeous Korean neighbor/childhood friend that Lena's in love with.

She sends me a gif of Santana from *Glee* fanning herself. If I wasn't so familiar with the show, I almost would have thought it was a gif of Lena herself.

LG: This is our year ...
LG: I can feel it

I vividly remember when she slammed her soda can down on the cafeteria table the day she decided to tell me about Jin Park. She launched into a detailed history of their families and their world travels together. She's not high-energy very often, but that day, it was like she'd channeled Cale. It was the first day I realized we were friends.

It's why her romantic flames go out so fast, I think. Jin's always been out of reach for her. He's only two years older, but that's been enough to stunt romantic progression, so she says.

While I am Team CaLena, part of me is already convinced she'll get what she wants and end up with Jin. Since he's been away at the University of Washington for two years, he's been just beyond her sights.

I'm starting to think that him being back for summer could be problematic for Cale...

I have yet to meet Jin, but I have seen his ridiculous mansion in the mountains because it's right next to Lena's ridiculous mansion in the mountains. They basically share a driveway, complete with a lighted fountain sculpture. The one I'll have to be careful not to crash into with my new-to-me vehicle.

That reminds me. I text her that I can take the dog-sitting job.

The three dots blink as I await her reply. I wonder if she'll think I'm dating him for the car... even though I am.

Her message pops up.

LG: No getting frisky w your bf in my house ;)

Oi. Good luck, Cale.

Track 03 - Starving

Well, the brakes work. They hold up when I pound them at every stop. Accelerator works fine, too. I don't crash into the Garcias' fountain, even though I could.

I *really* could.

I should have never told my brother that Cale gave me the car. Carson had a raging fit over it because guys only want "one thing."

So yeah, the brakes work.

Zero concern is elicited when the screeches announce my arrival at the Garcia estate. I don't care that I'm driving through the automatic gate to the freaking palace of the gods. I'm peeved about Carson's reaction to my "boyfriend." Mostly because he, himself, is one of *those* guys he went on about. He's such a hypocrite, but I knew that.

At least Dad was there, armed with his extreme work ethic. "She has a job to get to. Shut your trap."

It was honestly the most affectionate thing he's ever said.

The stupid part is that shame still hangs over me. I'm not being taken advantage of. But I am taking advantage of Cale. I'm lying for a car. But if I told Carson the truth, he'd just hold it over me. Guess I choose shame.

Just until summer's over. Then I can take this beater car on my way, guilt-free. Maybe Cale's plan will have worked by then, who knows?

I get out of my car. It's 10 AM and already mid-seventies outside. The summer morning reminds me that good things still exist. There's a breeze like God's gentle breath, trickling fountain water, rustling leaves from manicured bushes and trees, and the blue, hazy hills out on the horizon. The mountain air is clear, like a glass of water for my thirsty lungs. It's a terrible day to spend cooped up in an airplane. But at least the Garcias and the Parks will be in Italy at the end of it.

A limo gleams in the driveway. Rich people. Of course they'd get a limo up to this mountainside. I almost don't notice the silver and black Harley Davidson past the shine of pristine luxury cars.

I wonder if Lena's dad rides motorcycles. He seems the type.

No one's out here, so I grab all of my things myself. I'm one of those people who opts for one hard trip instead of multiple easy ones. I don't care that I'm over-encumbered. I *will* get into the house in one go.

My arms are fluffed full of my preteen dream pillow and blanket, one hand on the handle of my suitcase, and my stuffed Justin Bieber canvas bag dangling from my other arm. I can't manage a knock. I can push the door open, though.

They know I'm coming. I let me and my overfull arms into the massive foyer.

The suitcase wheels get stuck on the threshold. *Great.* I yank the handle and it gives way too easily. I barrel down and crash into the sparkling tile floor.

My pillow and blanket exit my arms like they're spring-loaded. My bag swings upside down and all my things plop one by one to the ground. Chapstick. Shampoo. Deodorant. Toothbrush. The YA romance novel slides across the floor.

My pitiful teenage existence is scattered around me as I lay on the floor, close my eyes, and question my life choices. I'll have a hip bruise to add to my summer edition of the "Joy is a Major Klutz" collection.

Sigh. This tile is nice and cool, at least. The beater is void of AC, and lugging my junk inside is way more exercise than I'm used to, so I'll just close my eyes and cool off for a sec—

"Uh..."

It's a male voice. I assume Fernando Garcia, the patriarch of this fine establishment. But when I peel my eyes open, I see a remarkably different male.

Whoa.

Like, *really* whoa.

His inquisitive face is the most good-looking thing I've seen, like, ever. An amused smile unfolds on perfect lips. "You okay?"

He offers his hand to me, so I take it. Was there a reason I was on the floor? The heat returns to me.

"I'm fine," I say after I'm upright. My word, this human is gorgeous. Smooth skin, long neck under a sharp jaw, black hair textured just enough to look effortless but not messy. His dark eyes squint slightly as he gives me a heart-melting smile. It's like a lipstick commercial, but in a masculine way.

This is definitely him.

"Jin Park," he says. I realize I had never let go of his hand. I take my hand back and laugh courteously. Or nervously. I'm not sure which.

"I know," I say. His eyebrows go up and I stammer. "I- I mean, I'm Lena's friend. I've heard of you. Joy!" I wince. "Joy is my *name*. Sorry."

His mid-range voice makes his laugh sound sultry and innocent at the same time. Is that even possible? "Don't be sorry. Nice to meet you, Joy."

I smile briefly before assessing the damage. Immediately, I gather my ridiculously embarrassing items. Jin bends down, but I tell him not to worry about it. Instead of listening, he lifts my pillow and blanket from the floor and moves them to the stairs.

He touched my hot pink fuzzy Barbie blanket. And Lisa Frank pillow. The blanket is from my tween days, but the pillow is a recent acquisition. Not that it matters. They're both very unsexy.

"I see you met our dog-sitter!"

Now *that* Puerto Rican voice I know belongs to Fernando Garcia. And the aroma that suddenly hits me is unmistakably his chocolate chip cookies.

I whip around to confirm.

"Are those for me?" I ask in desperation. I can always be distracted by cookies.

"No, they're for TSA," he replies in his thick accent, with a smirk on his goatee. I chuck my chapstick at him and he barely dodges.

"Resorting to violence, Miss Joy?" Mr. Garcia's eyes are playfully wide. We're both grinning.

"I'll keep your dog alive while you're in Italy!" I offer in a sing-song manner.

Jin chuckles. I'd forgotten he was standing there.

"Were we supposed to pay her in cookies?" he asks, his question directed at Fernando.

We?

"Oh, you're here!" The voice above is Lena's. She leans over the rail. Their bright foyer is two stories tall, with a chandelier and a massive window as the main features. Yet, Lena seems to sparkle far more. She bounds down the curving staircase, which is presently decorated by my garish middle-school bedding.

Her high ponytail sways as she bounces down the steps. She's in a casual pink tee, yoga leggings, Nikes, and Ray-Bans that complete the glamorous traveler look I'm sure she was going for.

She reaches the bottom and immediately places her hand on Jin's arm.

"Can you go up and get my luggage for me? It's a little heavy." Her smile is almost sweeter than the smell of brown sugar and chocolate and butter coming from the kitchen.

"Sure," he says. It's neither eager nor fake. He looks at me. "Should I take your stuff upstairs, Joy?"

I blink. He said my name so easily.

"Um… okay." I internally facepalm. *Yes, please take my unsexy bedding up to Lena's immaculate bedroom, thanks!*

"I'm so glad he's back," Lena whispers to me as she breezes past, tossing her sunglasses on top of her head.

I follow her into the kitchen. Nearing the cookies grounds me. I can see them through the archway, still radiating on the sheet pan Fernando placed on the granite-top island.

Lena reaches for one, but Fernando swats his spatula at her and she jumps back. He's wearing a frilly apron. Classic Mr. Garcia.

"Dad!" she scolds.

"I made a deal with the devil!" he says with exaggerated intensity. My generous laugh echoes throughout their immaculately clean and immaculately designed kitchen. I hover over the fresh-baked goods. These cookies are life. The gooey chocolate, browned butter, sugar, sea salt... I know they'll melt in my mouth. They probably *could have* paid me in cookies.

A pudgy ball of orange creamsicle fur waddles into the room. Diamond is the chillest corgi known to man. People would pay to hang with him, but I managed to get them to pay me for it. Don't say I'm not an evil genius.

The sight of the dog reminds me.

"I'm curious why Jin said 'were we supposed to pay her in cookies?' What did he mean by 'we?'" I ask Lena, as she attempts to grab another one.

Lena's eyes open a little wider. "I didn't tell you?"

Fernando overhears and swats at Lena's hand. "This is now a bribe! Hands off!"

She shoots him a mean look and drops the cookie back onto the pan. "I told the Parks you could watch their dog, too. I figured it wouldn't be that much more work for double the pay."

Double the pay? I'm already getting overpaid to spend the week in a pristine mansion, cuddle a fat corgi, marathon whatever I want on Starz, swim in their heated pool, and marvel at their view of the rolling hills and farmland during the best weather week in the Pacific Northwest.

Jin walks into the kitchen. "Are those—"

"They're a bribe!" Fernando says, attempting to look intimidating by pointing his spatula at Jin's surprised face.

"Oh, that reminds me," Jin says. He reaches into his back pocket, then holds out an envelope to me. "This is for watching Zany."

"Zany?" Interesting name for a dog...

"Joy didn't know she was watching two dogs," Lena informs him.

Slight disappointment manifests in his expression. "Oh."

"Oh no, no! It's fine!" I say, to ease any immediate worry. "You don't have to pay me. The cookie bribe is plenty."

Jin smiles and pushes the envelope forward again. "No, you saved us. Zany will be happier at home. And I can't bring this back to my mom." He whispers, "Take it."

Diamond bumps into my leg and I stumble forward, a little too close to Jin. Then, I pluck the envelope from him.

"Thanks," I say, backing away.

In the span of a few seconds, my earnings doubled and my workload barely got any heavier.

Cale's puppy love for Lena is really paying off.

♫

Once I've waved farewell to the limo filled with glamorous rich people on their luxurious trip to Rome and Tuscany, I head up to Lena's room with a mouthful of cookie. She has a fluffy queen bed with an indigo velvet upholstered headboard that made me drool the first time I saw it. Diamond has a castle dog bed. Dog panting echoes in the empty house.

Even though I ate, like, four huge cookies, I'm still starving. Food may be the first order of business.

...after I relax in my solitude for a second.

I can't believe I just earned fourteen hundred dollars to vacation in a mountain mansion. Two of them!

Hopefully Zany is as easy going as Diamond. He is already snoring in his comical dog bed. I copy him and fall back onto Lena's velvety, queen-size comforter.

My horizontal orientation reminds me of my introduction to Jin Park.

He's the first person I've ever met while lying down. So that was interesting.

And no freakin' wonder Lena's taken with Jin Park. He's Korean dreamy, like a K-pop idol who has a thousand gifs of him smiling. He doesn't seem to know it. The sight of his bony shoulders under that plain white tee lingers in my mind. Do I have a thing for shoulders?

All I can say is Cale's getting a run for his money.

The subtle way she touched his arm, the way her eyes lit up when he entered the room, I mean… I've never seen her like that. And they're on a literal Roman-tic trip together, right this second.

I'd be jealous, but I can't even believe my current fantastic situation.

I trace the Park's house-key with my fingertip. I briefly greeted Jin's mom, Jan-di Park, before they took off. She said, in her adorable broken English, that the instructions for Zany's care would be in the envelope with the money. I open it up.

Hmm. Sure looks like it's just cash. Okay…

It's just a dog. I mean, I can handle a dog without the instructions. Even if I've never technically done that until right this second.

Track 04 - One Call Away

W ell. Yeah. I was wrong. A few hours into this gig, and I'm already in way over my head.

Do black labs often growl? I'm too afraid to get close and find out why. When they joked that she got the name "Zany" for a reason, I was dumb enough to think they were teasing.

Nope. She's actually moody.

My butt's getting sore from sitting on this slate floor in the Parks' equally gorgeous kitchen. Their mansion is decked in different colors, with a contrastive palette of cream and mahogany. I think it's Korean influence with straight lines, solid wood and gold details. It's like an art exhibit or a lived-in antique shop.

Normally I like being alone, but massive immaculate mansions test the limits of my introverted nature. Maybe I'm more of an ambivert?

Zany yips from her kennel. My confidence in dog-sitting skills is dwindling. Fast.

I bite my lip. I could really use back-up. So I text Cale.

JB: You don't know anything about dogs, do you?

I watch for the three dots. Zany won't come out to eat. If I so much as put my hand near her kennel, her vocals rumble at me. I even carried Diamond over here to spread his calming energy, to no avail.

CT: *Yeah. My mom's a dog trainer, why?*

THANK THE GOOD LORD. I swiftly type out my message.

JB: *This dog I'm taking care of growls anytime I get close to her.*

CT: *Hungry? Hurt?*

JB: *Idk. I can't get close enough to her cage to figure it out. But she hasn't eaten in like a day.*

CT: *Did she mess her kennel?*

JB: *Don't think so*

CT: *She's prolly scared*

I peek at Zany through the crisscrossed grate. She's not showing teeth. No furrowed brow or snarling. I wish I could read dogs. Of humans and animals, Diamond is the only creature who makes sense to me.

CT: *I can come by if you want. Turn on my charms ;)*

JB: Do they ever turn off? lol

I hug my knees and set my phone on the floor. I *am* kinda craving human interaction. Lena's text about "getting frisky" echoes in my head and I blush. There's no chance of that, but still.

I send Cale the address and gate code, and I'm relieved already. Diamond snuggles up next to me and I pet the folds of his neck.

Twenty minutes go by, then the deep gong of the doorbell echoes into the high, crown-molded ceilings. Diamond skitters off my lap and beats me to the stained glass front door. I could not be more thankful for the bright, toothy grin that greets me when I open the door.

Cale's oversized t-shirt and basketball shorts are stark against the fanciful entry decor, which reminds me of those carved frames you see in museums. Basically, he looks like a gumball on fine china.

His whistle reverberates off the vaulted walls and the bronze chandelier that hovers over us. It's decorated with hummingbirds. The two-story wall opposite the entry is covered in a cherry blossom wallpaper with an apple red background.

Cale's Nikes squeak on the floor and I stop him. It's walnut and oat basket weave wood floor, far too shiny to lay a shoe on.

"You cannot wear those in here!" His surprise invites me to whisper, "They're *Korean.*"

His head snaps back. "Lena's Korean?"

I laugh. "No! I'll explain, just take your shoes off!"

As he unlaces his shoes, I think how strange it is to see my plastic-school-chairs, hamburgers-and-french-fries friend walk into this place. Then again, in my college sweatshirt, I probably look pretty foreign, too.

When I point to the kennel, Cale clicks his tongue repeatedly. Tip-toeing with his lanky fingers held out, she sniffs him. Zany growls.

"You scared, sweet girl?" says Cale, in a high pitch voice. He keeps his cool as she watches him swing the grate open slowly.

He's calmer than usual. I didn't know he could be so even-tempered.

I stand about ten feet away, with Diamond in my arms. His panting sends dog breath stinking up my personal bubble. Still, it's comforting.

"They got a fence outside?" Cale asks me.

I point to the door at the corner of the kitchen. "There's a dog run through there," I say. Cale nods.

With low energy like a gentle stream, he goes and opens the back door. Then he distances himself. There's a comforting smile on his face when he looks at me and I release a breath I'd been holding. Cale's usually bounding with puppy-like energy, which is something I like about him, but I had no idea he could come to my rescue. With calm.

Suddenly I hear the skittering sound of dog nails on the slate floor as Zany races out the door. She's a shiny black blur. Her kennel shifted back a foot in her speedy escape.

Cale steadily walks over and peeks out, confirming exactly what I hope he would. A report of abundant excrement and urine.

Then, he examines her bowl of food that I set out. He takes the time to *read the bag* and adds hot water like I should have done hours ago. He puts it right by the opening of the door and then takes a seat with me on the kitchen floor to observe.

Eventually, Zany sheepishly walks up and eats.

Cale gives me his cheesiest big smile.

Finally, I can relax. "I owe you one, Cale Salad."

"Nah! I'm happy to help." He scratches Diamond's ear. "But, uh, whose Korean?"

"Oh yeah. This house belongs to the Parks. Lena's is next door."

"Really?" He sounds intrigued.

"Yeah. They're super close, like one big family. They're on their trip to Italy together."

"Cool." His eyes wander as he places his lanky elbows on his knees.

Should I warn him about Jin? Or would that be pointless?

Cale turns his head to me. "So, what does a girl like you do with *two* huge mansions and a couple of mutts?"

"Excuse me, this is a purebred corgi."

Cale's deep, somewhat goofy laugh always puts me at ease.

"But, to answer your question," I continue, "I make full use of their pool and Starz subscription."

His laugh stops immediately and he startles me by getting up abruptly.

"Then let's go, girlfriend!" he says to me, and then stops in his tracks, turning around to give me a sly look, "Get it?"

"Ha, ha," I offer in consolation.

♫

June 21ˢᵗ

Floating in the vaguely cold pool would be much nicer if I were totally alone and not worried about an impending cannonball. But here I am, periodically opening my eyes at every twitch of the water surface so I can dodge Cale's manufactured tsunamis.

I'm failing, obviously.

These past few days have been way nicer with him here to help with Zany, but while I am seriously grateful for his last-minute heroism, I didn't expect he'd be by in his new-to-him car every day. However… my offering to watch all the Harry Potter movies with him might've insinuated an invitation. As much as this muggle loves HP, I kinda wish I hadn't committed to the marathon. The average person doesn't get the chance to live in a secluded mansion and soak up 100% autonomy.

Splash!

Fat drops of water spray me. Now I'm soaked. The beating midday sun had just dried my front.

"Cale!" I scold when that sparkly brown head pops up.

He pretends to be oblivious. "What?"

I wipe my face with my hand. "You're ruining my spa vibe."

"What's the point of a pool if you can't cannonball?"

I roll my eyes, but he has a point. He's here to have fun. And I feel kinda selfish for wanting this place to myself.

I'm just gonna call it quits and dry off with a towel.

The pool water cascades down my body when I lift myself out of the pool. My black one-piece catches a drift and cools me off. I grab a towel and dab my face.

"I'm gonna order a pizza."

"How many movies we got left?" He pulls himself out of the water too.

"I think there are four left."

He grabs a towel, too. "But I thought there were only 7 books."

"They made the last book into two movies. Which I still can't believe you haven't seen!"

"Take it up with my mom!"

Cale's mom is very kind... and *very* formidable. "No thanks," I laugh.

"No, you're right. Bad idea!" The way his laugh dwindles reminds me of a young Will Smith, *Fresh Prince* era. He stands a little close to me, the faint cologne that's mixed with the chlorine burns my nose. Lena's warning text rings in my head again. *No getting frisky.*

I swing my striped beach towel over my shoulders like a cape and cover up what's left of my exposed skin.

I hope I'm not blushing. Ihopeimnotblushing.

Briskly I walk into the house without another word because, even though Cale is my *friend*, it feels like there's some line we've crossed. Faking a relationship. Being alone in a glamorous mansion. Standing inches away in our sopping wet bathing suits.

That friendly smile just felt a little heavier than I expected it to.

"Hey, Joy?" He glistens, framed by the back door and harsh sun. "You're not mad, are you?"

I try to sound cheery. "No! I'm not mad."

He smiles. "Okay, just checkin'."

I remind myself that Cale is interested in Lena. That's the whole reason I'm even standing in this place. He gave me his car, I'm faking a romance with him, and the rest of it, the reality part, is that we're friends. Though, if I'd known Cale was going to come by as often as he is, I probably could've cut him into the deal as my chauffeur instead of doing the fake dating thing.

Then maybe I wouldn't be feeling my heartbeat in my face when he smiles at me.

Track 05 - Never Been In Love

L ight-filled pictures of my fantasy dreams pass under my thumb as I scroll. I'm finally back in my own room, lying on my white down blanket that is much homier than Lena's luxurious bedspread. I appreciate my naked walls and cotton sheets a lot more when I've been away from them for a week, even if I am daydreaming while searching AirBnBs on the Oregon Coast at nine in the morning.

It's easy to dream a bit more since I had an unexpected influx of dog-sitting cash. I offered some to Cale, but he said the intro to Harry Potter was more than payment enough. It doesn't seem fair since I probably couldn't have walked her by myself without his advice.

My house is super quiet now. Carson decided to stay at the Victoria Lake Resort so he could keep up with the appointments and injury-friendly resort jobs. I'm finally alone like I wanted. And bonus: the Cocoa Puffs last a lot longer.

I don't know what is so appealing about getting away by myself. I want to hear the ocean waves, smell the salty air, feel tiny grains of sand massage my feet. I'll spend my money on something boring and useful if I don't force myself to book something.

Lena sent me a long string of vacation pictures over the course of her trip, but I haven't had the chance to ask her how things went. I switch to that text chain and get lost in the images of her heavenly Italian excursion. Warm gradient sunsets, handmade pasta and deep red wine, and most notably, sunny selfies with a certain Korean gentleman. I saw lots of pictures of Jin around his house. A few in a neon-lit city in Korea at various ages. One of him riding a horse on a ranch, fishing in another, holding awards for piano competitions. My favorite was where he had a wide grin with surprised eyes, surrounded by Christmas wrapping paper like he'd opened some remarkable, long-awaited gift.

My new favorite is the one Lena sent me. He's super cute.

The phone buzzes, as if it's judging me. It's Lena complaining about jet lag.

I haven't forgotten about my sacred duty to Cale. I figure I can feel out where she's at if I ask how "things" went with Jin.

LG: Nothing romantic :/
LG: The mood never quite struck. Our parents were ALWAYS around.
LG: But, it was still…

She sends me a gif of Heidi Klum saying "Perfection."

JB: I'm glad you had a good time :)
JB: Too bad about the lack of mood haha
JB: You'll get another chance…

LG: True. It was fun to see Italy together.

LG: ...even if I am burning to make-out!!

I wonder if the yearning gets stronger for someone who *has* actually made-out before. I have no qualms about my lack of experience, but I kinda want to know what it's like to have a *real* kiss. The kind that's mutual and fun and... *burning*.

Maybe I'm not the *burning* type.

I've never met a guy I really wanted to kiss. At least, not enough to put him through my brother. It's risky enough that Cale's my fake boyfriend. I'm totally fine remaining unkissed at the moment.

Thinking about Lena has me mindlessly scrolling through her Italy pictures again. Impressive limestone fountains with detailed scenes. Impossible architecture. Food that belongs on Zeus's table. I find one of their two families. Two golden only-children and four parents. Jin's dad sticks out in this picture for some reason. I saw younger pictures of him at the house, but here he looks oddly familiar. Then again, he looks a lot like Jin.

I swipe back to my favorite pic. Lena in a wide-open smile and Jin playfully raising an eyebrow at the camera.

How can he look *that* cool and *that* goofy in one facial expression? It's unfair.

I put my phone down. I can't develop even a minuscule crush on this guy. He's cute and all, but he is off-limits. Lena has history with him, and I've been through enough to know how much that matters. Until she notices Cale, I refuse to be one of those girls that Lena told me about.

I should probably give the plot a nudge, though. My plan included getting them both to the State Fair with me and letting Cale's sparkly personality do some legwork. I gear up to text her.

Staring at Lena's most recent message, it suddenly occurs to me: is she going to wonder if Cale and I never kiss? My heart picks up pace as I rest my phone on my chest. She's *definitely* going to broach that territory.

So, either I give Cale my very first (fake) kiss, or I come up with a way to work around it. I don't *hate* the idea of kissing Cale. It might be kinda nice...

But I'm not sure I could go there for something that isn't real. No, I know I want genuine romance if I'm gonna kiss someone.

My phone buzzes. I flip it up and the soft light burns my tired eyes.

LG: We still on for the fair this weekend?

That was an easy way to broach the subject.

JB: Of course! You've never been! You NEED to

LG: K! Looking forward to it :D
LG: Be sure to bring your BF ;)

JB: Will do

My mission is clear: capitalize on the fun/lovey-dovey nature of both the State Fair and Cale Thomas.

Track 06 - Hold My Hand

June 27th

I am way too excited to care about my blistering steering wheel or the hot tornado that whips through my car on the drive to the fairgrounds. I park in the dead grass field next to other dusty cars. Windblown stray hairs stick out from my blonde *Anne of Green Gables* braids. I'm kinda channeling Anne today, with my freckled skin, bright eyes, and high spirits. I'm pretty sure I was in a similar state when I first came as a kid, braids and all.

I spot Lena's pink wheeled VW Golf, but I still have to roll up all four of my windows manually before I can head over there.

Still glad it's mine.

The dried-out grass scratches the exposed skin on my ankles as I walk. Aromatic waves of greasy food hit my nose and the sound of wailing fair-goers tugs my thrill. The Washington State Fair was a few hours drive from my hometown, but it was supposedly better than Oregon's and at a better time in the year. When I was ten, I tenaciously convinced my folks to make the trip.

Even though it's lost some of its luster, there's another kind of magic in the nostalgia.

I'm within a few feet of her car when Lena spots me and rolls her automatic window down.

Oh. She's not alone. Jin's in the passenger seat.

He half-salutes, half-waves at me and I wave back.

Lena's wearing her hair the same way as me. A more Dorothy-esque look with her blue gingham top, but I know two things for sure: 1) Lena is particular about her hair, and 2) she does not like to match looks.

I make quick work of taking mine out. I mind far less than she does.

Jin emerges from the car into the beating sun. "Why take them out? They're cute."

Cute?! Whoo, I'm sweating already. Is the temperature really that high today?

"It would be weird for the veteran to play twins with the State Fair virgin," I say, averting my eyes from the way his stretching lifts the hem of his shirt.

Lena turns her car off and steps out. I'm not sure she heard what I just said, but Jin chuckles.

"Where's Cale?" Lena asks. She playfully stabs my side with her finger. "You invited your boyfriend, right?"

I swat her hand away and my heart races a little because Jin now knows I'm not single.

Even though technically I still am.

"He's driving himself." I pull my hair up into a ponytail.

Lena's *Wizard of Oz* Dorothy-themed outfit is almost comical. Almost. She could wear grocery bags sewn together with seaweed and look runway-ready.

She breathes deep and coughs. "Is that grease?" Disgust flickers on her face.

"Get used to it," says Cale, weaving through parked cars from behind. "That glorious fair food is going to turn in your stomach all night."

Lena scrunches her face, then takes a drink from her glittery water bottle.

Cale reaches an open hand across the hood of Lena's car.

"Hey, I'm Cale Thomas. Boyfriend extraordinaire."

I sputter a laugh.

Jin receives Cale's hand. "Jin Park. I... uh... can legally ride a motorcycle in all fifty states."

"Oh, I see," Cale says, his face serious. He pulls his hand back. "A one-upper."

"Let's get this over with," Lena says, but when she looks at me, there's a side smile on her glossy pink lips.

♫

Cheap wristbands always stick to the little hairs on my arm, but the benefit of all-access to the fair activities is worth the few plucked hairs it costs me. It smells like dirt and fried fair food. Funnel cake, popcorn, french fries. The first layer of suntan sets in as people buzz around like bees, chomping shaved ice and corndogs. The Vegas plinking sounds from fair games and the creaking of rickety portable rides transport me to when I was tiny. Well, tinier.

I wore pigtails, not braids. Overall shorts and Carson's old t-shirt with the hole in the side. I lived in that outfit until the seams left indentations because I'd gotten so big.

But here I am, feeling like I'm in it all over again. I wish nostalgia wasn't so faintly soured by the reality of growing up.

"What should we do first? Games? Rides?" Cale asks, buzzing with excitement. "PETTING ZOO?!"

"Not before we eat, please," Lena says, her golden arms retreating close to her body.

Cale points at her. "Fair point, Ms. Garcia. More sanitary to eat first."

The crowd swerves around us. My feet are antsy to flow with them, but I don't know where I should end up. I spot an empty patch of dirt out of the stream and dash through fairgoers for it.

I expect the other three to follow, but I lost them. Scanning the crowd helps nothing.

Jin startles me by leaning in, his shirt brushing my shoulder. His scent is floral, but not feminine. Clean. Maybe peppery. I know this flower, but I can't name it.

"I should probably tell you I'm a State Fair virgin too," he says. His expression fakes embarrassment.

"Seriously? I have to teach *you* my ways too?" I say.

Jin shrugs with a grin on his face. I scratch my neck even though I don't itch. That smile was a lot like the first one he gave me. My nerves are jittery.

We're joined by Lena and Cale within a few seconds. I'm half-relieved that I'm no longer alone with Jin.

Why only half, I wonder?

What could a couple of State Fair pledges be compelled to do for initiation? My short stature makes my search difficult, but then I see the faded slate gray paint, rickety mechanisms, and depressing broken sign.

It's. Perfect.

"First, before we do anything else…" My sinister grin and pointed finger guide the helpless newbies. "Initiation."

♫

It's still early, so the line to get into the Haunted House is short. Cale waggles his eyebrows and rubs his hands together to set the mood. Those who exit the attraction leave with expressions that clearly say "one-star review," but I don't care. If they hate it, it will have done its job.

"No open-toed shoes," the mid-teens polo-clad staff member tells Lena. She points to the sign and raises her brow. The famous Garcia look of irritation settles on Lena's face. The teenager says, "I don't make the rules." And then waves her away.

This isn't good. I don't want to lose so early in the day, but I have no idea how to get Cale and Lena in this broken-down attraction.

"I've got sneakers in my car, it's fine. Can you guys wait, like, ten minutes?" Lena says.

Jin nods and Cale nods and I nod because I could use the extra time to craft a better plan. I'm thinking: air shotgun range. Cale could show Lena how to point the gun. It's cute. But it'd be awkward if Jin and I are also there.

Lena heads back to the parking lot and the rest of us stand near the Haunted House attraction. And then, genius hits me.

"You're telling me, in your *twenty years of life*, you've never been to a fair?!" Cale says to Jin.

"I went to Carnival in Brazil a few years—"

I interrupt by ushering Cale the other direction. "Go! Cale, now, go go go! Take Lena to the air shotgun thing."

"What?" He gives minimal resistance to my shoving, and then it suddenly hits him that I'm trying to help him out. *You're welcome.*

"Just tell her it's her punishment for being an unpre-pared pledge," I say. "Go!"

"Okay, okay! I got it!" Cale puts his hands up in defense and then walks the same direction as Lena. But my mission is only partially accomplished.

I glance at Jin and gesture back toward the line to the Haunted House. "Let's go! Hurry!"

"Um, okay," he says, like a compliant little kid with a hint of wariness.

My toothy smile makes the staff member eye-roll as she waves us forward in line. I feel like I discovered mom's chocolate stash and got away with taking one for myself. It may only be a few minutes, but Lena and Cale are stuck together. I'm not completely useless after all.

"It's not too scary, right?" Jin says to me. I nearly forgot about him in the thrill of my victory.

I know he's joking. "If you can handle your own reflection, you should survive."

He furrows his brow. "Uh-oh. There are mirrors? That's not good."

I eye him. "Why not?"

He whispers to me, "I'm a vampire."

"Too bad I never got into the vampire hype," I say, but now I'm thinking he might think I'm into him, or not into him, and I don't know how I feel about either of those. I probably should've chosen giggle over quip.

He's a gracious laugher, which helps curb the overthinking.

If I had to get stuck with one of Lena's crushes, at least it isn't one who's drooling over her. He seems excited about this mediocre attraction, which might actually make it fun.

The sweat inside my shoes builds as we step forward in line.

"What was that about, pushing Cale to take Lena shooting?" Jin asks.

I whip my body to face him, my eyes wide. "Uh... well..." Shoot! I'm not sure what I should say. Despite my false relationship status, I'm bad at lying.

I guess I could try the truth.

"I'll tell you inside," I say and I can't help but grin. I might have discovered another way to help Cale.

We approach the archway coated in peeling paint, which doesn't seem like an intentional part of the decoration. A bad speaker at the front blares a scream repeatedly as a strobe light flashes. We lift our wristbands and the guy at the front waves us into the darkness. I can make out faint images of green and purple skeletons, but that's it.

This first part is cringe-central because we have to feel around to get through it. It's gross thinking about all the unwashed hands that have grazed these walls, but I feel around to get my bearings. My fingers bump into some cotton fabric with flesh underneath.

Jin.

I jump. "Sorry!"

"No worries," he says, but I can only barely make out the outline of his figure. My right hand hits the wall, thank goodness.

And my left runs into his body again.

"Ah, sorry!"

"It's fine, Joy," he says with a small laugh. "Here."

His hand wraps around my left wrist and he pulls me along. Lena sure missed her chance, opting for open-toed wedges. She could've been unapologetically hand-in-hand with Jin in this chamber of low-grade scares. But, now it's Jin's hand holding *my*… wrist.

Who am I hoping ends up with Lena anyway? Jin or Cale?

Ah! A cackling plastic witch head jolts at me. I flinch and squeal, my heartbeat pounding in my limbs.

Jin squeezes my wrist a little tighter. I try to shake all of my nerves off.

We round the corner and dark blue light flows in. The opening to the hall of mirrors boasts poor quality thunder sounds and rain effects. The neon light distorts everything but the perfect curves and angles of Jin's face. He drops my wrist, but his touch lingers, and he gestures for me to go ahead.

I head into the maze and it's easy to navigate at first, but after a couple turns I'm stopped by glass panes. Jin follows shortly behind.

I tap on a transparent frame that's between us. "So you're not a vampire after all!" I yell through the panes. He shrugs. Adorably.

Next is the shifting floor beside gruesome cartoon jailbirds that do anything but frighten. Fake arms reach through prison bars as Jin and I find balance on the track.

I'm wobbly as a pirate ship in a monsoon.

I look back. Jin's black Converse hit the moving track confidently. Tall people find their balance so much easier. I'm relieved when I've gotten past this obstacle.

I wonder how Cale and Lena are doing. Jin and I have hit the halfway mark and I'm guessing there hasn't been much headway.

"So, you gonna let me in on why you made your boyfriend go after Lena?" Jin asks when he joins me on solid ground.

"Yes, but you have to keep it a secret," I tell him.

His endearing wariness resurfaces. "Okay…"

I bounce up the split stairs that alternate up-and-down. This ride is desperate to make a show of my clumsiness, I swear. "I'm trying to pin Cale and Lena together as much as possible."

Solid platform. We have to cross a footbridge made of chains. I turn around and face Jin. The chains rattle and shake as I walk backward.

My eyes catch his for a brief moment. "Cale is really into Lena."

Jin looks at me with a furrowed brow. "And you're encouraging it?"

My foot finds the landing. "Well, that part's the secret."

We climb down the spiral staircase to the ground level, me before him. "Cale and I are faking it. He's actually trying to spend time with her, so I'm just playing along until... I don't know, she sees him in a different light."

We ignore the pitiful jump-scares as we talk.

His angular eyes narrow at me. "That's kinda weird."

"Yeah, but Cale thought a ridiculous ploy might get her attention. Nothing else does."

Jin laughs. "True. But, why are you letting me in on this?"

"Because I could use your help."

Jin thinks about it, his eyes wandering to nowhere in particular. I bite my lip in anticipation.

"Okay," he says. "Sure, I can play accomplice."

There's a sigh in me that I didn't know was there. "Thank you!"

We make for the exit. My face probably says "two-and-a-half stars," at least.

Jin leaves ahead of me, and I completely miss the slight step down.

I crash into his back and grip onto his shirt. Before I realize it, Jin's turned around and steadying me.

By grabbing my hand.

"You okay?" he asks.

I nod and pull myself together so I'm upright. Guess that haunted house made a fool of me after all. I pull my hand from his and dust myself off.

Now, Cale's chances may be better than I thought.

And maybe it's a tiny, itty bitty relief that I have one other person I don't have to pretend with.

♫

Fair food is in a league of its own.

Our corn dogs don't last long. They're perfectly brown and crunchy on the outside, with a snap of salty pork flesh, lathered in corn-syrupy ketchup. Lena's prior disgust was clearly a facade. She inhales that thing.

After lunch, we head to the rodeo show and I finally get to ask Cale how it went at the shooting range.

He winks and says, "I let her win."

"I slaughtered him," she says as she leans over from Cale's other side. The show starts and Cale's focus becomes completely enraptured in rowdy cheering. One by one, the cowboys get flung into the dirt. Cale's ridiculous shrieking makes all of us laugh, but I think he's still nervous around Lena because he keeps asking *me* "did you see that?" or "wasn't that insane?"

I stealthily urge him the other direction. He hesitates but manages to get her attention a few times over the course of the show. His nerves are adorable.

Even though the fair food hits our stomachs like bricks, we ride a few rides before going to the petting zoo. Cale literally squeals at baby bunnies! Lena holds off, though. She's periodically staring at one flashing food cart, longing for the sugary sustenance of the Promised Land.

Funnel. Cake.

Oh, we sanitize! Lured by pictures of stacked pancake noodles topped with syrupy fruit and whipped cream, we buy ourselves some fried glory.

Funnel cake is always a bad idea. And I never regret it.

The sun is dipping low and the air finally feels bearable. Not bad weather for braving another grease-bomb. I dig in, but I'm already feeling my limits.

Jin gets his funnel cake and sniffs it.

He coughs, sending white powder out into the atmosphere like a dry firework. It peppers his arm and I have to turn from my plate as I laugh so I don't suffer the same fate.

Lena is in hysterics. Her cake slides off her floppy paper plate, jam-side down in the dirt.

Cale gasps. "The *humanity*!"

Jin wipes his face with a paper napkin and then offers his funnel cake to Lena. She lights up and accepts. He beams at her delight and I have two thoughts: a) either Jin enjoys being chivalrous more than eating funnel cake, or b) he likes making Lena happy.

Or both.

Cale holds a brief vigil for the poor, lost dessert. Despite how amusing that is, I can't take my attention off the electric Park-Garcia chemistry. They're so easy together. Like someone cast the two most beautiful people for this one scene at the fair to be best friends.

The lavender sky tells me sunset is fast approaching. The Ferris Wheel suddenly lights up like a beacon.

"We should go to the Ferris wheel right now," I tell them, with half my mouth full. "We'll get the sunset if we're lucky."

Lena nods, her pretty mouth dusted with powdered sugar and cheeks full of fried cake. I think we all feel that a few bites was enough, so we abandon our food in the trash. Lena and Jin walk ahead. The silhouette of them against the dotted lights of the wheel is like a movie poster.

Suddenly I feel a smooth palm slip into my hand. Cale's. I glance at him, but he keeps walking like it's nothing.

Without taking my hand away, I whisper, "What's this?"

"Keeping up the image," he says, his voice hushed.

How is he so natural at this? I hope I'm playing it cool. Holding his hand feels more than friendly, even in our context. I haven't built up the courage to talk about the limits of this "relationship," but I don't see a reason to object.

For a second, it feels real. And kind of sweet. Not the sickly sweet of sugary funnel cake. More like a summer blackberry, perfectly ripe. He squeezes my hand and grins, high on the fair atmosphere alone.

Keeping up the image. This is for show. For Lena. And that's fine. But it does make me wonder what it would feel like if it were real. I look up at him, and I can see him that way.

For Lena, I remind myself.

Cale and I catch up, approaching the line for the Ferris wheel. There are two side-by-side lines, separated by a rope. Lena is arguing with Jin over which line to get in.

"They take a person from *each* line," he insists. "So we have to split if we want to get on together." Once he sees me, he gives me the barest wink.

"Why would they do that?" Lena retorts in a high pitch.

"He's right, Lena," I say, leaving Cale's handhold. "We should get in each line so we don't get staggered."

It's not technically lying. It's opportunity-manufacturing. Cale should be the one to ride with her. We're leaving it to chance once we queue up. Jin stands in front of me in one line, Lena in front of Cale in the other. The four of us are next to each other.

Now I just pray they call on my line before Lena's.

By some heavenly divination, Jin and I end up ahead in line. One person stands in front of Lena when they summon Jin up to a car.

Right according to plan.

"Oh." He makes a show of false concern. I'm so glad I recruited him. "Sorry, Lena! Guess I was wrong."

All I manage is a shrug and a silent beg to God that she considers it an honest mistake.

"Joy!" Her shrill reprimand urges me to avoid looking back at all costs.

The metal safety bar falls on our laps and Jin leans over, waving and mouthing "sorry" at Lena before facing the tangerine sunset.

Cale and Lena are practically on the opposite side of the wheel when they board. It's like the fair gods were smiling on our sneakiness. If we're lucky, Cale will admit his feelings for her as they gaze on the gradient orange, rose and periwinkle sky.

I know it's a long shot, but I'm in a hopeful mood.

Breezes like this breathe peace onto me, coupling with the dull sounds of riders on coasters and plinking games in the fading day.

"Thanks for assisting me today," I say to my ride partner.

"I think it merits a high five," Jin says. My sunburned cheeks sting when I smirk. I give the man the high five he's owed. Then I return to soaking in the lavender and tangerine sky. There's no better vehicle for this meditation than a rickety seat on a Ferris wheel.

"So, tell me about yourself, Joy," Jin says. The sparkle in his eyes hasn't faded all day.

"College?" he asks.

"FredU. Finance major."

His eyebrows go up. "Exciting."

I laugh.

"So finance is your dream?" he asks more genuinely.

I fiddle with my ride belt. "No. But it's practical. I figure I'll have money if I work with money. Bakers aren't the first ones to go hungry. My mom always says that."

He nods in acknowledgment. "Okay, so, let's say you go impractical. What would you do?"

The wheel stops and we're suspended above people, under the orange sky.

"A singer. But that's not really—"

"That's not any more impractical than a baseball player."

My eyes widen. "How did you... did you know my brother plays?"

A sly smile appears. "Lena mentioned it."

"Well..." I start, gearing up for an argument. But, I don't exactly have one. "I guess you have a point. What about you?"

"Business Law, but I actually like it. I think I want to help small businesses. There's a lot of opportunity for translators, so I'm focusing on super boring law language in Korean and English. I have an internship opportunity in Seoul, actually. It would jumpstart my career, but I still haven't decided if I want to go yet."

"Wow." Actually, impressive. "Cale was right. You are a one-upper."

He laughs at my snarky observation.

A thought occurs to me. "Does Lena know? About the internship, I mean."

"No. I wasn't going to tell anyone until I made up my mind. So, I guess we're in each others' confidences now."

I smile and probably blush. "Guess so."

Wind combs the escaped strands of my dark blonde hair and the sky is slowly saturated with a blue hue. The ride lights cast a more striking glow. I didn't realize until now, but this feeling is what I'm chasing this summer. A collection of breezy, sunburned twilights.

"Thanks for all this, Joy," Jin says. His palms hold up his face as he admires the picturesque sunset. "Today was pretty perfect."

I can't keep from smiling. Today was more than perfect.

Track 07 - Better Now

June 28th

Ok but what happened on the Ferris Wheel?

This is how I start my text chain with Cale right when I wake up. I would have asked him right after I got home last night, but I experienced a hard post-fair crash. I haven't escaped the layers of my bed yet.

I *did* manage to talk to Lena before she got into her VW yesterday, though. When I apologized for the mixup, she smirked and said, "Well… Cale's Jim Halpert impression is impeccable." She kept giggling, even after she shut the door and waved goodbye to me before taking off.

So yeah, once I was conscious enough to text Cale, I did.

Thankfully he doesn't make me wait very long.

CT: Who wakes up before 7 in the summer SHEESH

JB: DETAILS MR. THOMAS

CT: Okay okay

In the minutes that follow, my eager heart pounds watching his ellipses flash on and off. Did my effort amount to anything? I guess it was kinda mine and Jin's effort. I'm glad he agreed to help.

Even if Jin is still probably the one who will end up with Lena.

Buzz.

CT: SO, we got on the ride and Lena was kinda pissed cuz I think she was jelly that you were riding with Jin. I figured I had two choices: 1) get my empathy card out and be a shoulder to cry on or 2) pull out the Caletastic charms. I went with 2, obviously. COMEDY is my specialty bb

CT: Anyway, I asked her what was wrong because PLOT TWIST I was gonna try 1

CT: She ignored me, but then there was a bee

CT: And I kinda freaked out and flailed around and rocked the gondola thing

CT: Then Lena flicked it away like it was NOTHING

CT: She also LAUGHED AT ME. THE NERVE.

I laugh at him too, right now. The texts come in one after the other. He must be fast at typing, but the progression cracks me up. I can totally picture it.

CT: We talked about fair food and The Office after that but... yeah

CT: I think Imma play the long game. Callin it a win :D

So, not as successful as I'd hoped. But it's not nothing. Like Cale said, probably a win.

JB: I'll keep thinking up schemes

CT: Your services are appreciated
CT: Thnx for inviting me

As if Cale has to thank me for that. I thank him for bringing himself. He's a force of hilarious nature. Even if I'm exhausted from all the walking and sun and human interaction, the aching is practically a trophy knowing he had a good time and inched a little closer to Lena.

I whip my white comforter off and relish the coolness of conditioned house air on my legs.

Today, I have zero plans. Carson's off at physical therapy and then odd jobs at Victoria Lake Resort. Willow Haven's claim to fame is "the town you pass through to get to Victoria Lake." We're not that big. But at least I feel like I'm included in "we" now.

I get to eat sugary cereal while browsing Hulu by my lonesome. It's amazing.

This is another feeling I'm chasing, I think. Lazy meals, binging shows I never got to watch during the school year, and soaking up the slightly wider edges of my solitude.

I break up my Nothing Day with more AirBnB browsing, paying particular attention to the long Independence Day weekend. One has a hot tub *with* an ocean view and a hipster cafe walking distance. Just have to make sure the beater can make it.

My phone buzzes.

LG: So how far have you and Cale gone?

JB: Omg Lena

I shouldn't be surprised, but I'm still beet red. I envision her sitting out by her glittering pool, wearing the pink bikini, or maybe the teal one-piece, having a second to herself before suddenly thinking, "I need to ask Joy about her sex life."

> *LG: What? You guys were good friends before it's not like you can't go a little faster*

> *JB: I haven't even kissed him yet*

So far I'm glad the topic hasn't come up between me and Cale. The hand-holding mishap was essentially the height of my mutual romantic affection experience. Actually, I hate to call it a mishap when it wasn't all that bad. It just wasn't *real*.

And I'm unsure how to address the rules of this game.

I wonder how many girls Cale has been with. He had a girlfriend at the beginning of the school year, but they broke it off early. He sang a few ballads at the time, but otherwise kept his usual class-clown composure. Apparently she thought they'd be better as friends, which isn't really surprising. Cale has a thousand friends.

And that's exactly why I shouldn't be wondering if he's going to try to kiss me during this deal. He's a great friend. He'll understand if I'm too nervous to hand over my first kiss for a fake relationship.

I just have to actually talk to him about it.

> *LG: OMG YOU CANT BE SERIOUS*
> *LG: I thought I taught you better than that*

> *JB: I like taking it slow*
> *JB: Not everyone is like you*

JB: Lol

I add the last text so she doesn't think I'm being judgy. What's wrong with taking things slow? It's not like I'm dysfunctional. I'm not even really dating him!

LG: Oh hey, you want another double dog-sitting job?

JB: YES!! Do you even have to ask??

LG: Awesome! The fams are taking an impromptu trip to Cabo :D
LG: You doing anything for the Fourth?

The Fourth? Meaning, the only week this amazing AirBnB is available? I flip over to my booking app to doublecheck. It's completely booked except a few days around the Fourth.

I was so close.

But I basically already accepted the dog-sitting job. I groan because I'd rather have money.

JB: Just eating hot dogs and reading magazines in bed like every year

LG: Mom said they'll pay you extra since its last minute, and the dogs might get freaked out. But I told her you could handle that :D

Oh yeah. I've neglected to mention Cale's whole part in the dog care last time. It seemed better unsaid after he'd seen her bedroom and noticed her collection of raunchy teen vampire novels (no, I'm not joking).

LG: And this time, IT IS ON
LG: I'm determined to get Jin to myself

JB: Good luck <3

It feels odd to wish her luck with Jin and then actively plot for her to be with Cale. Like he's psychic, I get a message from him.

CT: Sooooo, you got plans for the Fourth of July?

JB: Actually, I just took another dog-sitting job

CT: OOH! I am SO THERE

Ellipses pulse. Did he just invite himself over to Lena's house? He knows she won't be there, right?

CT: We def gotta hit up Americanafest!

I recall seeing the poster for that around town. Red, White, and Blues, it said. *Very original.* It looks promising enough. Lots of bands playing and food carts serving.

And Cale has a way of upping the ante in the fun department.

JB: Sounds great!
JB: But I feel like I should clarify that Lena will be out of town, so...

Ellipses.

CT: Girl like I don't love spending time with my FGF!
CT: We'll make her WISH she was in town
CT: I'm the party selfie MASTER, Becker

FGF = fake girlfriend. I laugh just reading his personality. I feel a little better about losing my beach house prospects. Now back to more urgent business: America's Next Top Model, Season 8 Finale.

♫

Okay, so my Nothing Day is not turning out as fun as I'd hoped. ANTM got repetitive, I snacked myself into a stomach ache, and a shower sounds like the worst way to distract myself on a hot day like this. Maybe the intense boredom is the reason I decided to text Carson.

CB: It's been hot out. No AC. Good though, shoulder's healing
CB: Lots of sexy girls to distract me

JB: Ew! Don't tell me that!

CB: Ur the one who asked

JB: I meant, like, how are you feeling? Is it fun? Does your name have the most gold stars yet?

CB: LOL u know it
CB: But I still miss you

Yeah right. Carson's not fooling me. He only misses me when I'm not serving his athlete's image. He's probably confusing me with pitching. Since I'm at all his games, he thinks my absence is the reason he feels off.

He's probably lonely. Probably because he drops people like bats and dashes for someone new.

Ugh. I'm too dried out and salty. Like a hot potato chip. If I don't text back, he'll just get mad.

JB: Miss you too

CB: Once ur at FredU we'll see each other all the time, don't worry

Perfect. Once I'm in the vicinity you can make demands of me and my schedule face-to-face instead of by rare text. I can even hand you your finished homework if you like! So much easier!

Gosh, I really am a salty potato chip.

But part of me knows he still needs me. That's really why I texted him. I can't forget that I needed him once. Even though he caused a hell of a lot of problems for our family, he protected me. And things are better now.

Out of nowhere, Lena calls me, which is highly suspect.

"Hello?"

"Oh my god, Joy! It's horrible!" Okay, she's panicking.

"What? Are you okay?" It's the dogs. No, the flights. I don't know. It's hard to tell on her tone alone.

"I'm fine, but..." She whimpers. It doesn't sound serious. Or, at least, not to anyone else but her.

"Jin broke his wrist! He said he's not coming to Cabo!" I hear a frustrated sigh.

"Oh," I manage to respond. So I was right. It's not actually an emergency.

"I can't convince my parents to let me stay behind," she tells me. "They don't want to waste the ticket. And they want to *bond*. That the whole point of this trip was to spend time *bonding*. Ugh!"

Poor Lena. Being forced to spend the holiday weekend in Cabo. I stifle a laugh.

"Sorry." Single-word answers are all I have at the moment.

I let her vent about the not-really-a-crisis until she's ready to hang up.

Once she's gone, it suddenly occurs to me that Jin will be home alone this weekend.

And, in the next house over, so will I.

July 1st

Oh gosh, the backroads to Lena's house make me so queasy. Why do I take them so fast?

The beater sputters into the curving shared driveway of the wealthiest families I know. Jin Park's petite mom, Jan-di, stands near the fountain in her cream blouse and bright fuchsia capris. She waves her hand wildly at me. There's an envelope in it.

Wow, she has a lot of energy for such a small person.

The hum of my car's engine turns off, leaving me in that calming split-second of quiet. Immediately, Jan-di is shouting my name.

"Joie!" My name almost sounds like "Joey" when she says it. It's kind of adorable. I step out of my car and slam my door. The air isn't cool this morning. Not hot, either. It's the perfect in-between, where you can't feel it at all.

Jan-di's straight, white teeth shine at me, so I smile back. She smells like orchids and orange peels.

"Thank you so much for help, Joie!" she says. Her accent is thick with mixed up consonants and improper emphasis. Jin has no accent. Or, I guess, he has a perfect Amer-ican accent. Jan-di's voice is high, soft, and smothered in Korean-influenced intonation.

I can't see her eyes through her sunglasses, but I know they are just like Jin's. Winged, flat, and colored like melted chocolate. I saw them in one of Lena's pictures. Kid's got good genes.

She hands me the envelope, but I push it away. "Oh, um, I thought since Jin was home, you wouldn't need my help."

She purses her lips and shakes her head tightly.

"No, no, no. Jin cannot take care Zany," she tells me. "His arm so bad. He can no walk her." The way she says his name is like a shiny metal sound. *Cheen!* It suits him.

Jan-di shoves the envelope at me again. I grab it to keep it from falling on the ground, but that apparently secures my acceptance.

"Thank you, Joie!"

I nod. "No problem."

"And make sure he eat! He forget so much!" Her dry, raven hair swirls in a short breeze. She looks too young and tiny to have sourced such a tall, 20-year-old son.

Said 20-year-old man steps out of the Park house, down the paved stone path. His cast is a blinding neon green and glows on his white t-shirt. Honestly, he could only own one shirt and I wouldn't know it.

I cast a shadow over my eyes with my hand and call out. "Hey there!"

"Hey, Joy. Do you need help with your stuff?" he asks. I'm certain it's a habit. I point to his cast as if he's unaware that his wrist is broken.

"I've got one good arm!" He waves the good one around a little.

"He's so good boy," says his mother. She pats his shoulder on the uninjured side, then skitters back down the path to her house. It's peculiar that she insisted Jin's arm was too broken for walking the dog but not for helping me with my stuff.

He walks up to my car as I rifle through my things. I feel like I should hand him the pillow and blanket since they're not heavy, but I'm still mortified that I own them. But, I guess he has seen them before. Damage is already done.

"Here." I push them toward him. His long, pale arm wraps around them, and I try not to notice that he examines them for a second. Lisa Frank and Barbie, like before.

I dive back into my car to hide my blushing.

"Apparently you're so crippled, you still need me to take care of the dog," I say as I pull my bags out of the beater.

He scoffs. "I don't know why. My legs work perfectly fine, and I can scoop with one hand."

"Oh no, please! I could use the money," I admit, hoping I don't sound nearly as desperate as I am.

"Oh, really? What for?"

I emerge, close my car door, and head to the Garcias' front door. "Well, I need *some* savings for stuff my scholarship doesn't cover. But, if you must know, I'm planning to buy myself a weekend alone."

"You like being alone?"

I feel my heart rate speed up. "No! …I mean, yes. But not all the time. It's just…"

It's hard to explain. I have an itch, sort of, but it's in that spot on my back that I can't reach. And a couple of days at a beach house is the backscratcher I need.

"Just… what?" he solicits. We stand on the Garcia porch, pausing in front of the double doors.

"It sounds refreshing. That's all."

Jin lifts his broken arm up, his exposed fingers rubbing his chin. I see one of his brows lift.

"Are you making fun of me?" I ask him. He immediately shakes his head.

"No! I just think you're interesting. You just got paid to spend a week alone at two huge houses, and yet your dream is to... pay for that very same thing."

"Ok, when you put it that way... I mean I wasn't *really* alone."

Shoot! It slipped out. I open the front door and hope the transition is enough distraction that he won't ask. Please don't ask.

"You mean the dogs, or... someone else?"

He asked.

I lower my voice. "Cale came by. Zany was freaked out. Cale's a dog person, so he helped with her. Plus, he'd never seen Harry Potter, so yeah. We spent some time together. Nothing crazy. Except for the two seconds he forgot to take his shoes off in your house."

Jin gives me an exaggerated expression of shock. "Betrayal!"

I laugh with him. He hands me my possessions and I hug them like a teddy bear. He still seems unfazed by the fact that I sleep on rainbow leopards.

"I should give you my number," he says, in a way that would inspire soft-focus and sparkles.

I gape at him. "What?"

"Um, just in case you need something," he amends, and scratches his head.

"Oh. Sure." I fumble for my phone and we exchange numbers.

"Guess I'll see ya 'round." Jin's voice is smooth. I catch myself biting my lip as I watch him leave.

I smell heaven on a cookie sheet and glance to the kitchen. Seeing Fernando in his frilly apron is like rewatching a favorite comedy. And this time I'm not splayed out on the floor, so it's even better.

Well, not for Lena. Nobody should be so upset to go on a vacation to Cabo.

She says nothing when she sees me. Unless you count a pitiful sigh as a greeting.

Fernando and her mom, Angela, assure me Diamond has never had issues with the Fourth of July fireworks. They head out to the limo that just arrived and Lena hangs back for a second.

She hesitates. "Jin's really friendly. Just… don't take advantage of that."

I blink, a bit shocked. "I won't."

Her shoulders relax and she smiles on one side. "Okay."

"Hey!" I gently push her shoulder. "Have fun, will ya?"

She rolls her eyes and fights a smile. "*Fine!*"

Then she slogs to the limo. Does she really think that something could happen between me and Jin? If she does, she's crazy. But, it could just be that I'm getting what she wanted, and I can't fix it. It's not as simple as taking braids out of my hair.

Lena will perk up when she hits the blue ocean under the Mexican sun. If not then, the tan, muscular beach men won't hurt.

I shut the door, enclosing myself in an echo chamber of silence. Apart from the soft scuttling of Diamond, who pants at my side.

I head straight for the kitchen.

The cookies are still warm and melty. Diamond follows and begs for a cookie with that goofy puppy smile.

If I could give him chocolate, I'd cave in negative two seconds.

"Hey pupperz," I say with a mouthful of cookie.

Eventually, the corgi and I snuggle up in the den. This Korean romance drama cheeses hard, but I can't stop watching. It has nothing to do with the fact that the lead love interest looks like the guy one house over.

Nope.

My go-to excuse is that reading subtitles forces me to pay attention to the screen instead of trying to multitask.

I'm a little stiff after a few hours of that. It's a good time to make myself dinner. When I peel the throw blanket off and rise from the supple couch, Diamond wakes into immediate jitters. He races to the stairs, probably heading for the kitchen. Fast for a corgi.

My bare feet touch the cold tile of the foyer.

Knock knock.

I see his distorted figure and neon green cast through the floral glass pattern on the door.

Should I open it?

What am I thinking? I can't leave him out there.

I open the door and perfectly warm air flows in with the evening sun.

"Hey, Jin."

He greets me with a warm smile. How can he just hand those out like they're nothing?

"Hey, um, I ordered too much Chinese food. Thought you might want some. Besides, you technically still have to feed Zany." His blush-color lips twitch in a smile for a second.

"Right! I should."

Oh my God. I just agreed to have dinner with him.

Diamond brushes against my leg. I look down at him and hope he's the only one who can see my nerves.

In an only-for-dogs voice, Jin says, "Come on boy!" Diamond happily waltzes out.

Ginger and red pepper in thick sauces send an aroma hovering in the air when we walk into his foyer. I still feel like we are way too casually dressed to be walking around in his museum of a house. Nevermind the goofy-looking corgi and hyper black lab.

"Do you like tea?" Jin asks me when we get to the kitchen. With one hand, he pulls out plates from the mahogany cupboards and then reaches back for a yellow box. He sets it down, and reads "Jasmine" in gold letters.

"Sure!" Wow, yeah. That enthusiastic attempt at lowering my awkwardness had the opposite effect.

The tea kettle hisses. I don't think I've ever had jasmine tea.

Jin attempts to shovel chow mein onto the plates. "Attempts" is a generous word, actually. I giggle cruelly, if that's possible.

"You can pour the tea, how about that?" I say, reaching for the white takeout boxes. I brush his arm. My senses are super haywire because I'm not sure if I should be here. Is this what Lena meant by taking advantage of his friendliness?

I choose to act like it didn't happen. Because, like, what the heck is the big deal about brushing arms, right? It doesn't mean I *like* him.

The hot water is done and Jin pours it into the mugs. I'm struck by the aroma of jasmine. Peppery, floral, and slightly citrus.

"Where have I smelled this?" I say as I pull the cup close to my nose. The steam hits my face.

I'm taken back to the fair. When Jin leaned in to tell me something. He totally smelled like jasmine.

"What is it? You remember?" he asks me. He sips from the edge of his cup, slurping to cool the tea.

Do I tell him? I mean, I *can*. This isn't a *thing*.

"It was you. At the fair." I desperately seek a segue. "Do you drink it a lot?"

He nods, and slurps his next sip. "I'm a tea nerd."

"Really?"

"My family in Korea sends me tea for my birthday. It's way better over there."

Jin opens a cupboard full of teas. He owns that fact about himself, along with many others, proving he's a good conversationalist. His wrist break story is a dull one, he tells me. He tripped on a porch step and landed wrong. I can relate. The cast should come off in less than two weeks, but he didn't "feel like" going to Cabo with it on. I mentally roll my eyes at the idea of a rich person not "feeling" like an exotic getaway.

Jin rubs his mug and sips. The halt in conversation is palpable.

"Was it really your wrist that made you not feel up to going?" I don't know why I ask, but it feels like there's more here.

"Ah, yeah. You got me," he says. "I've been worried about taking the Korea internship. I kinda wanted the head-space. But now that I have it, I just want... distraction."

I lean in. "What's bothering you about it?"

"It's a really great opportunity. I can do in a year what I'd get done here in two years. And I'd make connections with people over there, so jobs would be easier to find."

"But..." I prompt.

"I don't want to go. Or I guess, I don't want to leave. It doesn't feel right, I don't know."

"Can you put it off?"

"See, that's the thing. I can't, really. They want me to come in August. And it's an honor to get selected. They only pick five people in the whole country."

I get the sense that the pressure saddens him for some reason. I take a second to think about what I would do, but it's obvious to me.

"I mean, I would go," I say, but I kind of hate it when I try to be a fixer. "You should do what you think is best, but I wouldn't want to miss the chance, I guess."

He sighs. "Yeah. You're probably right."

We leave it there, and our conversation flows again, like we worked out a kink.

Jin gets out of me that I was vice president of the glee club at Willow Haven. I always think it's strange when people are impressed by what is essentially a compulsion. But I like that he thinks I'm cool.

And then he brings up Cale.

"So, it's definitely fake? Because I saw you two holding hands."

"All for show. I wasn't even expecting that." I have a bite of the spicy, tangy General Tso's chicken and keep talking with my mouth somewhat full. "I was relieved to tell someone, actually. Thanks for being my accomplice."

"Anytime." He smiles at me. Again.

"So, do you have plans for the Fourth?" I sip some tea. It's just barely not too hot to drink, and the flavor is delicious. Not near as soapy as I'd expected.

"Well, not anymore," he says.

"Clearly! Cale invited me to Americanafest, so I'm gonna go to that."

"Even though you're not dating?" There's a sly smile before he slurps more tea.

I automatically roll my eyes. "Friends can't hang out?"

"Of course they can. Just like this. We're friends, right?"

I nod. "Yeah, I could use another friend. You wanna come with on the Fourth?"

He pretends to give it some thought. "Yeah. Sounds fun!"

I sip my tea, hoping that Lena won't be too upset that I get to spend time with Jin. We just established *friendship*. Not taking advantage of friendliness, just reciprocating it.

I speed up our farewell by feeding Zany and washing dishes, which was basically just the two plates and two mugs we used for tea.

Diamond follows me back to Lena's. I wish I could stop thinking about Jin. My mind forces me to replay the various smiles he offered me this evening. My heart is a schoolgirl, and it just met a member of our favorite K-Pop idol group.

I need to calm down. He said it. We are just, *barely*, friends.

Track 09 - Woke Up Late

I wake up blissfully alone with the heavenly glow of morning to greet me. The tangible silence tells me I'm not at home. No road noise. No dad in the kitchen, whistling and crackling bacon in a pan. No Carson and whatever growl-inducing frustration hits him first in the day.

Lena's clock reads 9:09 AM in glowing teal block numbers. I yawn and stretch, relishing the puffiness of her blankets on my rested body. What should I do today? I check my phone, kinda wondering if Cale has texted me, but I didn't actually tell him I started dog-sitting yesterday. Hanging with him might be fun.

He didn't text me. But at 8:59, Jin did.

JP: Do you like french toast?

I think it's because I'm still half asleep. That must be why I text him back without reading his question as an invitation.

JB: Definitely

JP: Oh good! I need help cracking the eggs. I already made a mess of it so I gave up haha

Jan-di *did* say I should make sure he eats. Who am I to defy a strict Asian mother?

JB: Lol be right there

I pride myself on being ready in five minutes. I don't need much. My hair is post-sleep messy so I put it in a loose bun. I check myself in the mirror and brush my teeth. Put on a bra, some deodorant, a hoodie and yoga pants that have never once been used for yoga. Then I'm out into the blinding yet cool morning.

Jin answers the door with a lick of hair still sticking up. Did he look in a mirror after he got out of bed? Not that it matters with him.

In the kitchen, I witness the mess of egg guts and white shells in, and around, a metal mixing bowl. After examining the carnage, I make judgy eyes at the culprit. He scratches the back of his head with his good hand.

"My mom usually does the cooking," he says.

"You're hopeless." I waste no time making this mess right. First clean up, then ingredient prep. It's a good thing I make French toast for myself often. I whisk the eggs, milk, vanilla, nutmeg, and cinnamon with a fork.

"What are your big plans today?" Jin asks.

"Um, not much really. You?"

"Fighting boredom. I could use a break from Rocky movies."

I glance at him briefly before placing the soaked bread in the pan. It sizzles and my mouth is already watering. The mixed scent of vanilla and butter rises from the pan.

"Well, my plan is to binge the first season of The Walking Dead," I watch the edges of the toast for browning.

"Can I be honest?" he says. His tone is serious, like he's stepping away from our light conversation.

Our eyes meet. Why is my heart pounding? "Sure."

"I've never seen that show." He winces. "Is that bad?"

A stupid amount of relief washes over me. I laugh. "Oh my gosh! I thought something was wrong."

I hastily flip the bread over with a spatula. I didn't miss the perfect timing, thank goodness.

He apologizes for freaking me out. I get another piece of bread soaking in the egg mixture.

"I haven't seen it either. Figured I should start," I admit.

"So we have something in common! I was beginning to think you were more experienced than me." It's so casual and easy coming from him.

"Well, unless we watch it together, I will be," I say, and I feel my pulse in my face because that totally sounded like an invitation.

"Then I guess we're in it together," he says. I flip the French toast onto a plate. Then he smirks, and it's really cute, but I'm freaking out. I push the plate to him. He covers his toast in syrup and eats it, and compliments my French toast making skills and I AM STILL FREAKING OUT.

I feel sort of like I betrayed Lena, but it was just a comment. I didn't *mean* to invite him.

But I also don't stop him when he follows me back to Lena's house after breakfast.

♫

Zombies eating people is the most unromantic thing we could be watching together. Despite the brief hot and heavy scenes in the first episode—which are weird to watch with *anyone*, I remind myself—the show is nothing but gore and suspense. Harry Potter with Cale was more romantic, by a long shot.

Comfortably seated on the sectional, but keeping *friendly* distance, we watch three episodes without much interruption. Halfway through the first (oddly short) season, I pause it for a break.

"What? We have to watch the next one!" Jin says as if it's obvious.

"This is why I usually stop watching in the middle of an episode. You're not that invested in the middle."

Jin gives me a look of horror. "How can you do that?"

"I don't like the suspense of not knowing what's going to happen!"

"Really? I love that part." The way he says it makes me want to love that part, too.

Diamond waddles into the den. On that note...

"I should walk the dogs."

"Right. Forgot you were working."

We leave the den, and just when I'm convinced that Jin has had enough of me, he asks if he can join the walk. For fresh air. So I have him bring Zany over.

After securing the dogs on leashes, we take our walk. The sun's at a pleasant intensity, not too harsh but still causing a sheen of sweat. It's actually a bit too nice of a day for watching TV.

But somehow, I don't care.

Zany yanks hard on the leash, so I let Jin have Diamond. Jin jokes about Walkers racing out from the dense trees on the side of the road. I do kind of wonder what it would be like if zombie moaning interrupted the sweet bird songs.

We agree I'd probably kill more zombies. At least while he's still injured.

I really wanted to be alone for this long weekend. *Wanted.*

Now all I want is to finish the first season of The Walking Dead.

But when we get back to the house, I'm famished. I make him some boxed mac and cheese, despite that it's truly the one thing he could make with a broken wrist. I share my secret ingredient: salsa.

Yes, I'm serious. Jin's not buying it until I start eating from my own bowl. He wiggles his fingers for me to pass the salsa. Right when I do, my phone buzzes. His too, a second later.

It's a picture from Lena. Tan sand, harsh sun, teal waters in the background. Her black, sparkling bikini top holds her well. She gives the camera a rose-pink smile, with peace sign fingers. I don't know how many tries it took to get this picture just right, but she nailed it.

Guilt sinks in my abdomen. "It's Lena." I try to sound… happy?

Jin peeks at his phone screen.

"I bet you're wishing you were there right now," I say, with a pinch of regret. "Looks like she's having fun."

Jin pours a bit of salsa in his bowl of mac and cheese. "I'm having fun, too."

"It's not *Cabo.*"

"Eh. The Walking Dead is preferable in my state."

He makes eye contact for a second. Jin's eyes are so dark, they always have a twinkle in them.

I think I'm starting to enjoy his company too much.

"This is weirdly good," Jin says, chuckling with a mouth half-full of my odd food combo.

I stare at Lena's flawless picture. She's off in Mexico, trusting me with her dog and this guy that she's in love with.

I might've already crossed over into "taking advantage" territory.

"I should probably shower after this. What time is it?"

He checks his phone. "Whoa! It's almost 4!"

I stuff my mouth with the salty, rehydrated cheese noodles, relishing the vinegar tomato flavor that mingles with it. I don't know what else I should say. I may be okay at banter, but I've always been terrible at being blunt.

I don't want vagueness to get me in trouble again.

"We'll finish the season together, right?" Jin asks me.

"Yes! I'm not a Netflix cheater," I say, kind of surprised by how easily it comes out.

"Good to know, Joy. I'll remember that for later."

♫

Lena's shower is heaven. The water falls with just enough pressure, not the needle spray I get at home. Her iridescent tile makes me feel like I'm some kind of mermaid princess. When I'm good and done, I dry off with a fluffy, luxurious towel.

I used Lena's bluetooth speaker to listen to music and heard the text chime a couple times. I'm hoping it's Cale with details for the Fourth. I wonder if I should invite him to watch The Walking Dead with us (since I'm absolutely positive it also wasn't approved by his mom), but I hesitate before checking my phone.

I kind of like that I have a thing with Jin. And I kind of like that I have a thing with Cale, too.

I check my phone… it was Jin.

JP: It really has been fun not being in Cabo :)
JP: When should I come back over to finish TWD?

I didn't expect it would be him. Or that his words to send my mind spiraling into repeated visions of his perfect smile. A Jin Park tornado of happiness.

I shake my damp head. What's a good hour for a perfectly friendly friend to come over after I wake up? I'm almost settled on 11 when he messages me again.

JP: How about a late dinner? Like 8?

Wait, *tonight*? I bite the edge of my lip, kind of shocked at how badly I want to say "yes."

I was looking forward to spending my weekend with my waking hours heavy in the "alone" category, but I'm not peopled out. Or… not with Jin.

There's a sheer veil of worry on me about how Lena would take it if she knew that I spent more than half a day with Jin. But it's not like it's that different than Cale. Purely platonic.

I squeeze my eyes shut and press send.

JB: Sounds good :)

♫

One episode in and I'm invested hard. Wrappers from the pitas that Jin drove out to get are crumpled on the coffee table. We're both cozied up under *very separate* throw blankets on the couch. The huge TV screen fills the dark room with shifting light. OLED really does look better.

Sweating heavily, the zombie-fighters on the screen argue against the background of singing cicadas. It feels like a Southern summer came in through the TV. My eyes start to betray me near the end of episode five. But I can't stop! Jin was right; the suspense is the best part!

In the final seconds of the episode, a door dramatically opens for the dirt-covered characters. I jolt awake at the floodlight on the screen. Jin is glued to the screen.

I check my phone and it's not even ten PM yet. I should not be tired, and I'm definitely not stopping. The next one is the finale. We agree we have to watch it, so I let it play.

The AC blows in super lightly on my face, how I imagine floating on a cloud would feel. The blanket is silky soft...

I'm so warm... relaxed... the voices from the show are dull chants...

Shoot, I closed my eyes again. I try to refocus my attention on the show.

But the TV's off.

I wake all at once, barely registering the den in low light. As usual, watching TV is best done with eyes *open*.

There's a crick in my neck from the position I slept in on this couch. In the middle of my yawn, I look beside me. There's a tousled head of black hair lying still. *Jin.*

I bolt up! Where's my phone? *Gah!* Here, 6:03 AM. Oh my god.

Jin and I slept on the couch. Together. All night.

Shoot!

How the heck can he just *breathe* so *peacefully!?*

Okay, okay. I press the heel of my hand on my forehead. I have to figure out a way to keep Jin from telling Lena about this *without* revealing that she has feelings for him. She'll definitely be hurt if she finds out I let this happen.

I can't tell if I'm anxious or hungry or both, so I sneak out of the den and leave Jin to sleep. Once I have some cereal in my stomach, maybe I can handle this. When I get to the doorway, though, I look over at him. Sleeping Jin is so...

Nope. No way. I'm booking it to the kitchen.

Diamond is waiting for me, whimpering by the sliding door into the backyard, so I let him out. Zany's probably wondering what the heck happened to Jin.

Ugh, I'm a sore disappointment even to the dogs.

The stupid cereal box even feels heavy, which I know is literally impossible. I'm all nerves. I slam it down on the counter. *Nothing happened.*

Carson would freak if he found out. But he won't. There's no reason that would happen. God, I wish my brain didn't always try to process things through the Carson filter. I think it's my way of trying to control things ever since *that night.* But this is nothing like that.

It's over. Breathe.

It wasn't your fault. Everyone walked away.

Suddenly I'm sinking. Immersed in the icy pool of *that night.* The house party. Colored string lights, drinks I refused, the heavy beat of an unrecognizable song, and disorienting currents of wasted teenagers. *Breathe.* The dim hallway. That song shook the walls and I'm pinned to them. The beat pounds in sync with my heart.

Stop. Stop. Stop.

Tyler forces his drunk lips on my neck. I feel sick all over again.

The cereal bowl scrapes against the granite counter as I push it away. I'm not hungry anymore.

Diamond paws the door and I go let him back in, having barely resurfaced from drowning in my memory.

"Um... good morning." I swivel on my heels. Jin. Gorgeously disheveled and totally unaware that I was just underwater. *Breathe.*

Oh, God, but now I'm breathing like a fool!

"M-morning! Jin!" I stammer.

Diamond's in the house and I shut the door and HOLY CRAP what am I supposed to say?! Is he just gonna play it cool? Should I do that? No, I *hate* that! I'm so not cool right now! But I don't know how to play it down.

"I'm really sorry," Jin says. "For sleeping here. I should've gone home when I got tired. That's on me."

Wait. *He's taking the blame?*

"No, it's fine," I say. Diffusing is automatic. I don't control it. "I should've told you I was tired. I just wanted to finish the episode."

"No way. I was in the same boat and I should've gone home. Staying the night was not cool."

Wow, I'm really not used to a guy insisting it's his fault. I'm at a loss for words.

He stiffens, gathering courage. "Well, I mean! I don't mean it's 'not cool' like it was *horrible*. It wasn't!" He rubs his face and groans. "I'm sorry. I personally think it's a big deal to stay overnight with... a girl. So, you know..." He clears his throat. "I don't take it lightly."

Is he flustered? What is happening?

Am I just staring at him? Nod! Do *something*! Say something!

"It's okay. I don't blame you for conking out." *Conking out?* Oh my God, am I my dad?

Jin sighs in relief. "Are we okay, then?" he asks. And then he gives me a calm, friendly, hopeful smile that obviously I am no match for. Let's be real.

"Of course," I say, and I try to smile, but it hits me that I am already out of social energy. Finally met my quota. "But you should probably check on Zany."

"Right!" He nods once. Twice.

"Right," I echo and watch as he... doesn't leave.

Is he waiting for... "Oh! I'll text you the details for Americanafest tomorrow."

"Great," he says. That gets him moving and smiling that stupidly handsome smile again. "See you later, Joy."

"Bye…"

Apparently I was holding my breath because I heave a sigh when I hear the front door close.

I'm relieved to be alone, but I also feel guilty for it. He was so cute, waking up like that. Trying not to offend me by insisting he was wrong to stay over. *Insisting.* Carson would never insist he was wrong.

I feel this slight dethroning of turmoil in my heart. *It's over now.* The words are a fraction more tangible. He insisted it wasn't my fault, and suddenly the grip my past has on me is weaker. Can it be that simple? Are my demons just knots that can be tugged and loosened like thread?

Upstairs, I retrieve my phone. Cale's been texting me a bunch.

> *CT: There's a SINGING COMPETITION JOYYYYY*
> *CT: At Americanafest, forgot to mention that part*
> *CT: …and I already signed you up. :D :D*

Before I read his next message, dim anxiety rushes me. But it's the good kind. The kind that I ride like a wave right onto a stage before a performance.

> *CT: Think you can beat me???*

Shoot him the gif of Ice Cube saying "It's on" very intense-like. My pre-performance panic is always diminished when music gets involved. Or maybe when Cale gets involved.

I don't care if it's tomorrow and I haven't practiced anything. I'm already sounding off scales and imagining the bliss of belting out a ballad.

I will definitely beat Cale!

July 4th

Hopefully I'm not failing at channeling Lena's make-up sense. Effort is important on this day, the anniversary of our nation's founding. Good Lord. Is there a foundation that covers inherent dorkiness?

I weave my hair into a braid crown. The sunshine has given me lighter gold streaks, so the crossing of my strands is cooler than I'd expected. My patriotic foresight was actually in check this year because I actually have an outfit. A striped cherry red-and-white off-shoulder top, kind of a vintage 50s feel, with navy high-waisted (not-too-short) shorts with stars in place of polka dots.

When I check my made-over look in Lena's massive mirror, I like it. My freckles pop, and the green in my hazel eyes, too. Blood rushes to my already blush cheeks. I'm knocking on *his* door today. I wonder if he already texted me.

I pick up my phone, realizing it's on vibrate and there's half a dozen messages and a missed call from Cale.

CT: Hey, what time should we meet?

CT: The contest starts at 12. Check-in at 11.
CT: Should we drive together? I can pick you up from Lena's
CT: Actually, I don't trust that beater. I'll come get you
CT: ??? What time? Hello?
CT: Nvm, I'll be there at 10

It's 10:02 already!! I race down to the front door, and sure enough, he's on time. Or two minutes late, which feels like 20 minutes early as I mentally list my morning failures. One, I didn't prepare for Cale being this early. Two, I still haven't fed the dog. Three, I never ate breakfast.

And four, I haven't yet gotten to knock on Jin's door.

Chill! It's going to be a great day. The weather is perfection, I have two really awesome friends to hang with, and I'm going to a festival where there's a singing contest. All my nerves are like bubbles!

I wave to Cale once I notice he's spotted me, then check my phone again.

Apparently I missed Jin's texts too.

JP: Should we ride to the festival together? What time are you thinking you'll go?
JP: I'm an early riser so I'll be ready whenever ;)

My heart leaps a little at the winking face. It's just an emoji, *sheesh!*

I should go tell Cale I'm running behind schedule. I exit the house and walk up as his driver's side window slides down.

"Ooh, automatic windows are so nice," he says with feeling.

I laugh. "Wow, rub it in."

He slaps the outside of his car door. "So hey, since you weren't answering, I did the manly thing and decided for you."

"Sorry. My phone was on silent."

He tuts and rolls his eyes, but it's exaggerated enough I know he's kidding. "Well, you ready?"

"Um, almost. I still have to feed the dogs. And ask if Jin wants a ride or if he's driving himself."

Confusion registers on his face. "You mean Lena's Jin?"

Yeah. You know. Your romantic competition. I guess I forgot to mention that I invited him.

"Uh, yeah. Is it cool if I offer him a ride with us?"

Cale's playfulness dissipates as he considers it, which I wasn't expecting.

"I guess so." His tone sounds the tiniest bit offended, but maybe I'm reading him wrong.

I decide to ask Jin to drive himself. I don't want Cale to feel like he's playing chauffeur to the guy who could upend his chances with Lena. Cale agrees to wait and I head over to Jin's house.

I lift my knuckles to knock on his door, but he opens it before I make contact.

"Morning!" he says, extra cheery. I process him in pieces. Voice, then smile, then sunglasses, then cherry red tank. It reads "AMER" and then "ICAN" but in alternating blue and white, to emphasize "I CAN." I smile back at him.

"Morning..." I say, amused.

"Did you get my text?"

"Yeah, um, is it okay if you drive on the way there? We could ride back together and save Cale the trip."

He beams in the bright morning sun. "Sure! Guess I'll meet you there."

"Okay." I turn to leave.

"Joy?" he says, so I look back. "You look great, by the way." His grin lingers.

My feet and well, honestly, my entire body stay stuck for a second. Everything except my heart, which is freaking out. Can't this sunshine melt my frozen self a little faster?

"Thanks," I finally say. *Loosen up!* "You, too."

When regaining my agency, I resist the urge to run as I head to Lena's house.

I don't really catch my breath from his perfectly innocent compliment until after I get food into Diamond's bowl.

He said I looked great. Ugh. It's stupid to keep replaying it in my head. But I do.

I pile myself into Cale's car. There's a rising desire in my chest to share what just happened. But it was probably nothing. I'm sure he says that to Lena all the time.

Stay cool, Joy.

"Doesn't need a ride after all?" Cale's cheerfulness has mostly returned. I'm back to reality.

"Nope. He'll probably drive me back, though, if that's cool."

Cale nods. "That's cool, that's cool."

He'll probably drive me back. Just me and him.

♫

It wasn't just me who put some thought into patriotic dress. Even though that sounds obvious, I'm not just talking about other people. I'm talking about this whole "old town" part of town. Red, white, and blue striped Americana banners decorate the antique lamp posts. Main Street is closed for pedestrians and the shops have their doors wide open. Booths litter the sidewalks, covered in shiny patriotic balloons. The hum of the crowd and distant live jazz music fill the air.

We walk through the sea of people wearing America's colors. Occasionally, there's a rebel color like cotton candy pink or canary yellow. Jin's neon green cast sticks out that way.

Nothing is better than food carts. The smoke and salty, spicy aromas waft around us and my mouth waters. Since I was breakfastless, my nose is on high alert for something hot and probably meaty.

Part of me is sad to miss out on my family's baked beans and Dad's barbecue chicken, but I already told myself I'd settle for leftovers. It's the first Independence Day in which I'm claiming my own independence.

However, my stomach seriously expects some food right now. Hamburgers and hot dogs in red plaid cartons walk by me, in the hands of less worthy eaters. There's shaved ice and fritters and curly fries the perfect color of crispy, dark orange. I ache for them. Like almost literally.

"We gotta go check in!" Cale says, nudging me away from the blissful morsels of fried sustenance. Jin and I keep up with Cale's energetic pace.

"Did you eat yet, Joy?" Jin asks. I shake my head.

We head straight to the table labeled CHECK IN. The guy at the table is wearing a shirt far too small, and seems very uninterested in fun. He hands us a clipboard with a list of names and songs for us to choose from.

Cale writes his name with flare. He winks at me when he hands me the clipboard. I glance at it.

CALE THOMAS - TAKE ON ME

He literally couldn't have picked a better song for himself.

I write my name in my bubbly penmanship.

JOY BECKER -

I scan the setlist. It's all 80s karaoke. I want a song with power in it. Not just upbeat or punchy. Something to showcase my range. And wipe that smug look off of Cale's face.

Found it.

"You're goin down, Thomas!" I say as I pencil in my song choice.

I hand the clipboard back to the guy at the table. Completely monotone he says, "You must be present to accept the title after the competition. Results at 3pm." And then he sighs.

All I can say is *my* mood is the opposite of this guy's.

My stomach gurgles at me. I get that odd sucking feeling, like my stomach is trying to escape my body and get food on its own. I scan for nearby carts, but I notice Jin's missing.

"Where's Jin?" I ask Cale. He shrugs.

I turn around and search the crowd, trying to spot a lime green arm somewhere.

"Joy!" I hear on the side I haven't checked. Jin weaves through people. With a pulled pork sandwich on a flimsy paper plate that might as well be fine china.

"I got you some food," he says.

Who is this angel sent from Heaven? I close my gaping mouth, fearing drool might escape.

"Thanks." And I snag the food because I can't *not*.

"What about me?" Cale says, making a wide gesture at himself.

"I only got one hand, man."

I laugh because that's actually a good excuse.

The smoked meat is sweet with barbecue sauce, coupled with cold, dripping coleslaw in a pillow-soft bun. My mouth tingles. There's a bite of spice and a tomato-y tang. My stomach thanks me even though the food hasn't gotten there yet.

I could kiss him. At the moment, though, that would be a gross gesture.

The festival has filled out a lot for lunch. I'm loving the sun rays and soft breeze and this *perfect* sandwich. So far, the best Fourth ever!

Cale secures himself a couple of fish tacos, while Jin insists he's not hungry. As we chat and eat and laugh, I'm shocked that I'm here with two really awesome guys. *Me!* But Lena Garcia has a romantic monopoly on both. And she's not even in the United States of America right now.

I'm okay with it. I want all of these people to be happy, no matter how they arrange themselves. I just have to stay out of it, have fun, root for my friends, and head to college with an awesome summer in the books.

In a way, I feel more freedom without the pressure to impress either of the guys.

Bluegrass floats in the air as we walk around. There's a sign for upcoming shows and I'm locked onto it when I see the name of one of the bands.

The Crux Constellation. They're here? Despite the heavy rotation they have in my playlist, I've never seen them play because they hail from Seattle.

"Hey, you like them, right?" Cale says looking over my shoulder.

"Yeah, but… it says it's their farewell tour," I say. Wow, that puts a damper on things. But getting the chance to see them today is pretty cool.

"Guess we're sticking around!" Cale says. I'm so happy that he gets it.

"Guys, it's noon already," Jin interjects. I'm flooded with jitters. The competition!

We shuffle over to the tent, and free folding chairs near the stage. The MC, a tiny woman in her forties with excess perkiness, battles miserable feedback and gets the show up and running. It's not Broadway, but it's something.

Cale and I are a few down in the set, so we sit with the audience and watch. It's like bad karaoke. We politely cheer with the sparse spectators, but then there's this dangerously good twelve year old girl. How can someone that young handle ABBA like a pro? She calls herself Little Dragon.

"Because she breathes fire!" Cale says into my ear when she hits a particularly difficult note.

We join the applause for her as she bows and grins big with gleaming braces.

"Wow! What a fabulous performance! To follow *that* act, we have Cale Thomas!" the MC says.

His arms fly up and he moves for the stage. "Here we go!"

"Break a leg!" I call after him.

Once on stage, Cale yanks the microphone from the stand. Fake drums sound. Cheesy synth rolls in and his back faces the crowd. His only dance move is the snap of his finger to the drum.

Snap. Snap.

The song builds with a guitar strum and I giggle because I know what's coming.

Cale was *made* for "Take On Me."

The melody synth hits. He moves his hips, wide and flouncy. He swerves around, continuing his ridiculous but entirely appropriate dance.

He's definitely a Will Smith.

And his voice hits the speakers with the lyrics and cheers erupt for Cale. They didn't know what I knew. Cale owns his crystal clear voice like a pro. From the way he handles vibrato, you would not think he's breaking a sweat with that wiggly dance.

He's infected everyone in the crowd with his insanely entertaining energy.

Jin leans over. "He's good!"

I eye him. "I know!"

Cale delivers the smooth, long words of the chorus, and it leads up perfectly to the final word. That crisp high note garners intense cheers. He has them eating out of his absurd jazzy hand. There is no Left Shark in this kid.

I sing the echo in the second chorus. I catch Jin grinning at me.

When the karaoke-quality guitar solo hits, Cale starts half-break dancing.

We. Eat It. Up. His model poses, his perfectly timed robot, his *sprinkler*! Little Dragon has some serious competition.

The song slows for the third verse. He falls to his knees and I can hear in his voice that he overdid it. But he reaches his hand out to me and sings the words.

To me.

I pull my fists to my face and blush. He winks at me.

Cale Thomas. No wonder everyone in this crowd is into you!

He gets up and dances again for the upbeat ending. After he hits that brilliant, high note a few more times, it's over. He bows and the enthusiastic cheers prove his worth.

I'm beginning to doubt my ability to one-up him.

Once he's off stage, my pulse quickens. I'm next. Performing always gives me nervous energy, but I embrace it. That way it pulls my introverted self into scary places. I also have a jolt of Cale-induced energy to work with, like I was plugged into his electricity.

The little MC clears her throat. "Up next, Joy Becker!"

Before I know it, I'm on the stage. I take a measured breath.

The karaoke piano plays the lead up. I adjust the mic. Sharp inhale.

"Don't Stop Believin'" leaps from my throat. Journey's greatest hit. It was my life when I moved to this town a year ago. My one daily comfort. This song is muscle memory for me, so I play with vocalizations as I fall into the song. It's like home.

Armed with the surge I got from Cale, I claim the stage. I lean into the mic, not dancing with abandon, but tensing and pulling and pushing myself as I move through the emotion of it. It's not just the melody or the cheap synth of the karaoke version. The words, the way I command them, are my existence right now.

I love the way my heart bursts when I build up to the high note. That sweet echo of *my* voice reverberating in the speakers sends chills through my body.

I'm brimming with a songful of emotion and soul and vision, in sync with the power of music. It's like I have those wings on the cover of Journey's *Greatest Hits* album. For me, this is total freedom.

The guitar solo resounds and I have a few seconds to share it with the audience. My face hurts from smiling, Cale whoops, some even look starstruck... like Jin.

Holy... focus. I'm not done yet.

I hold the emotion until the last note. The outro ends and it's over. I fan myself while the people go nuts. I put myself out there, everything I had, and they loved it!

I descend from the stage, dripping with sweat, but I don't care. I run over to Cale and Jin. Cale wraps his arms around me and spins in a half circle.

"Girl, that was amazing!" he says as he releases me.

I'm out of breath, longing to be back in the middle of that song. I love and hate when it's over. I'm so harmonized with being alive when I sing.

In the corner of my eye, neon green. I look up and there's Jin, with a lingering look of awe. Brand new flutters wash over me.

"That was awesome," Jin says like he's catching his breath.

"Thanks!" I bite my lip and fan myself again. This heat, I swear.

My phone buzzes rhythmically in my shorts pocket, so I grab it to see who's calling.

MOM

There's a sudden drip of cold dread on my hot excitement. Buried deep is the part of me that knows she wouldn't call me like this without a motive. I brace myself when I answer.

"Hey, mom," I answer, scouting out a quieter space.

"Joy! Where are you?" she says, sharply.

I knew it.

I give the truth a shot. "I'm with my friends."

"You're supposed to be with your family! Or did you forget about us?"

Just like that, all the happiness I was feeling seconds ago escapes through the hole she just punctured in my ego.

"I didn't forget, I just…" I can't think of how to word it, but she jumps on me before I can.

"You *just* acted selfishly."

How dare I, *a grown adult*, make my own plans?

"Mom, I'm sorry. I didn't think it would make a difference if I was home or not."

The silence between our passes is super short when Mom is angry like this.

"You didn't *think* at all, Joy Diane!"

Psh. Middle name usage. It's pointless now.

She carries on. "Did you know your brother came home? When was the last time you called him?"

"Carson's home? Why is he home?" That doesn't sound good.

"Is everything okay?" Jin asks me. I turn and avoid him. My burning eyes land on a brown patch of grass.

"He lost his job! I can't believe you wouldn't even check on him!"

Yeah, right. Like the phone only works one way.

"What do you want me to do, Mom?" It always ends up with me asking this question, and obeying whatever she says. I hate it, but that's how it is.

"Just come home. I know you have to get back to the dogs, but at least spend a couple hours with your family. Your brother is really down."

I *really* wanted to stay here, but now I can't. I have no idea why Carson lost his job, but I know my brother. His feelings are as real, and definitely a lot more intense, than mine. There's no doubt he needs me. I have to go.

"Okay, Mom. I'll be there soon." I hang up and enter back into the world of Americanafest.

"Wait, what?" Cale starts, having heard my conversation. "You can't *leave*! You gotta stay to claim the prize."

But I can't win anything when my brother's involved.

"Are you really okay?" Jin asks again.

"Yeah," I sigh. "My brother just lost his job and my family wants me to spend the day with them. Can you drive me there?"

Jin nods, his brow still tense with concern.

"It can't wait?" says Cale, annoyed. "What about the prize? And that band you wanted to see?"

I shake my head. "You should stay, Cale. You beat me anyway, Mr. Glee Club President." I smile to lighten the mood. It doesn't really work. Cale lost some Joy.

"Hey, come here." Cale reaches his long arm around me and pulls out his phone with his other arm.

"Say 'singing champion!'" I see his big grin on the screen. I smile for the camera as best I can. It was fun while it lasted.

Cale kisses the top of my head and snaps the picture. My stomach does a mini-flip. He just kissed me. Once he has the selfie, I stare up at him.

"What?" he says with an oblivious smile.

I guess it's fine. Why not kiss your girlfriend on the head, right? It's more *keeping up the image.* Even though it caught me off guard, I feel better.

He quickly sends me the selfie.

"Selfie King's gotta selfie," he says with a grin.

I really don't want to abandon my friend with all this positive energy for the soul-sucking aura that Carson is no doubt emanating.

"Sorry, Cale. I really wish I could stay."

He makes eye contact. "Me, too."

The deepness of his voice makes me think he means it. Like he doesn't regret that I'm not Lena. Coupled with the disappointed look on his face, you'd think I was his real girlfriend. He even slaps Jin on the back and tells him to take care of me.

Am I letting these lines get too blurry?

I wave goodbye and walk to the car with Jin.

It's a shame I spend the car ride to my neighborhood doing mental circles around my frustration. Jin is polite in silence the whole way.

Carson always wins. I shouldn't have forgotten.

Still July 4th

My dead end street is packed with lawn chairs and charred remnants of used fireworks. Five minutes after Jin drops me off, Mom gives me a tight squeeze, then shoves barbecue chicken in my hand.

Food usually makes me very forgiving and she knows it.

In a way, I wish she would keep seething. That way I'd have a reason to ignore her. But she always forgives and forgets. Rinse and repeat.

"Hey, sis!" Carson says, opening his tanned, muscly arms wide for a brother bear hug. The curls of his head tickle my face. He doesn't seem depressed to me!

Carson didn't actually *lose* his job, I find out. He got caught making out with one of the girls staying at the resort. Her parents made some threats, but she was twenty (older than *him*), so they slapped him on the wrist for misconduct or something. He's on unpaid leave until that family leaves the resort.

Mom was embellishing. Shocker.

I'd wallow in anger, but there's no point. Actually, part of me feels guilty for assuming my family wouldn't want to see me today because I was "working."
Alas, I was wrong. Happens a lot these days.
As long as Dad keeps pumping out bratwurst and chicken, I'll try to be happy. Sparklers make me kinda happy, so I grab one.
My phone buzzes.

CT: GIRL YOU WON
CT: OBVIOUSLY
CT: They gave the title to the 12yo kid with the IN-SANE pipes
CT: And yours truly got 2nd place!!

My sparkler flickers and hisses. It's a bittersweet victory. Three dots appear.

CT: You were beautiful and amazing today

I stare at his words. It sounds weird, but for Cale, that text is understated. I'm used to his loud, elaborate compliments. Snarky gif wars. Exaggerated hand gestures emphasizing his enthusiasm. But somehow the simplicity feels... bigger.
I can't leave him on *read!* I should reply.
What does he even mean by that? I don't know what to say!

JB: Thanks :) so were you :D

Oh God, kill me now. Instantly I want to take it back. "So were you??" I squeeze my eyes shut and hope it's dorky enough that he'll take it as a joke.

CT: *Hahaha, you know it!*

I breathe. Was I holding my breath? Cale's into Lena. We're friends. I stare into my sparkler and remind myself of this plain fact.

"That's not from your boyfriend, is it?" Carson asks me. He's looking over my shoulder, waving his own sparkler close to me like it's a housefly.

"So what if it is?" I swat at his fizzing sparkler. "It's not like I'm sneaking around."

He scoffs. "Sexting counts, little sister."

"It's not! Here, see for yourself." I hand him my phone.

He examines the last few messages. He sees the picture, peers at me, and then hands my phone back.

"Um yeah, that was sexting if I've ever seen it."

"Are you crazy? How on earth was that 'sexting?'"

"I know what a guy is thinking when he calls a girl 'beautiful.' It's sexting." There's a smug look on his freckled face.

I roll my eyes. Carson thinks he knows everything about relationships and guys' intentions and how to woo girls, yet he's still single.

It's not near dark yet, but fireworks start going off. They ring in my ear, and I suddenly think about one, pudgy, slobbery face. Diamond. I hope he's not scared.

I say goodbye to my family. The fact that a paying job is on the line is enough to convince Dad to give me a ride all the way up to the boonies. I'm grateful it's him. Now I don't have to have any more anxiety-inducing conversations about boys with my brother. Or my mom.

In fact, the whole ride is completely silent and I'm 100% for it.

It's been an intense day. Up close explosives are not a necessity.

♫

The house is still and quiet, like it's been abandoned for years. Just the creak of the door gives it life. The leftover smoke and sun linger on my skin. I could fall asleep right here on the foyer floor. I'd probably summon Jin again if I did that, though.

Diamond is totally asleep. Guess I worried for nothing. I take a picture for my story with the caption "the chillest" and post it. The silence is barely broken by distant popping and shimmering. I bet I can see some sky flowers from up here.

My phone vibrates. It's Jin.

JP: You back?

JB: Yeah. Diamond is sleeping. How's Zany doing?

Ellipses.

JP: For how high-strung she usually is, fireworks don't seem to bother her.

More ellipses.

JP: There's a great view from my balcony.

Yes. That's the first thing that comes to mind. Even though I could just curl up under Lena's fluffy blankets and pass out, all I want to do is go to him. Can I do that?

I don't know where keeping it friendly ends and "taking advantage" begins. Actually, I doubt this twinge of guilt has anything to do with Jin's company.

I don't want to disappoint Lena. Which reminds me that I still have to make sure Jin doesn't let the couch sleeping incident slip.

Buzz buzz.

> *JP: It would be a shame if it were wasted on just me.*
>
> *JP: But it's okay if you're not up to it.*

He doesn't make it easy to say "no," does he?

> *JB: Be right over :)*

I'm hopeless. I like him. The evidence is right here on my screen. And blundering in my heartbeat.

God, I like him.

But I'll be careful. It'll be nothing more than watching explosions in a dark sky and agreeing that Lena doesn't find out about him accidentally staying over. That's all.

So… I'm walking over to his house now.

When he opens his front door, he greets me with a smile and I remove my flip-flops. Jin guides me up the stairs into a low-lit, pristine bedroom I haven't seen yet. His parents', probably. There's a balcony through French doors that are draped with sheer curtains. I see the first firework sprinkling over the horizon before I step outside.

Pop!

The loud booms and soft shimmers are muffled by distance. Jin leans on the edge of the iron rail. He looks peaceful in the dim flashes of color. That warm, summer night wind finds me, my heart rate lowers.

It really is a good view. Of course, the sky is only part of it. I have to pull myself together. GOODNESS.

"I wanted to clear something up, Jin," I start, all peace fleeing. "About yesterday."

"Sure," he says.

"If my brother found out you'd slept on the couch with me, he'd probably flip." It's easy to use Carson as an excuse. Easier than revealing Lena's feelings, anyway.

"I won't say anything," he says, while looking at the view. "Don't worry."

"Like, not even to Lena," I add, for posterity.

He smirks. "You don't have to say that again."

Okay. Good. He gets it. We're cleared up.

Pop! Fireworks are like champagne, spritzing the stars. Happy Birthday, America.

I glance at Jin's cast. "It's too bad you missed out on Americanafest *and* Cabo." I keep my eyes on the glittering sky. It's too pretty to look away.

"I'd rather be here," Jin says. I peek at his lit-up face, not expecting at all that he'd be looking at me.

But he is.

Oh man, I'm glad it's dark and he can't see me blush so hard. I land my eyes back on the sky, but I'm not really watching. I can't look at Jin.

Bang! Pop!

But I do say, "Me too."

Track 12 - Space Age Love Song

So far, my tactics for avoiding Jin have mostly succeeded. I pretend that the call feature doesn't work on my phone with Jin's contact. I have no reason to call him. Except that I want to.

When food or music aren't enough to distract me, I look at the listing for the beach house I booked for this weekend. Sometimes that helps. Mostly not.

The night of the Fourth, I acknowledged that I'm catching feelings for him. Which means I also have to avoid him. I've spent this week with the bulk of my focus on scheming again, even though I'm sure it'll fail. Given my own feelings about Cale's competition and all.

Jin has texted me a few times. More than a few.

But that's beside the point. The *point* is that I had to try really hard to accomplish three things:

1. Find some event that worked with both Lena and Cale's schedules,

2. Try to get them to cozy up at said event, and

3. Keep Jin away.

I expected the third would involve making him sit apart from Lena. I was wrong.

The first was simple. There's an 80s double feature night at the old Main Street Theater tonight, and they both are free. And so is my mopey brother. I invited him because he loves *Ferris Bueller's Day Off.* Also, he whined about being bored and wanting to hang out with me all day.

Dressing up for 80s night is encouraged, so I went with a simple Jennifer Grey *Dirty Dancing* look. High-waisted jean shorts and a white crop top. Lena showed up with a flamingo pink off-shoulder sweater, leggings, and a side ponytail. Even that doesn't look dumb on her.

The second task remains to be seen since we haven't seated ourselves yet. I just have to get them seated next to each other. I'm currently scanning the wine-colored velvet seats and formulating possible seating arrangements.

The third task turned out to be easy because even though I fully expected Lena to invite Jin, she didn't. I don't know why. It's taken a lot of mental energy for me not to ask where he is tonight. I might've been looking forward to having an accomplice, even if he's counterproductive to Cale's relationship goals.

I've limited texting with Jin. He told me more than once how impressed he was with my singing. Even though a lot of people tell me that, my heart still flutters with him. I've been really careful to keep responses to a single word or emoji. But not the winky emoji. Never the winky emoji.

Oh, I have an idea for how to arrange the seats!

Lena, Cale, and Carson are beside me in the aisle, the lines of each of their faces lit by the track lighting by our feet.

"Hey, I'm gonna use the bathroom real quick," I tell the others. "Squeeze in, I'll take the edge."

"I'm coming with you," Lena says without skipping a beat.

I deflate, hopefully not visibly. But my mission hasn't failed yet. I just hope that my bladder is full enough to keep up my deception.

We walk into the green tiled room with fluorescent lighting, but before the door fully shuts Lena says, "What's going on, Joy?"

I whip around. "What do you mean?"

"I *mean*, are you happy in your relationship?"

I frown. "Yeah, why?"

"Because... I don't know. I'm starting to wonder about you two."

Oh no oh no oh no.

"We're fine," I try to assure her.

"Was Cale really fine with inviting Jin to Americanafest?" She folds her arms. "I saw his neon green cast in your picture."

I freeze, looping between guilt and irritation. "Was there something wrong with that?"

"You told me nothing happened!"

Guilt is winning at the moment. "He had no plans, so I invited him. Cale didn't have a problem with it."

Her jaw tightens. "How did you *know* he had no plans?"

Irritation is winning now. "He told me. Was I not allowed to talk to him?"

She doesn't answer for a second. Her brow turns up and she releases tension. "You're right. I shouldn't have thought you wouldn't even talk. It's just..." She looks at herself in the mirror. Even under fluorescent lights, she's stunning. But past all that, where people don't often see, she's conflicted.

"I asked him to come. I didn't say it was a group thing, but he wasn't interested." She sighs. "Things aren't really happening between me and Jin. And I can't decide if I'm, like, scared it'll never happen, or if I'm fine with it because romance could wreck what we have." Lena looks at me, and then groans into the universe. "Ugh! But I want to kiss him so bad."

For once, I understand the feeling. I watch her eyes shift on her own reflection. I don't want to hope that she won't be with him. She's moving up to Seattle for him. I doubt he's told her about Korea, though. For once, I kind of pity Lena.

"By the way," she segues, "you and Cale have gone further, right?"

I look away, flush with nerves. "You have photo evidence of how far we've gone."

She puts up a judgmental finger. "Wait, that forehead kiss is how far you've gone? How can you hold back like that?" She grips her glittery phone and pulls up the picture. "Cale's so awesome. And he has *such* nice kissing lips."

I raise an eyebrow at her and turn to lean my hip against the garish bathroom counter. "Are you jealous of my boyfriend's nice kissing lips?"

To my surprise, Lena's eyes go wide. She blinks rapidly but says nothing.

My heart leaps for a second. *What if she actually is?*

"I'm not jealous," she finally says, "I just don't get how you can be so slow. It's torture!"

"Well maybe I'll invite him to my beach house this weekend," I say. Entirely joking. The mocking inflection and goofy expression convey it. There's no way I'd invite a boy to stay over with me.

I only do that by accident. Guilt wins again.

"You can't do that!" Lena says with an odd urgency.

It startles me. "Obviously I was joking."

"No! I mean, we have our lake trip this weekend."

I frown. "What lake trip?"

"Carson didn't tell you?"

"Carson? You made plans with Carson?"

"He texted me out of the blue and said we should book my cabin when he goes back to working at Victoria Lake. Our moms worked it out. They never told you?"

All at once, I'm fuming. It's suddenly very clear what happened. I storm out of the bathroom and head across the geometric carpet to Theater 1.

Carson whined about being bored all day. Carson texted Lena. Carson saw my beach house booking. Carson planned a family trip behind my back.

Carson definitely jacked my phone.

In the low, shifting light of the trailers, I find his spirally hair and bolt to him. He's shoveling popcorn in his mouth completely unaware of my fury. I reach the row.

"We need to talk," I say, not bothering to keep my voice or anger toned down.

He furls his eyebrows at me like there's no way I should be as mad as I am. Prick.

I yank him by his buttery hand out of the theater and into the hall, passing Lena as she sits next to Cale.

"So what's this I hear about a lake trip?" I accuse.

There's zero amusement in me, but he chuckles anyway.

"Damn. Lena ruined the surprise."

I roll my eyes. "You did it on purpose!"

He scoffs. "How could I do that when you never talk to me anymore?"

"I *know* you searched my phone. Find anything interesting?"

His brow goes up like he's the one who caught me in a lie. "Yeah, actually."

My stomach sinks. "What?"

He narrows his amber eyes at me. "Who's Jin?" He pronounces his name like *gin* instead of *gene*, which makes it more irritating. "You seem pretty cozy with him, for a girl with a boyfriend."

I can't tell if he's figured out that Cale and I aren't really dating or if he thinks I'm cheating.

Carson rubs the back of his neck, looking smug like he has me pegged. "Then you plan some secret trip to the beach. I *know* you didn't tell Mom about it."

I go slack-jawed. So he thinks I'm cheating. "Are you seriously trying—"

"Guys!" I hear, in a partial whisper coming from the entrance to the theater. It's Cale. My throat constricts. "You're missing the movie!"

Carson turns around, positioning himself directly in front of me. "We're fine, Cale. Be back in a minute." Carson doesn't exactly *sound* intimidating, but he is. It's all under his breath and in his stance. Cale definitely catches on.

"Okay, see you in there!" Cale flees, and I don't really blame him.

Deep breath. Carson turns back around.

"You had no right to go through my phone," I say. I keep almost all of my rage controlled, but there's still a tremor in my mouth and a worm in my chest.

He sighs, as if he's the one being reasonable. "Joy, when you don't tell me what's up, what choice do I have?"

He's infuriating! "You didn't even call me when you lost your freaking job, Carson!" I'm so exhausted trying to keep his feelings in check while weighing the risk of having my choices used against me. "You could have just asked me! I didn't think I had to tell you that I wanted a weekend to myself! You didn't have to sabotage it."

A tear rolls down my heated face. Normally I wouldn't unleash like this, but I'm so done with his games.

He throws up his hands as if he's tired of this. As if *he's* the victim. "I'm going back to the movie. We can do this later," he says.

As he swaggers back into the theater, it hits me. I'm not afraid he'll have an outburst. He already did all the damage he wanted to do.

No. I'm not staying in proximity to that jerk for the next four hours. Cale's romantic exploits be damned. I'm leaving.

I pass the muffled sounds of screeching brakes and explosions in some other movie. My stomach turns at the saturated smell of popcorn.

I don't look back even for a second when I walk into the parking lot. I slide into my car and drop my forehead onto my steering wheel. For once, I thought my brother and I might actually have a nice time. How idiotic of me.

I don't even know all of what Carson found out from stealing my phone, but I know I have to change my passcode. And worry a little bit about him texting Lena, now that he has her number. I seriously doubt she'll fall for his games (since she plays with the best of them), but I am worried he might make her think that I have a crush on Jin. Which is true, but I don't want her to *know*.

Honestly, I wonder if that would even matter anymore. In the short seconds between her doubting her own feelings and asking me about Cale, I was almost... happy.

You know, right up until I found out my brother purposely stole my phone and sabotaged my beach plans.

I sigh as I insert my keys into the ignition, but I pause before turning the beater on. The old-school theater lights flash into my car. It's not that I don't want to go to the Garcias' cabin at Victoria Lake, but I wanted some event to call my own. To think. I'm facing the drastic life change of starting college, with Carson around all the time.

The truth is, I'm likely to give in and go to Victoria Lake. Not to appease Carson, though. I'm *really* struggling to care about him right now. More because I want Lena and my mom to be happy. Canceling my solo trip isn't that hard. It's the kind of painful that's intense for a second, like ripping off a bandaid.

I try to start my car, but it just shudders.

My phone buzzes.

CB: *You better come back soon*

Jerk. I don't text him back. Instead I slam my phone on my passenger seat and groan in frustration. If I have to deal with him for at least the next week and half, I'm seizing this night for myself.

I try my engine again, but it just sputters and never lights.

I stare at the FredU phone case that sits in a flashing stream of yellow light.

I know I shouldn't call him. I was doing so great with all the avoiding.

Screw it. I call Jin.

The phone rings. He picks up right away.

"Hey, Joy," he answers, his voice as pleasant as ever.

I stifle the edge left in my voice. "Hey! Um, you aren't by chance up for giving me a ride, are you?"

It's quiet for a long second, but it might just be that my heart is pounding extra fast.

"Sure! Where are you?"

Wait, really? "Uh, at the movie theater. The one on Main Street."

I sniffle. He heard it. *Great.*

"Are you okay? Is something wrong?" I look out my windshield at the flashing bulbs of the vintage movie sign. 80S NIGHT DOUBLE FEATURE.

"Yeah, I'm fine. My dumb car just won't start."

"Oh, bummer. Well, I'm already downtown so I'll just be a few minutes."

"Oh. You are?"

"Yeah. I had a late dinner with my parents. See you soon, Joy."

"Bye." I hang up. Stare at my phone. Did that just happen?

I put my phone in Do Not Disturb. I don't really feel like dodging notifications tonight.

I get out and slam my door with residual anger. Then I see a glimmer in the driver's seat.

My keys. I locked them inside. Well, at least I'll have an excuse for why I left it here overnight.

Ugh. This is so me. I lean against the car and kick her with my heel.

A loud engine rumbles nearby. The kind that you know can't be an economical car.

Or a car at all.

I catch sight of the Harley that rolls into the parking lot, ridden by some guy covered in black leather and blue jeans, like James Dean. It's not until the motorcycle stops right in front of my car that I realize it's a Korean James Dean. Of course it is.

He cuts the engine and takes off his helmet. That does it. Jin's the sexiest guy I've seen in my life, no holds barred.

"Hi," I say, still dazed. "You didn't mention you'd be on a bike."

"It was the first day I could take it out after my cast came off. Oh, crap! Are you afraid of motorcycles?"

I shake my head, despite the fear that clearly grips me.

But that's not any worse than the dread that punches my gut when I see Carson jogging my way.

"Hold on," I say to Jin.

I meet my brother halfway. Oh, how I loathe his stern look of disdain. "What's this?" he accuses.

Any other day, I swear I would keep the peace. Not today. Not after what he did.

"Jin's taking me home," I tell him. I'm high-key frustrated. "I locked my keys in my car. And believe it or not, I don't *want* to go home with you right now. So let it go, okay? Go and enjoy the movie you were dying to see all day!"

"Hey!" He's offended. "I wanted to spend time with you! I should be the one to take you home!"

"Carson! Will you listen?! I don't want to go home with you!"

"What's the matter?" Jin says. He's off his bike. I've never seen him look this serious.

"He's my brother." It's not an answer to his question, but it also is.

"Is this that Gin guy?" Carson almost seems amused.

"Oh my god! It's *Jin*! He's my friend." This is so juvenile.

"No, no. I wanna meet the guy who begged my sister to come watch fireworks, even though she has a boyfriend." Carson steps forward. What an ass.

Jin doesn't shrivel backward like Cale did earlier.

I put my hand against Carson's chest. "Be cool! He's just my friend, okay?"

Carson looks down at me. "I can't let you go with him." He looks up at Jin. "Sorry."

"Shouldn't she decide that?" Jin asks, a small flame in his words.

"She's my *sister*," Carson fires back.

"Yeah, not your dog. You don't own her." Jin shakes his head like he shouldn't have to make that argument.

Carson presses his chest against my hand. I panic. "Carson. Carson! Please, don't."

He looks back at me, seeming at a loss for what to say. He's not angry with me. "You're not going, right?"

It's like he thinks we share one brain. One heart. But we don't.

I glance at Jin, then back at my brother. I can't believe I'm doing this. Because it's guaranteed to blow up in my face later.

"Yeah, I am," I say. And then I back away.

Carson stares at me, hurt that I didn't choose him. Eventually, he accepts it bitterly. "Okay, yeah. But you just tell *him*—" he points at Jin—"that he can look up my name if he wants to know what I do to guys who mess with my sister."

I look at Jin to gauge his reaction. His brow is up, like he wants to know if Carson is done yet.

"See you at home," Carson tells me, the words steeped in bitterness. And then he walks back to the theater, whipping the door open with all his force before he disappears.

I don't know what he'll do now. Probably dismantle everything.

Jin holds his helmet out for me. "Come on, I wanna take you somewhere."

Track 13 - Style

I'm not sure if I'm ready for the terrifying thrill of riding on the back of a motorcycle. I hold Jin's helmet in both hands and chew my lip at his proposition.

"If you're up for it," he adds.

I so am. It's at least a thousand times the thing I would rather do than go back inside the movie theater.

"Where would we go?" I ask.

"There's this place across the river that makes donuts fresh at night. I hung around after dinner so I could get some."

Late night donuts?

"It's my treat," he adds, with one of those irresistible smiles.

I nod. I motion to lift the heavy helmet on my head, but I pause. "Wait. Don't you need a helmet, too?"

Jin leans over the satchel attached to his bike and pulls out a smaller helmet. "That one's better protection. You should take it. Oh! And this, too."

He shakes off his jacket and gives it to me. Obviously he's wearing a white t-shirt. I put the jacket and helmet on, feeling about fifty pounds heavier. The helmet flattens my hair and muffles my hearing, but it's worth it when Jin gets close with that jasmine scent of his and secures it for me.

And it's even more worth it when I slide behind him on his Harley and wrap my arms around his waist before we lurch out onto the road.

Immediately I sense danger. It feels ridiculously insecure. Like, I feel more secure on a kitchen chair, and believe me, I fall off of those easy enough!

The violent wind races past, with the streetlights and cars that seem so much bigger from on top of a motorcycle. I cling to Jin for dear life every time we are near a semi-truck.

When I catch my breath, I think about how Jin feels under my arms. He's skinny. I can feel his ribs and flat stomach. I love how his fluttering t-shirt tickles my fingers

My stomach flips when another semi-truck passes us. I squeeze Jin and feel him laughing.

I've taken this route a dozen times, but not like this. Once I'm past the fear, there's a thrill that I've never experienced. We're suspended between life and death, tightly bound together by my flimsy muscles.

It's the closest to an adrenaline junkie I've ever been.

Once we exit the freeway, he finds a spot to park and the slow down feels like we're treading mud compared to the freeway. I'm desperate to take this helmet off and hear properly again.

But now that my physical body is safe, all I can think about is if Jin's going to ask me what Carson meant.

He can look up my name if he wants to know what I do to guys who mess with my sister.

My head feels light as a balloon once it's free of the helmet. Static and all. Jin carries it for me and gestures to the street block lit by yellow and pink neon signs. Our path to this niche donut shop.

Jin walks beside me, looking like a pillar of classic style. I look like I was swallowed by black cow hide and then electrocuted, most likely.

I'm just *waiting* for him to ask at this point. I'll be in a torturous mental loop until he does.

"You're not gonna ask?" I start.

"About what?" Obviously he wasn't obsessing over it like I was.

"About my brother. He only threatened you so you'd bring it up."

"Maybe that's why I'm not asking."

Hmm. That's nice. Someone who refuses to play Carson's game.

I examine the black sky. It's hard to see stars in the city's light pollution. As we walk, I wonder if I should just tell Jin what happened.

I see one tiny, flickering star. There are some that shine through all the fake light, I guess.

"Promise me you won't actually Google my brother's name."

Jin nods reassuringly. "I promise."

So far, he's been good on his promises. I should leave it there.

I see people lined up before I see the shop. This hole-in-the-wall place must be amazing. But the draw could be the novelty of donuts at night. Or both. This part of town looks too sketchy for this many people to crowd for mediocre donuts. Sure enough, I read the neon sign, in bubblegum pink: FRESH DONUTS NOW.

Once we're near the window, I catch a glimpse of the rotating display hosting tons of odd-looking donuts. Cereal, crushed oreos, pink, orange, purple. Some look normal and delicious. One of them has bacon on it.

It smells divine, like icing and grease with sugar dust in the air.

Most of the donut names on the chalkboard menu are innuendo or straight up profanity, yet people order like it's nothing. I go for the chocolate one with Cocoa Puffs on it. Jin grabs the Oreo one with peanut butter drizzle. Of course, the clerk with electric blue hair is pierced and tatted because it would be offensive if she weren't. She takes Jin's cash and barely even hands us our donuts before she shouts, "NEXT!"

We walk out and now I get the appeal. It looks delicious, but mostly it's weird. An escape from the mundane.

"So you were going to brave this by yourself?" I say to Jin.

"Yeah, but I'm glad I didn't have to."

We take the emptier blocks back to his Harley. I bite into my triple chocolate cake donut. It's soft and even warm, the cake gives to my teeth. I don't think two whole minutes go by before mine is gone.

I clear my throat and peek at Jin, halfway through his donut. To be fair, his donut was larger.

He's really not going to ask. Not even in the silence.

Here goes nothing.

"My brother beat up a guy that was forcing himself on me," I blurt.

Jin chokes on his donut.

"Oh my god!" I put my hands to my mouth. "Sorry! Sorry."

He puts his hand up. "It's okay! Don't be sorry. I just wasn't expecting you to say that."

"After what my brother said, I felt like I owed you some kind of explanation."

He clears his throat. "Joy, you don't owe me anything. I don't care what your brother said." I appreciate the sympathy in his eyes. "But I'm sorry for what happened to you."

I shrug. "It's over now. But it was a big deal at the time. The guy Carson beat up went into a coma for like a full day. Plus, he was the mayor's kid. The only reason Carson didn't go to jail was because our families reached an agreement. We'd all stay away from the media and none of us would press charges. It saved their reputation, I guess. Political people are obsessed with image, you know?"

He nods. "That was last year?"

"Yeah. In Salem."

His face is tense. He says "hmm" in acknowledgement but his mouth is shut tight.

"Anyway," I go on. "My mom worked for the mayor, so she left her job. And Carson lost his scholarship to OSU because even though we couldn't talk to the news, local media published stuff about him anyway. Which is totally bogus because they made him out to be some monster who unleashed his wrath on an innocent politician's kid. He's overprotective, but he's not a monster." I sigh. "That's why we moved up to Willow Haven last year."

It's easier than I thought, retelling my past to Jin. I can tell he's at a loss for words, so I point to his donut.

"You gonna finish that?"

"I'm really sorry, Joy."

"It's fine. It's your donut."

He shakes his head, catching up to my humor. "No, I mean... you know what I mean."

Even though I was kidding, he still offers me his donut. I refuse, but remain impressed with him. Continuously. The pink and yellow neon hues bounce off the perfect lines of his slightly sad face.

I'm happy for his concern, but sometimes it sucks to hear that people are sorry for something they have zero control over. They wish it never happened, I get it. But that's the burden of sharing. When someone believes you, you hurt them.

So, even though I was the victim, my autopilot reassures everyone who's sorry.

"I'm okay now. I mean, it still comes back. And I still feel guilty because I just watched, frozen, while my brother smashed a kid's head in at a party."

This part. This is the part that hurts the worst. No matter how many times my therapist told me to remember *it wasn't my fault*, I carry it that way.

"I always felt like I should have tried to stop him," I say, my voice a pitiful wisp. The echoes of therapy play in my head. *His mind was gone, his body was on a mission. You could not have stopped him.*

Always followed by a flicker of the shameful thought: I didn't *want* to stop him.

"He could've stopped himself," Jin says.

My heart stops for one beat. Somehow him saying it makes it feel true. Words coming from a guy who actually exhibits self-control, and remorse, and doesn't let himself get manipulated.

Jin Park is the opposite of me and my brother. I'm sure Carson will hate him for it.

But I love him for it.

I swallow. "I'm sorry my brother was such a jerk to you earlier."

Jin shakes his head with a mouthful of donut, like I shouldn't be apologizing for him. We arrive at his bike and he leans on it.

I continue trying to make up for Carson's failings. "He's protective, clearly. But I was really upset because I found out he was planning this lake trip with Lena next week—totally behind my back—and now I have to cancel the beach trip I just booked."

"Why do you have to cancel?"

Because I don't want to upset my brother. Because he'll tell Lena whatever he thinks he knows about me and Jin if I don't appease him, if he hasn't already.

But I can't exactly tell Jin that.

I cock my head. "It's not like I don't want to go, it was just a sucky thing for him to do. Carson's just... afraid of losing me, I guess."

It's really weird when the truth that's been under the surface just flows right from your own mouth and you weren't expecting it. But that's it. Carson doesn't want me to leave him.

Jin finishes his last bite of donut. "What if I said that my mom and I got invited to the cabin next week and I could, maybe, go too?"

My eyes go wide, feeling like my body is champagne bubbles. "Like, for real?" I sound the tiniest bit too eager, but if Jin's coming to the lake then I'll happily cancel my plans.

"Would you like that?" His question is adorably wary.

I can't say this out loud, but *hell yes, please stay in a cabin with me!*

"Yeah. I'd like that." I don't try to hide my smile.

Track 14 - Bad Liar

I'm beginning to think Lena was on to something with that whole "you can't pack for vacation in a couple hours" thing. It makes a big difference when you're *trying* to look cute. Mom and I are supposed to leave in an hour, but I'm skeptical of my ability to decide by then.

I'm about to give up on that and just pack all of Carson's hand-me-downs, since my vintage stuff is really not conducive to camping activities.

I don't think Carson said anything to Lena. She's been strangely silent on the subject of Jin, so I really don't know. But sitting with my traitorous romantic thoughts made me realize that I should try not to be so excited. Jin is still off limits and Lena is worth my loyalty.

I've had friends betray me before. I won't be one of them.

Oh, I give up. I stuff old sweatshirts and gym shorts into my suitcase.

I should probably just admit the truth to Lena. At least about Jin. Maybe Cale, too. I don't know. I don't want to foil Cale's plans, either.

Ugh! What do I do?

Like a silent movie on repeat in my brain, I see Jin's smile in the glow of neon signs. The flickering light of fireworks. The different times he opened his front door. I imagine what he looks like by the light of a bonfire.

Buzz buzz. It's Cale.

CT: *I've got a surprise for you, Becker!*

Ooh! I'm intrigued. I wonder what it could be.

CT: *I've been keeping it a secret for a while*

JB: *Well? What is it?*

Another car? One that doesn't need new spark plugs or a timing belt? Maybe one that doesn't need an oil change every three months just to run?

CT: *You will be graced with my presence*
CT: *AT VICTORIA LAKE*
CT: *BOOM*

He sends me a gif of a mic drop.

JB: *You're coming??? What?! How did I not know this?*

CT: *Me and Garcia have been keeping it quiet*
CT: *Imma cannonball that lake SO HARD*

My shoulders loosen when I laugh. That dork.
Wait. He schemed with Lena??

JB: I can't believe you connived with Lena!
JB: Does she know it's all a ploy to get her to like you?
JB: How's that going, btw?

Ellipses. Ellipses.

CT: It's hard to get the girl you like to notice you

He sends me a gif of Jim Carrey, arms outstretched, saying "LOVE ME" which is definitely something I could imagine Cale doing in real life.

JB: Lol good thing you'll have lots of time with her at the lake

CT: good thing indeed :D

Maybe he'll pull it off. Getting himself inserted into our multi-family vacation is a genius move.

"You're not packed? What, you don't want to go?" Carson says, leaning in my doorway. His tone is like I'm twelve years younger and not twelve months.

"No, I do. Just…" I turn away from scattered clothes to face him. "Did you say anything to Lena on eighties night?"

He drops the arm that was propped up. "I didn't tell her anything. I just said you started to feel sick so I was taking you home. Then I left."

He *covered* for me? "Why?"

"Why do you care what I said to Lena? What if I said something to your boyfriend?"

"Because… Cale won't misunderstand. But Lena will."

"Why? 'Cause she likes that guy… Jin whatever?"

"God, Carson! I'm not going to explain it. You're the worst person to tell secrets to."

"She does, right?" he solicits, but I ignore him.

I stand up and gesture to the door. "Just get out. Please."

He suddenly registers my words. "What do you mean I'm the 'worst' person to tell secrets to?"

I glare at him. "Seriously? You constantly hold stuff over me! I can't tell you anything without you bringing it up as some sort of collateral."

He doesn't leave. "What are you keeping from me now?"

I'm so exhausted with him. "Get out!"

He doesn't. He bolts into my room and grabs the suitcase so freaking fast.

Slam! Oh my God! He threw it against the wall.

When did my hands cover my face? I don't remember doing that. I'm tense all over. My clothes have littered my room.

"Dammit, Joy! What are you keeping from me, huh?" His voice booms, but it also rings with fear. I bring myself to look at him.

It's not anger on his face. It *is* fear.

"Carson..." I mutter.

He folds, crouching to the floor. "I'm sorry."

My pulse calms down. What does he think I'm keeping from him?

Mom crashes into the room, her mouth and eyes round. "What happened?" she says repeatedly, placing her hands on Carson's shoulders.

"It's nothing. I'm okay. I'm fine."

I'm confused. Those words are coming from his mouth, not mine.

What's with him? First he *doesn't* tell Lena or Cale about Jin picking me up and actually covers for me. Then he flips out when he thinks I'm hiding something from him. And then he... calms himself?

This isn't my brother.

♫

Sitting shotgun next to my mom reminds me of the time the whole family visited Victoria Lake when I was little. But this time, my ears have grown AirPods and we don't play the alphabet game the whole way.

The trees pass by to my summer playlist, keeping me company for the hour drive. Then we arrive.

Victoria Lake.

Vintage-style signs direct our car to the lodge, swim park, and lakefront. Mom follows the arrows for Cabins 91-130.

The further we are from the resort entrance, the more nature takes over. The cedars tower high and the roads are less manicured. I see some gravel roads leading to the cabins. I had no clue the Garcias would settle for an unpaved driveway.

Familiar cars are parked by the cabin. Lena's mom's Land Rover. Jin's Mazda. Cale's Hyundai. Now my mom's car is parked among them.

When I get out, it sounds like the moms are competing to see who can greet with the highest pitch voice. Normally I'd eavesdrop like a proper introvert, but this cabin...

I mean, it's not a cabin. It's a mini cedar mansion. Lena's family must like double story windows, because the angular panes reach into the sky. So big, you can see right through the house to the backyard.

I grab my things from the car. Angela, Lena's mom, directs everyone. She has a handle on life that I can't comprehend. I don't know how we're made of the same chemicals.

And there's a reason Lena is gorgeous: because her mom is. Angela is the Greek side, with black hair in shiny, loose curls and the same bright green eyes as her daughter.

Lena bounds down from the front deck to greet me, her hair swinging behind her like *Baywatch*. "The boys are getting my room since it has two twin beds. The moms have the other two guest rooms, so you and I get to share the pullout in the basement. Promise it's not drab *at all*."

I laugh because I love it when Lena pretends to care about things like whether or not I care about a basement being drab. "Great," I say. "Where's…"

I hope I don't seem eager as I look for him.

"Cale?" she finishes. I nod. *Sure. I meant to say Cale.*

Angela overhears and says, "Oh, he's in the kitchen with Jin. Cutting watermelon, if you're hungry."

"I am so hungry, it's not even funny," I say to Angela, and she scrunches her nose at me in acknowledgement. Her attention goes right back to my mom's probably invasive questions.

"Go ahead and find the boys. I gotta talk to my mom," Lena says.

The boys. Of course she lumps all of the male species into one term.

I run inside because I really want to see… the fruit. Just the fruit.

The place is gorgeous. I feel like I'm constantly entering beautiful homes with arms full of my unworthy belongings. Yes, I did bring my trademark pillow and blanket.

This cabin is huge and airy, with exposed beams in the super high walls. That pleasant brown-red of cedar colors the inside, until the white and black fur floor coverings break the scene. The grey boulders of the fireplace climb one side of the living room.

"There she is!" Cale's voice bounces against the walls and I look over to see his two lanky arms open in reception. One of his hands holds a watermelon triangle. I drop my stuff on the espresso leather couch. The contrast of it is ridiculous. Fashion Barbie, enjoying a luxurious leather couch. I mean, she's a billionaire, so why not?

I smile at Cale but... I'm distracted by Jin putting force into the chef's knife as he cuts the watermelon. I approach the kitchen island and he has the nerve to smile at me.

I pluck a triangle for myself and take a bite. It's so perfectly sweet, firm, and overly juicy. At least food is also distracting.

Jin's eyes flit up at me for a second. He makes another cut, smirking. "I see you brought your usual things."

"Of course!" I say with a mouthful of watermelon. It's already dripping down my fingers.

Cale snags a new piece. "Clearly, she's not a shy one," he says to Jin.

Jin laughs. "No. I knew that already."

Oh, goodness. It seems I have a reputation among *the boys*.

The front door shuts and Lena walks in. She beckons me to leave my snack and check out the basement, so I grab my things and follow.

Down here is certainly darker, but the track lighting gives it a movie lounge vibe. There's a huge black leather sectional that should really be two couches. Lena's already pulled out the bed. The beams make it seem like the walls are higher than they are.

"Movie nights are so fun here!" says Lena. "Perfect for *cuddling*."

"If it comes to cuddling," I say. "I'm glacial, remember?"

"I wasn't talking about you," she says with a laugh. "But jeez, get a move on. You can't even cuddle?"

"I can't even flirt yet. I don't know how I ended up in a relationship."

Yikes. Lying still stings. I kind of don't want to do it anymore.

"Lena, can we talk?" She gives me her attention. And I freak out internally. I can't do it yet.

"It wasn't too awkward when I left you at the movies with Cale, was it?" I say.

"No! We're buddy-buddy now," she smiles. "Actually, that's how I set up your surprise."

Yes. The surprise.

"Oh, really? Thank you! It's a good surprise." I hope I'm selling the *I'm happy my boyfriend is here* thing. I mean, I am happy to have Cale around, but Jin was the bigger prize.

Ugh, I wish I didn't feel so guilty right now.

She flashes a smile. "I'm also super glad Jan-di convinced Jin to come. At first he said he didn't want to ruin a girl's trip, you know, when it was just you and me and all the moms. Guess he changed his mind."

He did? Holy crap, *he did?!* Was that for me?

The hopeful part of me wants to think so. Because if he even has a sliver of the same feelings as me, I'd be over the moon. And really conflicted. Now I'm not sure which feeling is right.

But the fearful part—the greater part—watches Lena tap the spines DVD cases on the shelf. She's in love with him. She picked her college so she could be near him. Even if Cale did get her to notice him, he'll be at FredU with me. Honestly, we'd probably all be better off if Jin and Lena end up together. Cale would survive the rejection and so will I.

But that hopeful part of me is a lot bigger than it was yesterday.

♫

We spent the day swimming at the lake, and I can't wait to spend long hours doing that all over again. I had a pineapple snow cone hand delivered to me by my brother. For a while, Lena and I just tanned and watched Jin and Cale race across the strip of sand, crash into the lake, swim to the buoys and back. I had my bets on Jin, but Lena bet on Cale and she was right. Jin lagged a tiny bit behind. It was wildly amusing. Among other things.

One perfect lake day down, four to go. I'm actually glad I cancelled my plans.

Lena walks up fresh from her shower, interrupting my reading. I'm not really paying attention to the magazine, though because I keep thinking about college. I don't know why I'm starting to question my choices now. In my head, my major was always finance because it made good sense. But now I'm wondering if I should've explored other schools. I bring it up to Lena.

"God! We have at least a year before we have to figure out that crap, Joy."

Lena stands over the bed, fluffing the down blankets and smoothing them so we can get to sleep. The basement carries more of Fernando's taste than Angela's. I think this is the only place he's allowed to display Dallas Cowboys paraphernalia. I get up and drape the Cowboys throw over my arm, dark blue with a silver star. I wait for Lena to tidy our bed.

"And that plan is approved by your mom?" I ask.

She grabs the blanket from me. "I tell her Portuguese. But when she really interrogates me, I stick with political science."

"Political science?"

"I mean, I'll take a class to see if I like it. When Mr. Allen did Puerto Rican week in Lit, I started to really wonder about the politics of my heritage. So *yeah*, I'll double major in poli-sci and dance." Her laugh is like caramel, sweet and smooth and a little sultry. "You still majoring in *finance?*" she asks, using some awful form of a British accent conveying mockery and fanciness.

I throw a pillow at her. "At least I never argue with my mom about it."

Lena finishes making the bed, then turns and drops backward onto it. "I wish I had your mom."

My right brow goes up. "No. You really don't. I wish I had *your* mom."

"Oh my god, Joy. You have no idea how wrong you are. My mom has a deep, deep dark side."

Lena always talks about it, but I sure haven't seen the "dark side" of Angela Garcia. She's treated me wonderfully. She's a pillar of success in the community with her commercial real estate business. She even told me that I'm her favorite of Lena's friends.

And seriously, as if Fernando Garcia, keeper of the world's best chocolate chip cookies, would stay married to someone with a "deep, deep dark side."

I plop next to Lena on the just-made bed. "Can I ask you something?"

"Mmhmm." I can tell she's sleepy.

"When did you know you'd fallen for Jin?"

I feel kind of bad for gauging my own feelings against hers, but that's why I'm asking.

Lena bolts up to sitting. "Don't be so loud! Oh my God!" She rakes her hair with her fingers, laughing at the nerves.

And then she tells me the story.

It started with her getting her braces off in middle school. She was a kid when she got them on and a woman when they came off. The sudden sex appeal was brutal on her self-esteem, which surprises me. She got a lot of attention, good and bad.

"All fake," she says. "I got asked out every day. It was like a game to them. No matter what I did, I lost."

Oof. I've never related more to her.

Going into the summer before high school, Jin's family decided to take Lena with them to Korea. Lena lights up when she talks about it. I can picture the scenes as she describes them: the top-notch, steaming Korean food, being bombarded by different customs, learning ritual phrases and making them laugh when she mispronounced things. I'm not jealous that she's well-traveled, but going abroad with people who take care of you like family makes me wish I were her.

Her brightness fades. "Then came the first day of high school. It was a freaking horror show."

She takes a deep breath, like I do when I'm steadying myself.

"What made it so bad?" I ask.

"I'm not stupid, you know?" She's not really asking me. "I know what I look like. But the first day of classes, word spread that there was a *new hot chick* in school. People flooded the halls during first period just so they could get a look at me through that stupid slitty window in the door, like goddamn paparazzi. I thought it was gonna be eighth grade all over again. But, then I found Jin at lunch and sat with his friends to eat. He knew what was up, so he just told people to back off and they did because they respected him." I don't usually hear Lena's voice so low or genuine like this. "There's no other guy out there I respect as much as Jin. I don't really know when it happened, but... I realized that I can't lose him."

Wow, that makes me feel selfish. Here I am with a schoolgirl crush like all those other girls Lena mentioned and here she is way beyond just *loving* Jin Park. He changed the whole game for her.

I fixate on one corner in the ceiling, where the crown moulding doesn't quite meet. Is Jin worried what Lena will think of his opportunity in Korea?

I wonder if she's the reason he's struggling to decide.

"Anyway," she says, yawning. "I'm wiped out."

"Me too," I say, though it's not really true. But it doesn't matter what I say. The dark lashes of her eyes are already closed even though the lights are still on.

It doesn't matter if I'm a bad liar or a good one. I doubt I'll ever have a chance with Jin.

Track 15 - Forever Young

July 18th

There's something so wonderful about the way summer leaves a layer of different things on your skin. Smoke from a bonfire, sweat and tan from direct sun, the musty smell of lake water in your hair.

And if we're talking about me, the dried watermelon juice on my arms.

For hours, Cale and I have been swimming in the lake like we're a pair of preteens. With adult-sized cannonballs. I beat him breath-holding, he's clearly a faster swimmer, I'm better at Marco Polo, and we're about matched in splash wars.

He's definitely got me beat in the bright smile department, though.

I'm not sure if you can call the sand patch a beach, but it's packed with swimmers and tanners. The docks, too. I'm out by the boundary of buoys around the swimming area. I can see out into the grander portion of Victoria Lake, where people fish and zip around on jet skis or sit in swan-shaped pedal boats. I definitely want to learn to water ski someday.

Bobbing in the cool lakewater, I glance over to land and witness squealing little kids in adorable baby rashguards, ketchup-covered hot dogs in their pudgy hands. Lunch sounds like a good idea. Especially once I spot my brother walking to the snow cone stand to start his shift.

"I'm heading landward," I tell Cale, and paddle myself in that direction.

"Understood, Almond Joy! I'm gonna float on for a bit." Sure enough, he splays himself out and relaxes on the water surface.

I make eye contact with my brother and he smiles at me from beyond the dude so clearly flirting with him. Even if he was a jerk for upending my plans, I can't stay mad at him. I still see the kid who grew up with me. The one who smashed ice cream in my face as often as he willingly shared a single cone. He adjusts his hat and does "the nod."

It's our thing. At baseball games, he finds me and nods from the pitcher's mound.

I nod back. I always will.

Water from the swim drips down the length of my body, tickling my legs. I slick back my dirty blond hair and run toward our group's spot. The sand sticks to my feet, then the hot concrete path pricks them, and then my soles are caressed by supple green grass. I don't blame the moms for not swimming among overeager kids.

Jin claims he forgot his bathing suit, but I overheard Jan-di say she wanted to spend time with him because "she never see him when he at school." It seems like he's engaging the moms pretty well.

Lena clearly prefers sunbathing to swimming. Might more accurately be called "summertime man-catching." But, even with her bright pink bikini that hugs her youthful Latina curves, she straight up ignores how "nice" the men are toward her today. The guy she fell for is probably the least superficial guy in her life, maybe apart from Cale.

But even he makes elaborate plans to get her attention, I guess.

I yank the blue striped towel from the ground and use it to dry my face and scrunch excess water out of my hair.

A toddler in a forest green swim diaper waddles up and touches my leg. He has adorable round eyes with impossibly long eyelashes, big rosy cheeks, and brown curly hair that reminds me of Carson.

"Hawoh!" he says, looking up at me with a toothy smile. What did I do to deserve such a cute smile? Seriously, I've been getting way more than my fair share lately.

Jin kneels down to him and holds up his hand for a high-five. "Hey, little guy," he says, and the boy slaps his hand.

Awwwww! I feel like Kristen Bell seeing a cuddly little sloth.

"Oh my gosh! I'm so sorry!" says the mom. She's a petite woman with long wavy hair, who snatches the boy up with a confident grasp that only moms seem to have.

"It's okay!" I tell her. I kind of love when kids break social boundaries like that.

Jin stands up and says with utmost charm, "I hope my future kids are as cute as yours."

"Ha, thank you," she says graciously, and I know she blushes because, like, *how could you not?!* I'm blushing behind my towel and it's not even my kid!

So Jin Park wants kids someday. Noted. Man, I didn't think that sort of thing got to me.

"Your boyfriend is really nice, Joy," says Angela, and I revert back to reality. She's stretched out in a lounge chair with her wide-brim hat, flipping through a home decor magazine.

"Where did you meet him?" she asks.

"Glee club," I answer. Jin takes a breath to say something, but Angela commands the verbal baton.

"Your bathing suit is so cute," she says, like my answer didn't even register.

"Really? Thanks." Her comment surprises me. It's just a plain and modest navy one-piece with a sweetheart neckline. I mean, it's fine. Lena's is way more glamorous.

"You should dress more like her, Lena," says Angela, not skipping a beat.

"Mom!" Lena says, like a bite. She turns her head the other way, having none of it.

"You dress too sexy. Guys minds go crazy—"

"Mom!"

Angela doesn't stop for even half a second. "Jin knows! Tell her."

My mouth drops open, but I close it right back up. Jin cocks his head and I notice he's stopped breathing. He lets out air with a small laugh.

He doesn't dare remain unresponsive. "I don't think it should matter what girls wear. Guys will always think things." Safe answer. I'd verbally agree with him if it wouldn't offend the Garcia matriarch.

"What do you *prefer*, though?" she asks him, pulling her sunglasses down to peek at his face.

His brow lifts. "Mrs. Garcia, I don't think—"

"Oh come on, Jin. You're like my own kid. Like a brother to Lena. Your opinion matters to us. Come on."

There's the dark side.

Lena is stoic, with arms folded and glare in the opposite direction. No matter what he says, Jin is doomed at this point, I think.

"I prefer a girl who's confident, no matter what she wears," he answers.

This guy. Pulling a rescue move on a collision course. I hinder a smile and wipe my neck of the sweat beads I earned during this conversation.

Angela pulls her sunglasses back into place. "Well, I don't know who raised you, but she did a pretty good job."

Lena uncrosses her arms mouths "thank you" to Jin.

So maybe it wasn't "deep, deep dark" like Lena had described, but I see now why Angela Garcia is not to be messed with. Unless, of course, you're the irresistibly benevolent Jin Park.

♫

I slam cards on the glass coffee table. "Told you not to mess with me, Thomas!"

"Again!?" Cale groans.

"Tired of being slaughtered at this game?" I taunt.

Jin laughs, still shuffling the cards in his hand as if I didn't just beat him, too. Three times in a row.

Our second lake day was a success. Once we finished hamburger dinner at the cabin, the moms cleaned up and called it a night, presumably to read similar romance novels. Lena went for her nightly shower, so I got left with *the boys*. I did what all teenage girls would do and hustled them into a game I'm good at.

The smell of fresh shampoo hits me and I notice Lena's walked up. She shakes her damp hair, dressed in a cute fluffy cardigan and leggings. It's the opposite of me with my post-swim blonde mess and hand-me-down hoodie and gym shorts.

"We're doing s'mores, right?" she asks.

"Did you say *s'mores*?" Cale asks in monotone. He smacks the table, startling the cards right out of my hands, and darts to the kitchen.

"Guess that's a 'yes'?" Jin says with a grin and I just laugh. He helps me pick up the scattered cards. And our hands touch. I feel electricity. That's the only word I have to describe it. I'm staring at the table and Jin's hand takes a second too long touching mine, or is that me?

I retreat.

"Sorry," we say in unison.

"I got this," he offers. I nod. I'll let him take clean up. Yep. I'm gonna go outside and shake this tingling feeling off my hand.

Before I reach the sliding door to the backyard, though, I pass by the mudroom. Out of the corner of my eye, I see Lena reaching for something in a cupboard.

Cale is with her. I seriously doubt s'mores ingredients are in the mudroom, but right away I sense that they're having a private conversation. I won't eavesdrop, but...

Sometimes I overhear.

"You know you've got game, Cale. There's no need to hold back."

What?! I fumble opening the sliding door. Is she... is this actually working? I dash outside and try to forget about what I just heard but also I'm obsessing over it.

In the twilight, I start the fire with some old newspaper and a lighter. I always hold my breath in the moment before a small fire grows into a blaze. I wait for it to catch.

Cale and Lena were just *whispering* in private. Maybe I've been too pessimistic and Lena's hesitation is because of Cale.

I sink into a fabric lawn chair coated with pollen and dirt. The bonfire glow flickers and I'm the sole admirer for a minute. Closing my eyes, I breathe in the faint smoke in the air. The image in my mind is Cale hand-in-hand with Lena.

"Hey," I hear. It's Cale. "I got something I wanna tell you."

"Yeah?" I say. *That the girl of your dreams finally noticed you??*

His mouth twitches to and from a smile before he pulls his hand out of his pocket and holds a small paper out to me.

I take it. "A business card?"

???

"Yeah. Read the name."

The Crux Constellation. Robbie Gonzalez, Manager.

"What's this for?" I turn it in my hand. It has their constellation logo.

Cale takes a seat next to me. "They saw us at the festival. Well, and they saw you sing. They said you should call them." He smiles with his pearly white teeth, then bites his plump bottom lip.

They want *me* to call them?

"Weren't they doing a farewell show?" I ask.

Cale shrugs. "You know, kid, I don't know everything! But I think they liked what they saw." He looks into his lap and says reservedly, "What's not to like?"

I catch his dark eyes. He looks away.

"Well, anyway…" he says, scratching his head.

"She's not out here, you know. You don't have to pretend to like me."

"I don't pretend to like you, Joy." The fire pops.

Was that a confession or… just him saying he likes me in general? I can't tell.

I open my mouth to say something, even though I'm not sure what, but the cabin door slides open. Jin and Lena walk into the backyard, and she shakes the ingredients to show us that they have all been acquired.

Food. Distraction. Thank God!

I grab a poker and secure a marshmallow on it. I try my best to attain perfection. Tan all the way around. Cale is the burn and bubble type.

I'm still so confused by his mood. By what Lena whispered to him. Was she flirting? It sounded like flirting. But what the heck did he mean by "I don't pretend to like you?"

Did his feelings change? This whole time, this has been about him and her. Not me. That "surprise" was nothing more than him doing legwork on his own plan. He came here for Lena.

Even though he's been spending all of his time with me. Sitting next to *me*. Waggling his eyebrows at *me* as he eats his chocolate-and-graham-cracker sandwich. He's goofy and fun and adorable...

My marshmallow catches.

"Shoot!" I blow it out. Though a tiny bit charred, it's still perfect. I put my s'more together, and then glance across the fire at Lena and Jin. They talk in some attractive, orange-glow conversation that I can't hear. It's unreal the way her hair falls on her shoulder, dark and long and just messy enough. She's way beyond "league." The amber flickers of light caress her cheekbones and soft lips. I'm just the girl who's thumb fiddles with a new hole in the sleeve of her brother's rejected sweater.

Jin laughs generously at something she says out of the side of her mouth. It's probably one of the hundreds of inside jokes they have. They're primed for each other.

God, I have no chance. He's just a fantasy and I've already hurt Lena by letting my feelings get to this point.

Cale grabs my s'more hand, breaking me out of the trance I was in. He's leading it. *My* dessert. To *his* mouth.

I resist. "Hey! You have your own!"

He smiles with a full mouth, a small piece of melted marshmallow on his face. "Mine's not sweet enough!"

In what universe is it possible for a s'more to not be sweet enough?

Suddenly he pulls my arm hard and with the momentum, lands a kiss on my cheek. My heart feels like a book getting all its pages flipped at once.

I don't pretend to like you, Joy.

Lena noticed and she grins, eyes sparkling with satisfaction. There's no way she's jealous.

I yank my arm back, but remember to turn on the courtesy. Nervous laugh. Force a smile.

"You really shouldn't mess with a girl's s'mores," I tell him.

"But they're *my* girl's s'mores." His dark eyes glimmer with a smile.

That was real. Wasn't it? Is he playing still or was that real?

Nervous laugh. Force a smile.

I stick another marshmallow on a stick and start roasting again. Pretending I'm not freaking out is the best course of action. This could still be an act, so… yeah. Play it cool.

Cale's lips move in a circle while he chews. He grins at me, having won my first s'more.

Crap! This one's set ablaze too. I continue making another sandwich with it anyway. Please distract me, little dessert!

I peek over at Cale and he's giving me his best impression of a sad puppy.

"Make. Your. Own," I say as I lift my s'more to *my own* mouth.

He snatches my wrist and I instantly resist. "Cale!"

I pull away and start giggling, mostly because his wide open mouth is goofy enough for me to know he's being playful. Back and forth, I give it all my effort and then…

My s'more flies out of my hand.

It smacks Cale square on his cheek on the way down. He tries to catch it with his big, pink tongue, but misses. It plops sadly on the ground.

Cale whimpers, positively dejected.

The image of his tongue contorting to catch the food replays in my head and I cannot stop laughing! I snort, which makes me crack up even more! *Wheeze!*

"I'm glad to know my massive fail was so amusing," Cale says sarcastically.

My stomach hurts! There was no chance for that poor tongue! I snort again.

"Okay, okay! I'll make one for *you* now!" Cale says. I nod, fighting residual laughs.

I'm glad *something* calmed my nerves. I look over at Jin and they come back.

He was watching me, if that grin means anything. Lena garners his attention back to her.

One thing is really unclear to me right now: Cale's actual feelings.

But two things are very clear. One, that I've definitely fallen for Jin.

And two, I can't have him.

If Cale has somehow shifted focus onto me, that might change things. I mean, Jin will be gone no matter what. Cale's around. Maybe it makes more sense to choose him.

I just never thought there might be a choice.

"There we have it," Cale announces. I lean out of my lawn chair to grab it, but he holds it out of reach.

"Mmm, I think I need payment."

I stand up. "Um, no! You owe me that sugar sandwich."

His finger points into the air. "But this one was made with love. It can only be bought with a kiss." He taps his cheek.

I shake my head and giggle. "No!"

"Fine," he says, and holds it out to me. But once I reach for it, he pulls it away again.

And then his free arm is wrapped around my back, pulling me up close to his body. My heart flutters and I look up at him in surprise.

And then he kisses me. And not just a peck on the cheek. His mouth is warm on mine, lingering, sending sparks through me like the embers of the fire pit.

A *real* kiss. My first real kiss.

My eyes blink rapidly as my brain catches up. I feel his exhale on my cheek as his hand presses my back, bringing me closer to him.

My heart is leaping and in shock, all at once.

"She said NO!" Jin's commanding voice cuts through the crackling fire.

Cale suddenly releases me and I stumble back. Smoke and crickets color the tension.

Jin's standing up, glaring at Cale, who's frozen in Jin's smoldering anger.

"Jin! Jeez," Lena says, rising from her chair and pulling her cardigan more closed.

Cale looks between me and Jin, a little panicked and unsure. Jin's stern look is harsh by the firelight.

"It's okay," I assure Jin. Keep the peace.

Don't let him get out of control.

My old turmoil swirls up from my stomach like vomit. Jin's not Carson. Cale's not Tyler.

It's not going to happen again.

"S-sorry… Joy," Cale says. The s'more cracked in his hand a little, but he holds it out to me as a peace offering.

I take it and thank him. Eat it. Nothing happened. *We're all walking away.*

Jin quickly simmers down from battle-ready to annoyed, which is relieving. When he turns to me, his eyes ask if I'm really okay. I nod. I am okay. But my heart feels like it just got tilled. I don't think I have room for Cale. Real or fake. I want Jin so much. It's clearer than ever.

But I know I can't have him. So I have to get over him somehow.

Track 16 - Rainbow Connection

It would be an understatement to say that I didn't sleep well, because my dramatic, thumping heart didn't really let me sleep at all. What a *pain!*

It would be an understatement, then, to say I "woke up" early. Or is that an overstatement? Really, I got out of my borrowed pullout bed around 5:50 AM, praying that no one else would get up at such a crazy hour and I could finally be alone. I cannot sort through my feelings and socialize at the same time. Apparently.

When I was a kid, my family came to Victoria Lake for almost 3 weeks. For an eleven year old from the most boring part of Oregon (other than Boring, OR), the mid-summer break from life at a lake resort might as well have been years in a magical hidden kingdom. We memorized every trail, counted a hundred ant hills, learned how silly we could make campfire stories if there was enough Pepsi to keep us awake.

One thing I remember vividly is the Secret Pond. It might more accurately be a secluded pond with a waterfall, since I doubt the only people who discovered it were a couple of kids. But it's off the beaten path, enough that I doubt anyone will be there this early. So, now's as good a time as any to find it.

After putting my bathing suit on under gym shorts and a baseball tee, I pack my mustard yellow Fjallraven backpack with a towel and a water bottle. I'm planning to bring some snacks, and then I'm gone for a couple of hours.

Alone. The only way to sort my heart out.

I head upstairs into the fresh dawn coming in through the massive windows.

The fridge door closes and my heart throbs. *Now* I remember that there's one other person who gets up this early.

Jin.

He stares at me, holding an orange juice carton and glass. "Good morning," he says, looking like a deer in the headlights.

"Morning." I try not to make conversation as I head to the sink to fill up my water bottle. The granola bars are on the counter behind him and so I'm, um, not gonna pack those.

"Going somewhere?" he asks.

"Yeah. Going on a hike. Be back before breakfast, probably." I purposely use as few words as possible. I've already spent way too much time with Jin on my mind. Like, his face, or the way his voice sounded, or his stance when Cale kissed me.

He downs a glass of orange juice faster than my water bottle gets filled.

Get out before he says something!

"Bye!" I say. I walk fast, trying not to seem like I'm escaping. Probably failing at that. Oh, well.

I hit the pavement and try to find peace in the quiet drum of my sneakers. What brings it is the birdsong and sun rays that warm up the leftover coolness of night.

There's the sign. CAPER TRAIL. Carson once said it was named after an unsolved mystery involving stolen jewelry they found buried here. He also said the jewelry belonged to Queen Victoria and that's why they named the resort after her. My kid-brain marveled at his twelve extra months of wisdom. Even though that was bogus.

Something about this place brings out a lot of memories of Carson. The good ones first, when we were best friends. The sour ones where he suddenly became obsessed with his image. The bad ones, then the really bad ones. *Breathe.*

It strikes me as odd that, right after he slammed my suitcase against the wall before coming here, he didn't storm off or scream profanities.

I'm okay. I'm fine.

Rubbing his eyes with the heels of his hands. The anger actually leaving. Something was different.

My shoes crunch on the gravel and I trace the edge of the path with my eyes, searching for the split boulder. That's my marker. My legs are already warm from trekking up the hill. I can already tell from the bright sun rays that it's going to be hot. I doubt it's even 7 AM yet.

The split rock emerges into view. I remember Carson jumped up and perched like a grasshopper. Then he leaped off and clung to the side of the hill. It's maybe a 70-degree angle, covered in ferns and trees and some weed-like plants.

I bet I can beat you to the top, that boy told me.

Bet not! I was always up for a challenge. Carson launched up the side, gaining traction with his grip strength and determination. I don't call him "Racecar" for nothing.

My feet stop right in front of it. Maybe this hill can help me feel better like it did back then.

I didn't come here to think about my big brother, yet I can't stop. Maybe this is what I've been putting off. At the end of summer it'll be me and him again. College classes, baseball, vague commitments to associations and an excess amount of Northwest coffee. It feels like a lot. These feelings I have… they've been a welcome distraction.

I've been staring at this hillside for a little too long. I'm still gathering the courage to climb it. Even though little Carson is long gone and he won't be reaching his hand down to help me up, this hill reminded me how much I love him. And maybe, I can still love him even if I don't want—

"Joy?"

I jerk my head to the left. It's Jin, in his AMER-I-CAN tank that flaunts his shoulders at me. What is he doing here?

And why did it have to be him?

He jogs closer.

"Why are you staring at this…" He can't think of a word to describe what I'm looking at. Probably because I'm not staring at anything in particular. I'm just gaping at a wall of plant matter covered in dew.

"Lost in thought, I guess. Why are you here?"

He scratches the back of his neck. "I, um… I don't really have a good reason." There's blush around his shy smile.

Maybe it's selfish, but I laugh. He's nervous. Questions flutter around me like butterflies. Should he really be here? Should I really want him to be? Does he like me the same way I like him?

Am I really going to ignore Lena's feelings and let this go on?

Though it should all be answered with "no," my soul is yearning for "yes."

Burning for *yes*. So maybe I am the burning type.

I point to the part where the hill curves to a stop. "There's a pond up there. I don't know how else to get there except climb up from this rock."

"How do you know?" His curiosity is achingly endearing.

I grip the straps of my backpack. "I stayed here one summer when I was a kid."

He nods and examines the same hillside. "Then let's go find it," he says and he doesn't wait for me. I follow him like the fool I am.

Jin scales it like it's nothing. I'm not nearly as nimble or long-limbed. And believe it or not, vines and ferns are not great for climbing. They tend to break under the weight of any-size human. Jin clears the top while I continue to struggle. I'll fall if I'm not careful.

If only tumbling down the hill were the only danger.

"Here." His hand descends to me. It's just within reach.

A flood of those feelings race back to me. When I was a kid, I couldn't imagine anyone better to lift me up. It's no different right now.

Jin Park is the person I lend my weight to, guiding me to the point of no return.

Who am I kidding? That point was long ago.

Coated in dirt and sweat, I pull myself over the edge, into another world that is seldom broached. There's no path, no disturbance. Just the singing birds and sunbeams, the smell of earth and drying dew, and the flush of excitement.

"I hear it," Jin says, smiling on one side. The faint rushing of a waterfall. I look around. Nature rarely lends to familiarity, but this feels the same as it did years ago. We tread through the brush toward the sound and I spot the rocky clearing.

I race there like I'm eleven again, snagging Jin's hand on the way. I didn't think about it.

I've had butterflies with Jin for a while, but I don't remember when I crashed so hard in love. It could have been when he reached for my hand a second ago. It could have been when he stood up for me last night. It could have been when he showed up on his motorcycle or when he invited me to watch fireworks. It could have been when he grabbed my hand and helped me up from the tile foyer floor. It doesn't seem to matter now. I'm already done for.

I drop his hand.

"Sorry," I say, assuring him with a small smile. "I got carried away."

He shakes his head, then beams at me. "It's fine."

Then, the sight captures him. I'm taken with his impressed expression. It's almost as enrapturing as this place is.

There's the small waterfall, the fence of trees, the rocky shore, and the glittering pond reflecting a pale blue sky. Jin walks to the water and the reflecting sunlight gleams onto him like he's some kind of angel.

My backpack crashes to the pebble-covered ground. I lift my baseball tee off and bend down to unlace my shoes. Jin's steps are wobbly on the rocks as he walks toward me. He pulls his shirt off in one swift motion.

"You're not dressed to swim," I say. That was his excuse for not swimming last time.

"I don't care about that." He grins and uses his toes to remove each of his shoes. Then he dashes to the water and crashes into it without a care.

It looked like an ocean when I was a kid, but now... it only feels that way.

Smooth, water-worn rocks massage my feet as I walk to the pond. Jin lays facing the sky, floating atop the settling ripples.

I shuffle into the cool water, my steps wavering on the rocky ground. Soon I let the coldness envelope me and go under. Water falls away from my face when I surface and a shiver travels through my entire being. I position myself to float on my back like Jin, allowing my legs to float up. A breeze blankets me as I stare into the clear morning sky.

I'd stay here forever if I could.

The water beneath me shifts. It feels like a giant fish and freaks me out! I squeal and fold, instinct kicking in. I try to escape before using reason.

Jin breaks the surface looking as smug as I've ever seen him. His black hair lays flat and shiny, his cheeks round in laughter.

"You scared me!" I splash a wave at him. He pushes a bigger wave back at me and it hits my face, pulling my hair in a wet sheet over my face.

I laugh at myself. At this crazy circumstance. This beautiful morning, where Jin Park followed me to a secret paradise and smiled when I grabbed his hand. Where he made fun of me and now looks at me as if I'm the best part of all of it.

Without a doubt, I share that look.

He bites his wet lip. My heart races even more than it did when I was on the back of his motorcycle. Like we're suspended in danger all over again.

Am I really doing this?

Yes.

This is all I want. Maybe I never wanted to be alone. Maybe I always wanted him to show up, unexpectedly, and fill my days with this.

But... *Lena.* I know why she's head over heels with him now. Everything about him is inviting, not just his perfect, genuine smile or his warm laugh. It's the way he approaches you with respect and obvious desire for connection. His infectious happiness. His refusal to shy away from conflict and confidence that shows up even when he doesn't know what to do.

I wish I could be like him. But I'm not. I can't escape the image of deep hurt I might see on Lena's face if she knew everything. I'm not ready to disappoint her.

Diving under, I drown my thoughts in white noise. *Get out. It's not too late yet.* With droplets racing down my limbs, I brave the stones, which are gaining heat in the aging day. Upon reaching my backpack, I open it and pull out the towel and dry off. Why haven't I stopped this already? I've already betrayed Lena's trust far beyond the boundary of forgiveness. I look over my shoulder and Jin's following me out, slicking back his hair. Smiling.

Maybe... I'm starting not to care what Lena thinks.

I shake the towel open and lay it over the pebbles. It's rock hard and lumpy, but it'll do. I sit, placing my abdomen against my thighs, laying the side of my face on my knees, letting the hot sun wick away the pond-water from my body.

Jin walks over to me.

"You didn't have to get out just because I did," I say. He takes a seat next to me.

"I wanted to." His words are so simple, yet for me, they're loaded.

His arms are wrapped loosely around his knees and he looks distantly at the waterfall.

"I really want to hear you sing again," he says like it's a thought escaping.

I turn my face into my knees, blocking the sun, hiding my blush. "Really?" My voice is muffled by my legs.

"Well, yeah. You're amazing."

I turn my face again and meet his eyes.

I give him a courtesy smile. I'm lost for any other type of reaction that might be appropriate because my heart is losing it's cool, *for real.*

"Please?"

I lift my head. "What, like now?"

"Are you doing anything else?" There's a hint of wariness in his request and it's adorable.

I push my legs out in front of me and lean back on my hands. A flood of joy washes over me. "I guess not."

But his anticipatory stare chickens me out.

"You can't look at me like that!" I protest.

"Okay, fine!" Jin shuts his eyes, the anticipation still ever-present.

What should I sing to him? It sounds childish, but there's one song that feels perfect. *Rainbow Connection.* It's Kermit the Frog, yes, but he's existential and magical. He tugged on my spirit when I was a kid. I could sing it then, and just as passionately now.

Slow, soothing. In my head, guitar strums and violin sings, but just my voice pours out...

Rainbows. Shining, full-spectrum, their essence visible to everyone. It's a song about how people desire deep beauty and meaning, yet it's still elusive.

No wonder this song is on my heart.

At some point in the verse, I close my eyes, too. A vision of a glittering rainbow tickles my mind.

I give in to the song like it's just me. Singing to the earth, the moss, the water, the trees. Giving them life with the vibrations of my voice.

This feeling is probably magic...

The last word spreads out, growing, pulling my soul open. Then the sun is eclipsed by something. I open my eyes. Jin is close, staring. Longing.

"Can I kiss you?" he asks desperately.

Time stops. I nod. "Yes," I hear myself say, matching his desperation.

This distance, it's gloriously gone. He's kissing me, softly at first, palming my face and pulling me closer.

The music goes on in my head, the orchestra, the voice someone else's, serenading this moment. I'm floating, flying, kissing *him.*

His lips are the sparks of fireworks, the smoldering of a bonfire, the sweet taste of summer fruit. He's kissing *me!* I graze his shoulder with my fingertips.

Jin sends chills of wonder throughout me. Each move he makes, I'm further lost in a wilderness of magic. This is what my first kiss should have been. What every first kiss should be. The long-awaited relief of yearning I've been feeling for I don't know how long.

He pulls away and I witness him anew. This is the Jin Park I don't have to question anymore. I have my answer.

But I also have a brand new problem. My bliss wavers. I can't.

Jin leans to kiss me again, but I push my hand on his chest. He doesn't hesitate to respond.

"What's wrong?" Now his bliss wavers too.

I can't do this to Lena. I told myself I would never be a traitor like my old friends were. If she loves Jin at all like I do... I can't keep doing this.

Regret burrows in, a little at first, then a tidal wave.

"I'm sorry," I whisper.

"Why?"

My heart shatters. I shake my head. I should have stopped this a long time ago. Maybe she'll forgive me if she gets him.

I get up and distance myself. Jin stands up with me, confused. "Joy, what's wrong?"

I haphazardly stuff my shirt and damp towel in my backpack while searching for the point of exit.

Why does this have to hurt so much? It was so perfect.

These sharp rocks prevent me from running. I slip my sneakers on without lacing them. They hang loosely on my hasty feet.

"Where are you going?"

"I can't do this," I tell him without stopping.

"Why not?" I hear his slight exasperation. Bless him for being angry. Even that is perfect.

Don't look back.

It's time to tell Lena the truth. I should not have been so selfish. Ever. Couldn't I have just told him "no"? Why did I have to let everything be "yes" today?

I try to keep steady. I'm almost to the brush. Almost to the hill's edge.

Jin's hand lands on my shoulder and I whip around. He breathes heavy with a stern expression... no, that's hurt. His dark eyes secure mine.

"Don't run," he tells me. "Please, stay with me."

"I'm sorry." I break into a run toward the edge. I almost reach it, but I pause. *Don't run.* I don't want to. What am I supposed to do?

I turn and see him standing there, shirt in hand, his chest still glistening. He takes one step, so I do, too. Backward.

Not my first mistake of the day.

Track 17 - I'm Down

When my body figures out that I need air to survive, I suck in a breath. My ankle screams in pain so bad that my other muscles are tense. I tumbled down the hillside and landed my ankle on the split boulder at a weird angle. I'm also covered in scrapes from all the sticks that brush that I rolled down on.

I guess that's just the Joy Becker way. Give something your best shot, wind up injuring yourself. Trademarked.

My ankle throbs as I try breathing evenly. Jin slides down the hillside on his feet, as a stable person does. It looks like he grabbed the shoes that flew off my feet when I lost balance and rolled down here.

Of course he offers to carry me. It's like poetic justice. I try to avoid his affection, only to be unable to refuse being held by him immediately thereafter.

Jin helps me up on my good leg and I put my backpack on, tears streaming down my face. Then I pull myself onto his back, gripping his shoulders and collarbone as he wraps his arms around my legs. It feels like our hearts are too close and tangled.

The persistent pain in my ankle isn't as difficult to handle as the fact that I like being close to him. The bliss of being held hurts because I know it's fleeting.

He carries me silently down the path. The scent of dirt and pond water is on his skin, like fresh rain. I lay my head on his shoulder and try not to think at all. Not about how he holds me. Not about how hurt Lena will be. Not about how complicated Cale makes this, or Carson, or the fact that once summer is over, none of it will matter anyway.

"Did you follow me?" I ask him, my tone muted.

He sighs. "Yes."

There's an extra vibrant tick of my heart. "Why?"

"Because I wanted to. I wanted to be alone with you, and I didn't realize it until I was already on the path."

I don't respond, because that's exactly what I thought. What I hoped.

The sun is intense now.

"I'm sorry. That sounds creepy," he admits.

"No, it's okay. We've been alone a lot already. It's not like I don't trust you." I feel his tense shoulders relax.

Twittering birds and Jin's shuffling feet are all I hear for a minute. My lips tingle, replaying the kiss. It still feels unreal. It's also another thing I have to tell Lena.

There's a bench a little ways off, under some tree shade. Jin asks, "Is it okay if we stop?"

"Mmhmm," I say.

Though Jin is careful about setting me down, hitting the bench makes the pain shoot up my leg. I wonder what I did to it. I've never broken anything before. The radiating pain is unrelenting.

"Do you have any ice?" Jin asks me, grabbing my backpack. I don't. When he finds my water bottle, he kneels to the ground and holds it to my ankle.

"Why'd you run?" His question punches me in the abdomen.

I can't tell him about Lena. And anything else just doesn't seem like enough of a reason.

"I don't have a simple answer, I guess."

He makes eye contact. "Are you trying to protect Lena's feelings?"

I hesitate, but it's pointless. "You know about that?"

"She's not subtle."

I let out a knowing laugh.

"But I don't feel that way about her." I can tell it's hard for him, but also definitive. "She's like my sister."

"Right. A supermodel sister who isn't in any way blood related to you." My word, was that a twinge of jealousy in my voice?

Jin doesn't skip a beat. "It's not just that. I appreciate her and everything she's done for me. But, even if we had no history, she's not my type."

I don't mean to say it out loud, but I say, "And I am?"

"Is that so hard to believe?" And then he checks me out. Not subtly.

Goodness.

I laugh off my nervousness. He's been so chivalrous this *whole* time! Have I been too dense to see that he's attracted to me?

"What is it about me, then?" I ask. I don't know why Lena isn't better. She's been beside him forever. She's packing up and moving near him. She's ready, willing, gorgeous, fun, strong.

"Your confidence. Definitely." Wow, that took zero time for him to think about.

"What confidence?"

He looks up at me with a furrowed brow and adorably conflicted smile. "How do you not see it, Joy? You laugh openly, you sing freely. And share yourself with everyone. You wear what you want, eat what you want, and you fully enjoy things that Lena wouldn't bother with because it's too basic or some dumb reason."

"Did you just call me *basic*, Jin?" I ask, amused.

He laughs, then sets the water bottle down. He sits on the bench, really close to me. Touching. Making eye contact.

"Joy, you're adorable." His look is most definitely *adoring.*

A breeze brushes by us. I'm still a bit in awe of all this.

But then he switches gear. "What I can't figure out is how you keep sacrificing so much for everyone else. Even your running away was for Lena's sake, right? Unless… you don't *want* to be with me."

"Are you crazy? Of course I do!" And I mean it. So much. "And it's not just because you're amazingly handsome. You… Jin, you are a rare kind of wonderful."

He seems kind of stunned as if my words are particularly meaningful. "Wow. That makes me happy."

I'm lost in the look of his flushed cheeks and perfect lips and exquisitely messy, damp hair. His hand brushes my cheek and he draws closer.

Jin smirks. "Because I've been holding back."

My eyes flutter wide. I almost don't register what he's said before he kisses me again, deeper and more commanding. Like there was a longing he held back before. All the blood leaves the sharp pain in my ankle and rushes to where his hands are. The back of my neck tangled in my hair and firm on my hip, keeping me from floating away.

Jin pulls away, but it's like there's an invisible rope tying us together. And the best part of it all is how he looks at me. Like, how is this happening?

How did I get to this incredible moment of time? With *him*?!

I don't care if I'm injured. I could be suspended here forever, pain and all.

Like a slamming door, our moment stops. His mood shifts and he scoots away.

"What is it?" I ask.

"I'm still holding back," he says, frustrated.

"*That* was holding back?"

"No! I mean, there's still that whole deal with you and..."

"Cale," I finish. "Right."

Jin rubs his temple. "I've been so upset over it. And until now, I just felt like I didn't deserve to be. We met, like, a month ago."

Wait, *for real?* It's hard to believe.

Those dark brown eyes latch onto mine. "I know I'll intervene if he touches you. I can't play along, Joy."

I grasp his arm. "I get it. I don't want you to. Just, give me time to talk to him."

Worry burrows into me, though. I lace my fingers together. "I don't know if it's all fake to him anymore, though."

"That's more reason to end it." His words are confident and definitely at least a little jealous.

I wonder if I couldn't bring myself to talk boundaries with Cale because I didn't want to let him down. Maybe I sensed that things were different. He'll forgive me, but that's not all there is to it.

"It's not just Cale, though..."

Jin squares himself to me. "Lena is going to get hurt either way. Let me worry about her."

"You weren't the one who betrayed her trust. I was. I have to talk to her."

Jin grabs my hand. "Let's do it together, then. You don't have to do everything yourself."

We make eye contact. These peaks and valleys of emotion, like the terrain we're on, torture me and heal me. I want him so much, but traversing this won't be easy.

"You're a rare kind of wonderful, too, Joy. I don't mind fighting for that." Though he doesn't smile, I sense his happiness. It's the same as mine, hidden in some secluded, vibrant place. Like the pond where we finally kissed.

"How's your ankle?" he asks.

"Throbbing." I sigh. "Just like my heart, Jin Park."

He laughs and looks off. "I love that you say things like that."

Huh. He actually likes my dorky commentary. I take an eyeful of him. "I can't believe you exist."

He turns to me, drawing close as he says, "Do you need further proof?"

I smile in the moment between him leaning in and his lips pressing on mine again. Okay, I believe it. He's real.

It stops too soon. How does anyone ever let go?

Jin thumbs my cheek. "I'm saving the next one for when there's nothing in the way."

I'm spinning, but I somehow still have a quip. "That's a shame."

"Good motivation, though," he replies. I nod.

One really good thing about being clumsy: when you fall, you fall hard.

Track 18 - Sucker

The official diagnosis is that nothing is broken, but it still feels like everything's on fire. My ankle. My sunburned shoulders. My fear of telling Lena. My heart when I see Jin. My lungs when I think about breathing a word of this to Cale.

At least the ankle will heal.

When Jin and I came back from the First Aid Center, explaining what happened was… a balancing act of truth. We said we went on a hike together.

Not untrue. Not really enough to calm the radiating heat of Lena's anger at seeing us return to the cabin together. At least Cale was eager to believe it and move on to being my dedicated helper, ice packs at the ready.

Since I'm really good at ruining things today, I break it to Carson that roller skating is not on my agenda. He's working at the skate rental desk today after seeing the resort's physical therapist. His response was "that sucks," so it could've been worse.

So I am doing my part insisting everyone else still go while I watch. Frankly, I don't feel the need to prove just how ungraceful I am. Point's been made.

The moms, who have become the Sisterhood of the Trading Romance Novels, tell us to go on our own. I'm starting to think I should bring Angela and Jan-di to distract Mom on all family vacations.

All over the resort are staff clad in dark green t-shirts driving golf carts to get people around. We snag a ride, which isn't the easiest on my ankle, but it's less torturous than walking.

Carson is waiting at the rink, leaning against the rail that goes around the outside. It's an open air rink, covered by a gazebo. Brown pillars hold up the roof. You can feel the wind, smell the evergreens, and even inhale the dust from the gravel parking lot while you skate.

I hobble over to Carson on my recently procured crutches. He scrolls on his phone, then looks up. I messaged him about my ankle so he wouldn't be surprised, but something feels off about his expression. Like he wants to frown, but he's trying not to.

He even smiles at me. But his eyebrow twitches when he sees Jin.

My internal danger meter goes off. I forgot they met once before.

I'm pleading with God to keep this light and airy.

"Glad you still came," Carson finally says to me. Not cheerful, but not about to burst.

"I'd hate to ruin everyone else's day. I don't mind the sidelines."

Carson breathes a bitter laugh, but I don't know why. I'm always on the sidelines for him.

"Well, I'm going to leave you all in the dust," Lena announces as she passes by us. She heads to the skate rental counter, Jin following.

My heart rate bounces rapidly, but I resist the urge to look at him.

Cale's hand falls on my shoulder. "Can I get you a concession, Almond Joy?"

Oof. His light touch cuts deep today. "Just a soda," I say with a smile. He obliges my request.

"Hey!" Carson grabs Cale's attention. "I'll take first shift with her. I'm not on duty for another 30 minutes. You go get some skates."

Cale's eyes bounce to me, but he nods. I'm pretty sure Carson scares him.

"You don't have to babysit me," I tell my brother.

"I wanna talk." But it doesn't sound like he wants a friendly chat. It's a command.

I don't resist, but maybe I should. What's up with him? Maybe it's selfish, but I don't want this day to be soured by my brother.

We grab a table right next to the rink, where there's a half-wall separating tables and the skaters. There's a beat from the mid-grade speakers. The Jonas Brothers' "Sucker," but some kind of remix with more synths and bass. I'm alone for a second while Carson grabs my soda from Cale. Lena hits the vinyl floor like some kind of pro. Her hair whips behind her as she floats along with the grace of an Olympic ice skater.

She wasn't joking.

Jin looks like a toddler learning to walk, but with lanky limbs. I chuckle. He doesn't look at me though, because all of his concentration is taken up by trying not to fall.

Cale is somewhere in between them. Not miserable like Jin, but not the smooth glider that Lena is either.

The paper soda cup slams on the table. Beyond the blue PEPSI label, all of Carson's facial muscles are tense just short of revealing a specific emotion.

I grab the soda slowly. "Thanks."

"So, how are things with your boyfriend?" he pries.

"Fine." I want to keep this as minimal as possible.

But part of me knows it's not going to be a small conversation.

He squints at me. "Are you cheating on him with that Asian guy?"

I choke on my soda and start coughing. Once I catch my breath, I say, "N-no."

It's technically true. I'm not cheating. I'm just not actually dating the guy he thinks I'm dating.

Carson grits his teeth.

No. *No no no.*

"Why are you lying to me, Joy?" His mouth is a tense, straight line.

"What makes you think I'm lying?"

He knows. I'm petrified watching him pull out his phone, thumb through something with purpose. He flips the screen over to me.

A picture of me and Jin, kissing on the bench. From this morning.

I'm too stunned for words. How could he have gotten this?

"There's a PDA channel on our work Discord. I was checkin' the channels and woke right up when I saw this, y'know?"

"Carson, please let me explain this."

"Sure. Tell me why you've been lying about that guy?"

I glance out, certain there's worry all over my face. They're rounding the rink, close to passing me and my brother by.

Fake a smile. *Fakeasmile!*

Lena whips past us and smiles back, enjoying herself too much to pick up on the ominous air. Cale keeps a hefty amount of distance, which basically proves to me that he's afraid of Carson.

Jin catches on. I'm sure he does. His eyes are tuned into mine for the second that he passes us by.

Carson's eyes burn into me. "Now they're gone, Joy. Talk."

My voice is hushed. "Cale and I are faking it. He said he liked Lena and wanted to spend summer with her, so I went along with it. That's all, I sw—"

Slam! Carson's hands hit the table and my soda falls over, spilling everywhere. I jolt all over. My heart is pounding in my head.

"I'm not an idiot!" he yells.

I hold my breath and shake my head. I know he's not an idiot. If this were flipped, I would think he was lying, too.

Carson lifts his hands off the table and reveals his freshly cracked phone screen, the image of me and Jin still displayed.

Jin's body slams against the barrier. "Everything okay?"

Carson's jaw juts out in anger. But he sighs deep and meets Jin's solid gaze.

"Carson," I beg. *God, don't throw a punch.* I look at Jin. "It's okay, you can go."

"Yeah, we're fine," Carson says. Even though I fully expected him to fight, he doesn't. He just walks away, leaving the rink for the parking lot, not even turning over a chair as he goes.

Carson has been suspicious for a while. *What are you keeping from me, huh?* He thought I was cheating on Cale. And now, he thinks he's got proof.

"You sure you're okay?" Jin asks me. Soon, Cale and Lena crowd around him.

"What's with him?" Lena asks, judgment thick in her voice.

My hands cover my face.

It echoes in my head, over and over again.

Carson always, always, always wins.

But this time, when he could've bested me, he walked away.

Track 19 - Rewrite The Stars

While I'm stuck figuring what the heck I should do about my brother, Jin cleans up the spilled soda. He kneels on the ground, dabbing it with a wad of paper towels.

"Seriously, what the heck? He invited us here," Lena says, still standing in the rink with her arms folded.

"I'm gonna rest at home, I think." It's the first thing I've said since Carson left.

Jin looks up at me. "Should I come with you?"

"Jin! Come on," Lena says, "It's not like she needs a babysitter."

"You can stay if you want, Lena," Jin argues. "I'm trying to be nice."

Cale walks up to the table, skates in hand. "You're a real MVP, Jin, but I think I should escort the lady. It's kind of my duty."

Lena scoffs. "Gosh, now you're all ready to leave because Carson had a hissy fit. Guys, he's a jerk. We shouldn't let him ruin our day."

"You're right, Lena," I say, "But I kinda want to be alone. You guys should stay. Have a good time."

I'm wobbly getting up, mostly because this chair is so unstable. *Everything's* unstable.

They let me go, and I'm grateful for the lack of resistance. I don't think it's been even an hour since I left the cabin, but it feels like I lived through two weeks of turmoil and bliss today. I take a bitterly quiet golf cart ride back. It's not even one o'clock when I walk into the empty cabin.

I flop myself onto the living room couch, right in the direct afternoon sun that shines through the giant window.

Carson could wreck a lot of hearts with that picture. I finally let myself cry about it.

At least now I'm actually alone.

♫

I wake up. My tears left a dried trail to my ears. For a second, I'm not sure where I am. Every crevice of the ceiling and piece of furniture or decor is mysterious. I've never known this leather couch I woke up on.

As soon as I realize where I am, I also realize none of today was a dream.

Even though seeing Jin makes me feel like it must be.

"Hey, you're up," he says.

I unstick myself from the couch and clear my throat. Jin's in the armchair next to me with a gentle smile and every wonderful emotion hits me like that waterfall.

A muffled laugh sounds and I notice that everyone else is eating outside. Cale is doing some silly dance with his hands, which seems like something he'd do when surrounded by women.

"What time is it?" I ask with a yawn.

"Past six. How are you feeling?"

I heave a sigh. "That's complicated."

Lena waltzes into the cabin. "Oh hey, you're awake! Guess what we're gonna watch for movie night? It's one you've been begging me to watch."

Cale follows after, grinning. "The *best* movie of the decade!"

"We'll see about that," Lena bites back.

I furrow my brow, wondering what movie… I hazard a guess. "*Greatest Showman?*"

Cale claps his hands and points to me. "Yes! Thank you! Can you believe Lena's so uncultured?"

Lena scoffs. "I'm gonna go make sure we have it." She crosses through the living room and heads downstairs.

I swing my injured leg off the couch and wince. Still tender. "I could use some help."

Jin grabs my arm and drags it around his neck. His fingers are warm on my hand and his neck muscles make my arm tingle. He slides his other arm around my waist sending sparks along the path.

"No problem, Joy."

His voice is so cool, my heart flutters.

"Thanks," I half-exhale.

It isn't until Cale is at my side that I remember he was literally right behind us.

"I got your right, Almond Joy!" His hold is sloppier and he pinches my side trying to maneuver around Jin's arm. When I'm secured, I glance at Cale, whose close-mouthed smile and wandering eyes make my stomach do flips. He's too eager to mistake the gesture as just friendly.

How did I end up like this? Between two guys who both seem like they *want* to hold me?

"I'll start the popcorn!" Lena calls as she bounces up the stairs. She pauses when she sees us.

I give her a crooked smile.

Why do I feel about as unlucky as I am lucky?

♫

The popcorn wafts with a strong buttery aroma and my mouth waters. I should want more sustenance than just this over-salted movie snack, but I reach into Cale's bowl and grab another fistful.

The orientation of the young adults on this sectional is as follows: Lena on the right end of the couch, leaning against the armrest with her legs folded neatly under her. She intermittently scolds Cale for humming along. Jin sits next to her, quiet and still (other than blinking). I can't tell if he's paying attention to the movie or desperately trying to not look at me the same way I'm (failing at) trying to not look at him. He's only about an inch away from my injured, outstretched leg, meaning my petite self is taking up most of the couch. Cale is on my left, confined to the corner, hogging both the bowl of popcorn and the Cowboys throw blanket.

"You don't have to be such a blanket hog," I chide as I pluck more popcorn from the bowl.

He raises his eyebrows far too high. "Oh, really? We're goin' there?"

I giggle and stuff my face with popcorn. Plead the fifth.

He sets the popcorn on the coffee table and opens the corner of the blanket. "Well, then, snuggle on up, Becker. Or are you all talk?"

I hold my breath. I can't *snuggle*! But we're still technically faking and Lena is eyeing me.

But… Jin. We both brushed it off when Cale grabbed my other side and helped me down the stairs. Jin didn't seem jealous, but he also told me in no uncertain terms that he couldn't stand by and watch our little charade go on.

"Oh God, Joy! We don't care!" Lena assures me.

But I care! And I avoid looking at Jin because I *know* he does.

Cale flashes a goofy grin at me. "Come on! We can be cuddle buddies."

And the waggling his eyebrows makes me question if this young man has ever been serious a day in his life. My laugh relieves some of the tension, but I still feel wrong obliging.

And I still don't want to disappoint him.

We're at the part of the movie where Hugh Jackman holds out his hand to Zac Efron in an attempt to strike a deal.

Jin finally looks at me and raises his brow, expectant of my choice. Unlike Zac Efron's character, I'm not going to compromise.

It's clear who I'd rather not disappoint.

"Actually, I kinda have to use the bathroom," I say. "Could you give me a hand, Lena?"

"Oh, sure." Lena doesn't bother to pause the movie as she gets up to help me. I leave my crutches and hop into the hall, keeping steady with a grip on her shoulder. The bathroom is at the end of the hall, the movie noises becoming faint whines.

I'm glad to be out of sight of the boys. One makes my heart flip because I'm still buzzing with thrill at our shared feelings, while the other makes my heart flop because he's my friend and I don't know how to make him happy.

Distance is good right now.

I let go of Lena's shoulder. "Thanks."

"You're having second thoughts, aren't you?" she asks.

The urge to release it all rises up in me. Second thoughts? I never had first thoughts. But I'd far prefer having this conversation with Cale first.

"Yeah, maybe," I say. It's only a slight bluff. Not a full-blown lie.

"Why?" She sounds annoyed.

"Because I am. I like Cale a lot but… I don't know if our thing is working." Not a lie.

"Oh my God, Joy. Is *that* why you were with Jin this morning?"

I'm stiff. And kinda peeved she's acting all superior. "No!"

She folds her arms. "Do you like him? Just tell me."

Lena has always intimidated me, even when we shared chocolate chip cookies or cracked up at some dumb meme or studied together in a subject that I know better. She's used to getting what she wants. Now I see she can also be very patient to that end.

She's waited years for Jin. I've tried over and over not to take her jealousy personally.

But I didn't have to wait years for him. We fell together like a chord falls out of a guitar when the fingers press the right strings.

Lena's going to get hurt either way.

"Maybe I do like him," I say.

She throws her arms down and uses a hushed voice. "What? Joy!"

Then she rubs her forehead and sighs like she's handling a disobedient child. "You know he's just nice, right? Like he helps people because he cares about everyone?"

I blink at her with my mouth ajar. She thinks I'm Jin's *charity case?!* It takes everything in me not to shove it in her face that Jin came onto *me*.

But then she dabs her eyes, careful to preserve her mascara. I soften. I've never actually seen her cry before.

"Lena," I say as tenderly as I can. "I *tried* not to."

185

She wipes another tear away and launches into rambling. "When he went to Willow Haven and I was, like, a sophomore, girls were *all* over him, okay? Jin totally just doesn't realize that being so nice comes off as, like, flirting. You know?"

"I know. I get that." *Shut up.*

She sniffles. "The point is that he turned them all down. He's not a player. So, like, I just don't want you to get hurt because, you know, he's sweet and everything. If Jin *actually* likes someone..."

The next words out of her mouth are basically slow-motion. Here's a bona fide expert on Jin Park, about to tell me what he's made of. If he *actually* likes me.

"...he's obvious. And by then he's serious." She takes a deep breath and wipes her cheek again. "Being friendly is, like, his default."

He's obvious. And by then he's serious.

I fake a knowing nod. I have to pretend like her words didn't just send my heart beating into a frenzy.

Jin was certainly obvious. Kissing-me-three-times obvious.

Miraculously, I speak monotone. "Okay, well. Thanks for the info. Still gotta pee."

"Oh God, sorry!" she says, and she turns around to walk back to the movie, but she stops. "Hey, Joy?"

I crack the door open and turn to her. "Yeah?"

"I just... I care about you. Other than him, you're my only real friend."

I feel like I'm punched in the gut. Lena's only real friends are conspiring to break her heart.

Locked in the bathroom, I pull out my phone. There's at least one variable I can try to control.

JB: *Let's talk tomorrow, I'll tell you everything*

JB: I just don't want the pic to hurt my only friends

CB: K, I'll listen

Track 20 - Feel It Twice

Well, this is an unexpected turn of events. Cale's leaving. Tomorrow.

Cale stuffs his backpack full of crumpled t-shirts and attempts to zip it up, without success. I lean against the doorway to his and Jin's shared room, trying to decide if I should make the effort to break off our deal or wait until I see him again.

After the movie, I came upstairs to eat some leftover tacos (you know, *proper* food) and asked Cale if we could talk. He told me he still had to pack and the whole intended conversation got derailed.

"Why are you leaving tomorrow?" I ask him as I watch him fumble with his belongings. Jin's bed is the neat one, looking as if he never slept in it. Cale's looks like a failed omelet flip.

He pauses packing. "My mom only let me come because it's halfway to my sister's wedding. Can't believe she's gettin' hitched tomorrow." He wipes a false tear. "They grow up so fast!"

"Isn't she older than you?"

"Not the point!" He points at me for a second. Then goes back to frantic stuff-gathering. "I'm sorry I didn't say anything. I would have taken you as a plus one but Dee's keepin' it small."

Now it's like he's not even trying to cover up that it's me. I'm worried that breaking things off could sour his sister's wedding. My hesitation, with the butterflies fluttering in my still empty stomach, make me wonder if *my* feelings are also more than just fake.

I'm so confused. But I came here for a reason.

"So what did you wanna talk about?" he asks.

I open my mouth but can't speak. I want Cale to be happy so much it hurts. I'd give up the car, if it would keep that silly demeanor chugging on. I guess he must want me to be happy too, since he actually did give me his car.

"Oh, nothing serious. Just wondering if you were going on the jet skis tomorrow, but…"

I sigh. Lying doesn't ease the butterflies at all.

"If I wasn't heading off very first thing, I'd sip iced tea and watch Jin and Lena wipe out all day long with you, Almond Joy."

Cale snaps his fingers when something else occurs to him. "Hey, but we got Carson's practice game next week, right? Your mom said I should go with you."

I stiffen. "Wait up, *my* mom told you about Carson's game? She didn't even tell me."

"Oh, really?" Cale looks worried, but a sly smile curls on his lips. "Am I becoming a favorite?"

"Trust me, Carson has a monopoly on 'favorite.'" I should try not to sound so bitter in front of Cale, but being polite seems like an excessive burden. Carson literally threw my suitcase at a wall and broke his phone because I was "keeping something" from him, but he can't tell me that he's playing again? And Mom assumes I'm able and willing to go?

Cale furrows his brow in my direction. "Hey, you okay?"

I meet his round, gentle eyes. He can tell that I'm not.

"We don't have to go, Joy. I know things get tense with your brother."

I sigh. "No, I'll go. I don't really have a choice."

"Of course you have a choice," he argues, like it's simple and there's nothing more to it.

Cale doesn't get it. I know I have a choice, but the worse choice is *not* going. That choice would mean Carson would get God-knows-how angry. Since Mom babies him and Dad ignores him like he does everything else, I would have zero support in that decision. Except maybe from Cale, but he's got a wimpy track record with my brother. Not to mention that I'm the sister. Siblings are the only people who can really get it when life hands you a bad card.

I have to choose going.

I clear my throat. "No. I want to support Carson, I'm just annoyed I found out secondhand. That's all."

Cale's busy hands give up on his overstuffed backpack. He walks over to me carrying the scent of his laundry detergent. My eyes strain looking up at him, he's so much taller than me.

And then he puts his finger on my chin.

"Look up, Joy," he says. And he's smiling, like he's taking the gentle approach to cheer me up for a change.

Don't do this, Cale. Don't kiss me.

Along the soft edges of his features, his skin glows and I wonder if I should've been honest. Almost every second of the day, Cale is kind and thoughtful and hilarious. He's so good.

Why can't I tell him about Jin? Even now I'm wondering what Jin is doing, what he's thinking. I don't want him to catch sight of me and Cale.

I pull my chin from his finger, which lingers in the air like a tree branch that's lost a blossom.

"You don't have to worry about me, Cale Salad," I tell him, grabbing the crutches that lean against the wall. I hobble off, still pondering these butterflies. They're there, but they dwindle.

I don't think I'm sparing Cale because I'm falling for him. I think it's because I'm loyal to him. Maybe a romantic spark could've started with that before Jin.

But I'm not before Jin anymore.

When I enter the living room, I find Jin sitting on the couch next to Lena. He looks up with hidden hopefulness. Before I can give him a sorrowful, bare shake of my head, Lena looks up from her magazine. "Everything cool?" she asks.

I try to sound happy, but not too happy so Jin doesn't think we're in the clear. Because we are not. "Yeah, but I'm gonna go to bed. I'm pretty wiped."

Jin gets off the couch. "Let me help you."

"I got her, Jin!" Lena says, quite literally shoving him down into the leather. "God, do you always have to be so chivalrous?" Her tone is like a grapefruit: kinda sweet, kinda bitter.

Neither of us resist her. Maybe Jin feels the same way about telling Lena as I do about Cale. It's so hard to ignore that I'm crazy about him.

I doubt I'll be able to sleep much.

♫

July 20th

I did sleep. Minimally. By the time I check my phone and see that it's just past five in the morning, I can't get back to sleep.

Jin texted me last night.

> *JP: So, you talked to Cale... How'd that go?*

My fingers wake up before my brain does.

> *JB: We talked about my brother. And no other subject, unfortunately.*

I know he's not going to read it yet, but I owed him that much.

Lena is still snoring like a dainty pug. It's as good a time as any to get out of bed and test my ankle.

Better. Still aching like someone took a nail file to the muscle, but better.

I'm parched. Orange juice is calling my name. I discover I can hop up the stairs one-legged. The living room is dressed in a nice shade of robin's egg blue, light enough to see everything.

I bounce over to the armchair and rest my overworked healthy leg. Is it too early for Jin to be up?

As soon as I hear faint footsteps, I have my answer. Seeing him sets my heart smoldering like a campfire. His mussed hair, foggy eyes, wearing that same plain t-shirt crumpled a bit from sleep. I want to kiss him again. And run my fingers along the nape of his neck. And sing to him under the sky and watch the sunset on a Ferris wheel and listen to him talk about his childhood.

I'm bombarded by these desires crashing together like bursts of fireworks. I love it.

"Morning, Joy." He grins and his eyes tell me he feels it, too.

I respond with a similar grin. "Morning, Jin."

As he walks past me, he catches a bit of my hair and lets it slide through his fingers in the sexiest way possible. His eyes linger on mine, even though he walks farther away.

It almost aches to watch him pour juice from a carafe into a glass.

"You hungry?" he says.

"Oh, always."

My answer makes him laugh a little. He pours a second glass and puts the juice back, then brings it over to me.

"For your effort," he says. There's a sad smile.

I don't take the glass. "I'm sorry."

"It's okay." He stretches his juice offering out more and I take it. "I know it's not easy to break news."

Jin averts his eyes. He must be struggling with letting Lena know. How can I blame him?

"Eggs?" he asks, heading back to the kitchen.

I sip my juice and give it a thought. "French toast?"

"Whoa, that's a bit romantic. What will our moms think?" He smirks and I laugh thinking of when I took over making French toast for him.

We have inside jokes. Me and Jin. I could get used to that.

"What's romantic?" Angela emerges from the hall. She pulls her black curls into a ponytail as she walks toward the kitchen.

My laugh halts. "Nothing," I answer, trying to sound light.

"It's a joke," Jin says, sounding far lighter than I did.

"Because it's French?" she asks, then reaches into the fridge to get the eggs.

Sheesh. She was totally eavesdropping.

"Yeah," Jin says. Maybe it's because I know him a little better now, but there's a hint of reservation in his answer. He totally suspects that she was listening, too.

I'm actually happy when my mom's clueless energy enters the open space and offers to whip up German style crepes instead of French toast. It's weird that she's up so early, but I'm not asking questions. Conflict-avoidance is my specialty these days.

We all end up at the dining table while my mom does her 1-2-3 crepe recipe: one cup of flour, two cups of milk, three eggs.

The others are a bit slower to rise. Jan-di is the first after about an hour, Lena about a half-hour after that. She doesn't speak a word to me. Or to anyone else. She grunts for a mug of coffee as her first conversation of the day in exactly the same way her dad does.

As soon as she has her *second* cup, we'll have the Lena we all know and love. Too bad she drinks it like a caffeine-addicted sloth. At least the conversation, or rather debate, the moms are having about the staying power of *shiplap* is riveting entertainment.

Finally, an hour later, Cale gets up. He practically darts into the living room like he's hopped up on six shots of espresso.

"ImlateImlateImlate!!" He plucks a rolled up jelly crepe and it dangles out of his mouth while his backpack swings around on one shoulder. He slides his feet into his sneakers and takes the floppy crepe out of his mouth.

"I'd give a speech about how grateful I am for all this, but I've already wasted too much time explaining why I'm *not* giving a speech, so THANK YOU and GOOD DAY!"

This kid really needs to learn how to utilize the alarm feature on his phone.

Cale stuffs the crepe back in his mouth, cheeks full like a chipmunk's.

We ring in a chorus of polite goodbyes. The door slams and leaves us in an awkward quiet.

Now that he's gone, I regret putting off the conversation. Sometimes you don't know if you made the right choice until there isn't a choice anymore.

"Cale really is something, Joy," my mom says with admiration. She glances at Jin's empty coffee mug and offers to pour him more. With his mug in one hand and the coffee in the other, she says, "How do you like it?"

"Oh, I'll take it how you like it, Mrs. Becker," he says with an insane amount of charm.

Angela slices a bite of her crepe and lifts the fork just in front of her mouth. "Isn't he just a dream, Karen?" She eyes him and bites. "I wonder why you're still single."

"Give break to my boy, Angela!" Jan-di says with her own mouthful of crepe.

"So, Joy, think you and Cale are gonna last?" Lena blurts out before blowing the steam off her coffee.

We all kind of stare in shock at her.

"I'm not sure where my daughter left her tact," Angela says, "but I'm sure she just means to ask how things are going with you two."

Sure. That's why her comment was juxtaposed with the topic of Jin's relationship status.

"Things are fine," I answer safely. "We get along really well."

"You must be kinda sad he's gone now," Lena says.

If only she knew why.

I stab my eggy pancake with my fork. "I don't think I'm more upset than his mom would be if he missed his sister's wedding, so I'm okay."

"Oh," she says, finally straightening her back from the gollum hunch she had over her coffee. "Well, I'm sad you'll be missing out on the jet skis today."

I sigh. Today is jet ski day.

Yay.

♫

Lena's less snooty when we get to the rental shack. It's probably because she gets to ride a jet ski with her arms around Jin.

Now I *really* regret running from him.

The moms decide they'll take turns keeping me company (which is wildly unnecessary, but there is no talking these women down). The off-duty moms, starting with Jan-di and my mom, ride a tandem paddle boat.

This clear, 85-degree Saturday afternoon was apparently very tempting to the local population, because all of them are at this lake spot. Lots of little kids run around and squeal and cry. There's an ice cream puddle on the pavement and hardly any sand peeking out from under all the laid out towels on the manufactured beach. I'm lounging in a fabric folding chair on the grassy section, failing to get lost in my book.

I can't keep my eyes from wandering over to Jin in his navy swim trunks and bright orange life vest. His slight slouch is more obvious from this distance.

Maybe it's just me, but that K-Pop idol of mine sure glitters in the sunshine.

Lena rides up on a sunflower yellow jet ski, wearing an apple red life vest. Her glistening skin reminds me of the shining coats of mustangs in classic paintings, especially with her high ponytail whipping behind her like a majestic tail.

Angela sits next to me, sipping an iced coffee through an emerald green straw and flipping through a magazine in the shade.

"The Parks are leaving early tomorrow. Yuno's back from his business trip already," Angela says, without even looking up, though it's hard to tell what her eyes are doing under the wide sunglasses that cover half her face.

Yuno. Jin's dad, the lawyer, and the reason he's studying law. That sensation of recognition hits me again.

My eyes fall on the bright blue paddle boat in the distant part of the lake. Mom's laughing while Jan-di's arms flail about.

"They seem like they get along well," I say without much thought.

"Hmm?" Angela says. My gaze is on my mom and Jan-di, but somehow she traces it to Jin and Lena. He's helping Lena off the yellow jet ski onto the dock.

"Oh yes. They always have. Jin and Lena," says Angela.

I look at her. She takes another sip and smiles. "They'll be good together."

What now?

I stiffen. "What do you mean?"

She clears her throat and puts her drink in the grass. "They're suited to each other. Life's gotten in the way, but it's just a matter of time. Lena's never stuck to any other guy before. It's always been Jin."

I square my shoulders to her, eyeing her with subtle frustration. "What if they don't want to be together?"

She takes her sunglasses off and pierces me with her bright green eyes.

"Why do you care, Joy Becker?" She says my name like I'm a lowly peasant and Jin and Lena are royalty.

Lena was totally right. Her mom is a piece of work.

It's odd to be stuck in a public place, where your world stops, but the rest of the world still goes on around you. Kids lick melty ice cream, teenagers laugh in fits, someone lathers sunscreen on someone else. And here I am, an inch from unraveling.

I want my seams to give and throw every contradictory punch I have at her. *Actually, Jin chose me and has never looked at your daughter that way, so THERE!*

Jin's voice echoes in my head, though. *It's not easy to break news.* I owe it to him, even to Lena, to let Angela have her assumptions and play her games. I won't bite.

I want to run, but that's literally impossible at the moment, so I lie.

"I *don't* care."

Angela folds up her magazine and places it beside her. "Joy, you may think that us moms don't pay much attention to what goes on with you guys. But we do. We have to." She folds her sunglasses, knowing she has my attention. "We have to protect our kids. Our homes. You didn't think I would let some random friend of Lena's have total control of my house without some checking, did you?"

A sharp breath escapes me. Tears manifest and I dread whatever hangs on Mrs. Garcia's lips.

It had to happen. Sooner or later.

But why the hell now?

"I am well aware of your family's past, Joy. And it didn't bother me. You are not your brother and you've been a good friend to Lena. And I spoke with your mom about it. She told me everything."

I can't stop the trembling in my lips, or the tears that trail down and sting my sunburned cheeks. I feel like a wrecking ball collided with my chest, hearing that my mom shared my past. I know it affected all of us but... it *happened* to me.

"Don't worry, I never said anything to Lena. But, there's something else you should know."

No venom is on my teeth, but I wish it were, because I'm buzzing with hatred.

I was *trying* to make things right. Trying to work past the scar tissue and be happy without tearing anyone down because I've been down enough for a lifetime. Now I feel it twice. Inadequate. Hateful. Worthless.

My burning, wet eyes glare at her, waiting for her to finish. "What?" My voice is coated in anger and hurt.

She sighs, her shoulders relax, and she looks at me with pity.

"Jin's dad is one of the Mayor's lawyers. *Tyler Fuller's* lawyer."

Unsteady air escapes me. I cover my face. *No.* Jin was new. The one who pulled me out of that pit.

How is it possible that his dad protected the monster that derailed my life?

That's why I couldn't shake his name or his face. *Yuno Park.* I only saw him one time, at the end of the hospital hall, in a crisp black suit. Standing next to Mayor Fuller and his wife, while their unconscious son was wheeled into the hospital room.

It's like a puzzle piece of my memory fills in the picture where his face wasn't clear. It was him.

God, this whole time my past was chasing me.

I can't stay here. My shaky arms lift me off the lounge chair and I grab my crutches.

"Where are you going, honey?" she says, not bothering to move a muscle.

What a calculating opportunist Angela is. She definitely had suspicions about Jin and I, and she saved this game piece.

Well, I guess she wins.

Maybe it's not that Carson always wins. Maybe I just always lose.

I honestly don't even care that she dug around my past and got my mom to reveal personal details of the night I was violated. It stings, but that pain is so trivial now.

Before I get far, I search for him standing on the dock. He gleams.

I trusted him.

Jin waves at me and my world falls apart like someone's deforesting the evergreen woods in the background. His hand drops. He knows something's wrong.

And it really is. Because the last person I thought would lie to me was Jin Park.

That was last year?

There was no reason for him to know the timing. He suspected. He knew.

And he never said anything.

Track 21 - Somebody That I Used To Know

I'm only going so I can keep you from doing something stupid."

I grinned at him, my cheeks dusted with glitter, a lace choker around my neck to go with my black sequin dress that wasn't too short, or so I thought. It was the pride of my closet before that night.

"You know I never make a fool of myself, Joy Bear," Carson said to me. He wore a sly grin and an ocean blue tank that he knew garnered female attention.

His shirt would be covered in blood before midnight.

The memory is almost like a ghost's whisper. "No d r i n k i n g ..."

Tyler Fuller was the golden boy of the whole town. I'd known him since I was a kid because my mom had worked for the Mayor for a really long time. We had roots in that godforsaken place. Tyler had asked me to be his girlfriend more times than I could count. I always rejected him, but I tried to be friendly for my mom's sake.

I wasn't expecting him to be at Molly Hannigan's house party. He said he'd never get caught dead partying.

God, the irony. It's the kind that stabs and hurts and isn't funny at all.

The beat was far too heavy to know what song was actually playing. I found the punch bowl, which reeked of whiskey, I think. I didn't bother to taste it. Molly made the rounds like an overly chipper *maitre'd* dressed in a yellow knit crop top and tight burgundy leather skirt. Way more revealing than me. Her matte lipstick smile greeted me and my brother, before she insisted she had to go to another part of her massive, unsupervised house.

That was the last moment I considered her a friend.

Carson made it to the string-lighted backyard before I had two seconds to get my bearings. Parties were not my thing, but Carson was finishing his senior year and wanted to go. I didn't know anyone there except him and Molly.

And Tyler.

He came up behind me smelling like booze and inappropriate thoughts.

"Joy, didn't think you'd come!" I remember his curly smile as clear as a bell.

I may have politely smiled back, but inside I was in shock. "Hey, Tyler."

"You look really good tonight." I watched his eyes cover me and immediately made plans to burn my outfit later.

"Thanks."

Thanks. Ugh. I wish I never said that.

I don't know what else we said. The next few minutes felt like hours as far as memory serves. I was on edge, I know that. I refused drink offers. And he drew in closer. And closer.

His arm was around my shoulders and his breath was hot in my ear. "Hey, let me show you something."

"I don't know, Tyler." My shoulders felt like they were up to my ears.

"Come on!"

"...okay."

I didn't stop him. I followed because I wanted to be nice. I didn't think it would end the way it did.

I realized later that Tyler didn't know Carson was at the party. They hated each other and everyone knew it. I had always tried to play peacemaker, which gave Tyler the wrong idea. Despite the post-trauma counseling I got in the plea deal, it's hard to feel like it wasn't my fault.

Even though I rejected him so many times before. Even though I resisted when he pushed his body against mine in the dark. Even though Molly walked by, saw my look of desperation, and continued to the bathroom.

Everyone else would figure Carson snapped because he was drunk.

He wasn't drunk, but I guess he did snap.

Tyler had me pinned against a wall in a dark hallway, and during that time Carson was looking for me. He was already angry about something. But then, he caught my voice. Whimpering, stuffing my crying down, trying not to move as Tyler pressed his unwanted lips on my neck.

His hands wandered too far. Criminally far.

Carson ripped him away from me by the collar of his polo. I was stuck in an elongated moment. I watched Tyler slam to the ground. I saw the terror on his face before Carson's first punch landed.

And I was so... relieved. For a very short fraction of a second, I was relieved it was over.

But it had really just begun.

My brother brutally beat him, landing blows with all the accuracy and muscle he'd earned pitching baseballs. The bones of Tyler's face cracked under Carson's knuckles.

Tyler managed to stand up in an attempt to flee. His face filled with fear as blood and saliva fell from his mouth like thick red threads. Carson yanked on Tyler's shirt and shoved him down again, eyes wilder than I'd ever seen. Carson didn't let up even after Tyler went unconscious. I watched and listened as people struggled to decide who to side with: the golden child of the mayor or the promising baseball star. They chose the one who wasn't conscious.

Some of the brawnier partiers finally lifted my brother off and held him down until police came. Tyler's face was bloodied and swollen and, most of all, unmoving. A few people swore he was dead.

The next twenty-four hours were the most grueling of my life. My brother was in police custody. I wasn't sure if Tyler was going to live or die. I held a deep pain that I wasn't sure I could ever talk about. My mouth was shut tight every moment I wasn't forced to speak.

Then I started to pray that Tyler would live because his death would've made it all worse.

I talked to police officers and lawyers. I felt like I wasn't really the one talking, though. I observed myself re-counting what happened. They found witnesses, though I'm not sure who they all were. I was both glad they corroborated my story and furious they did nothing to stop it. It was and still is conflicting.

But most confusing was how desperate I was for none of it to balance out. I didn't want justice for my brother, or justice for Tyler, or justice for myself. I wanted us all to walk away. That's it.

In the end, it was actually Tyler's mom who convinced me to press charges. She knew what her son had done. I've thought about what her reasons were for encouraging me to do it. Maybe she was ashamed. Or maybe it was because, even though he hurt me, I still valued his life. I've wondered if she might've known what I was feeling. Maybe she went through it herself before.

"You have power here, Joy. You should use it. If you don't, they will learn nothing," she told me.

I knew she was right, but I told myself it wasn't enough. These men didn't deserve to learn from this! They didn't deserve to become better people at my expense, to be saved from the consequences of nearly killing someone or to be spared a reputation with a plea bargain. For it to work, I'd have to be willing to share my side in court, if Tyler was stubborn enough to fight it. And I was convinced that he was.

But then I realized that Mrs. Fuller wasn't just talking about Tyler and Carson. She was talking about *every* on-looker. The Mayor, the rest of my family, other women who were in positions like me, my friends, maybe even my future children.

I willed myself to stop thinking about it and just do it.

I told the Fullers that I would press charges against Tyler if they pressed charges against Carson. I was 100% ready to face court. But, in the end, they settled.

We all walked away. Even Tyler.

The media doesn't like settlements wrapped in shiny red bows, though. They like to rip things apart so public scrutiny runs free like blood from a prey. It was illegal for them to report anything about my part, since I was a minor, so Carson got the brunt of it. Lost his baseball scholarship to OSU. Forced us to move from Oregon to southwest Washington. Never quite healed from it all.

At least Tyler lived. When he woke up, my relief was mostly for his mom. I don't wish him dead, but I hope I never see him again.

It was one of those events that you find yourself measuring everything else against. What's really so bad when your brother almost killed someone and it was your fault? But, I know it wasn't my fault. *He could've stopped himself.* Now, I'm sitting outside the locker rooms at Victoria Lake, reliving it. But it's different this time. Like I'm more sober. When Jin told me *they* could've stopped, it changed me. But in the end, he still lied by omission. There's no possible way he didn't make the connection. How many mayor's kids get beat into a coma?

I run my fingers through my sweat-damp hair and suddenly understand why people pull it out when they're frustrated.

I'm so tired of feeling elated just to get stuck in a self-destructive loop, debating whether or not I'm worth such amazing feelings. I'm so tired of crying over it. I just want to be done already!

Maybe I'm allowed to just sit in my twisted up feelings while I process the crazy curveball that got thrown at me. Maybe I finally *know* I wasn't the one to blame.

Maybe, even though my heart is broken, I'm still resilient.

"Joy?" Carson says as he exits the locker room. "You finally talking to me?"

Track 22 - Say Something

Sometimes I hate that I'm so close to Carson. It's hard not to be attached when you have no memory of a world without someone. We share brokenness because we're a pair. The Becker kids. Even if I heal, there's always an ache in my soul over him.

"There's something you deserve to know," I say. Carson takes a seat on the metal bench just outside the locker rooms. His curls are dark and damp from his post-shift shower. The shade is still so hot, it's like I'm watching him dry.

"About time," he says. I involuntarily roll my eyes.

"I don't care if you don't believe me. I never cheated."

"Bull—"

"Shut up! Can you listen for once?"

His brow turns annoyed but I'm sure my expression reflects it back. He folds his arms over his chest and slumps back.

Deep breath. "I was telling you the truth. I made a deal with Cale, that we'd fake a relationship because he's got a crush on Lena. That's why he gave me his car."

"You really think he gave you his car because he has 'fake' feelings for you?" He uses air quotes around "fake" because, well, he has a point.

"I'm not sure anymore."

He studies my face. "You were really faking it?"

"Yeah. But I care a lot more that you believe I wasn't cheating."

Carson sighs and sits up to put his elbows on his knees like the athlete he is. "It's not that I don't believe you. It just sounds so... stupid."

He's not wrong. But him saying that is a healthy portion of relief for me.

"I still don't like that other guy," he says.

I smirk. "Only because he stood up to you."

"No, it's because he freakin' seduced you when you had a boyfriend! Fake or not!"

"Carson, obviously I told him!"

"Pfft! And he believed you?" Carson grins as if he's just witnessed something supremely idiotic. His scoffing makes me realize how easily Jin accepted my word. We didn't even know each other that well.

Is that a good trait or a bad one?

The warm breeze brushes against us. The woods that surround the employee locker rooms are a mix of quiet stillness and bustling nature. On any other day, I'd drink up the summer heat and fresh air, paying no mind to the impressions this metal bench is leaving on my bare legs.

Today, though, the forest's serenity offers no escape from reality.

"I didn't actually come here to defend myself, Carson."

"What else is there?" he asks with the vague annoyance that's a staple of his utterances.

I tell him about Jin's dad. As I do, every hint of his usual smugness fades and his amber eyes go distant into the trees. He didn't expect this to catch up to us again, either.

"Guess it's not gonna work out after all, huh?" he finally says.

I fight tears hard and say, "Guess not."

But I wasn't ready to say that. I wasn't ready to call it because I never gave Jin the chance to explain. Carson and I are so interconnected that he spoke for both of us. I can't dangle his livelihood over spikes just because Jin's smile won't leave my mind.

"You really like him, don't you?" I'm surprised he's watching me. He hardly ever leaves his own head.

I sniffle. "More than I thought I would. A lot more."

"Well then, screw it!"

My head whips to face him. "What?"

"Figure it out! You don't always have to spare me. I can take one for the team sometimes."

I gape at Carson, in a spiral of emotions that's going both up and down at the same time.

"He lied to me, Carson! He knew about our past and said nothing. I don't blame him for who his dad is but... he should've told me."

"Oh." Now he gets it. "That sucks."

I pat my face dry with my wrist. "It's not like it stops there. Lena's been in love with him forever, so it's just way too complicated."

He looks a bit skeptical. "I thought she went through flings like crazy."

"Yeah. Jin's the reason for that."

"Huh." He sits in this place of wondering about everything. The level of emotional investment he's putting into it surprises me.

Then I have to rewind. "Were you really about to let me date a guy that you hated? Like what have you done with my actual brother?"

Carson chuckles. "My old techniques weren't working so I'm flexing new ones."

I furrow my brow. "Techniques for what?"

"Protecting you."

That's the first grain of sweetness I've gotten on a long, bitter train of conversations with Carson. I smile. *He's finally learning.* Took his sweet time, but Carson is getting there.

"When were you gonna tell me about your *game* next week, huh?" I punch his firm upper arm and he laughs.

At least one thing in my life doesn't have to be beyond repair.

♫

The hot wind from the golf cart ride heals my swollen face, like it's taming the flames of my uncertain heart. Carson drops me off at the cabin so I don't have to hobble all the way back from the locker rooms by the lake. My armpits are so sore from the crutches. Profuse sweating is zero help when attempting to balance on metal sticks.

Carson helps me into the air conditioned cabin, but he has to go to physical therapy again. So, once again, I'm alone. With my thoughts. I take my usual spot on the leather couch. It's been imprinted with my body and turmoil. I'm a lot antsier than usual, though, so I get up and hop to the kitchen for ice water. It's all I can stomach with these balled up nerves.

The cold water traveling down my throat reminds me of being enveloped in the pond. Alone with Jin. I'd stopped fighting for long enough to fall. The bliss was explosive, but ignorant.

Maybe he wanted to tell me, but couldn't. Like how I was with Cale.

I know it's hard to break news.

Was he talking about this? Even if he was, does that change anything? He still kept it from me. He still kissed me. He knew who I was and he let me fall. But maybe I shouldn't blame him.

No. I *know* the right thing was to say something.

I stare at the vaulted ceiling. My breath feels shallow, not just because I'm lying down again. I have to talk to him. But how?

My mom's voice enters the cabin before she does. Heat radiates inside the cabin when she opens the door. Jan-di gives me a sun-kissed smile and waves at me as if she's not only fifteen feet away.

And they don't ask me why I came back early.

Angela walks in after them, her towel and hat under one arm and clear vinyl tote back dangling from the other. She says "hello" but clearly she's keeping our last conversation under wraps. Judging by how everyone else acts when they see me, I'm sure she covered up what actually happened.

What an ugly woman.

Lena follows after her, thumbing her phone. "Oh hey, Joy! Get too much sun?"

I nod, but her eyes are already back on her screen.

And then Jin walks in. Whatever lingering smile was on his face fades entirely when we make eye contact.

I can't keep it. I look away immediately.

Don't cry.

His hand falls onto the couch back.

"Hey," he says in a low voice. "You okay?"

DO NOT CRY.

I don't look at him. "Fine."

He lingers on my monotone answer.

Everyone else goes on about the fabulous weather, the amazing nature, some guy with a weird tan line. They loved every minute of today.

Feels like I'm on another planet.

"You wanna help me start a fire?" Jin asks in almost a whisper.

I finally meet his eyes and I don't know how to feel. I caught insane feelings for him. I still dream of our next kiss. I'm still twisted up with hurt. I can't answer him.

He shakes off my silence, but I can't decide if he knows. He goes into the backyard and starts fiddling with the fire pit. The other women have barely stopped talking. Not really surprising that none of them perceive my actual state of being.

Jan-di leans on the back of the couch, the edge of her bob tickling her jawline.

"Joey, you should go to talk with Jin," she says, with a small, courteous smile.

Or is it something other than courtesy? Maybe Jin actually talks to his mom.

She holds her hand out. "Come up." I take her hand and strain to get off the couch. She carries my crutches as I limp to the door.

The sun casts a harsh glow on everything. Jan-di shuts the door behind me. Jin lifts his head. He's tense, so he knows *something*. I take a seat and my crutches crash to the ground.

Jin pulls newspaper out of the cardboard box labeled "BONFIRE" and crumples it into balls. I hate that I'm watching him. How can he be so beautiful as ink spreads onto his fingers?

"When were you gonna tell me about your dad?" I ask.

Eye contact. Yep. He knew. He squeezes his eyes shut and his shoulders fall forward.

"I'm so sorry." He's quieter than the rustling of newspaper in his hands.

"It had to come from *Angela,* right after she goes off about how you and Lena are meant to be together." My lip trembles. There's a wavering anger in me that I never expected would be directed at Jin.

I don't want to scold him. "How long did you know, Jin?"

"When you told me last week. Donuts. First time I made the connection." He drops what he's doing and kneels down in front of me with urgency. "I swear I was gonna tell you. That's why I followed you yesterday."

I can't tell if it hurts or not, knowing it wasn't just blind affection that drove him to come after me. "So why didn't you?"

He opens his mouth to talk but nothing comes out for a second. "How was I supposed to tell the girl I like that my dad almost ruined her life?"

My stomach flips. He'd been trying to figure it out because he liked me. His remorse softens me. I'm weak for his weakness.

He keeps talking. "Everything was too perfect, Joy. And then you ran and I just... I didn't want to give you another reason."

I shudder, but it's because it makes sense. I doubted him and I shouldn't have. *Deep breath.* "It's okay. I get it. I don't blame you."

Is it that easy to forgive him? I want it to be. But there's still worry in his brow when he bites his lip. He stands up and gets back to his forgotten task of lighting the fire, fiddling with the lighter.

"What is it, Jin?"

He throws the lighter in the unlit pit. "I'm stuck on you, Joy. I meant it when I said I would fight for this. If you want me to."

There's something foreboding in the way he says it. Like I still don't know everything we're fighting against.

I frown. "Jin…"

"There's something else I have to tell you," he says, avoiding eye contact. My heart is in my throat. I'm caught in that suspense and I hate it. I've always hated it. How can someone love this part?

It pains him to get it out. "I accepted the internship." Now he looks at me. "I fly out in two weeks."

My eyes fall closed, my face gets hot. I'm awash with unforeseen despair.

He's leaving.

Jin draws near again, and I sink further into the chair. The daylight has faded and everything is turning blue. He grabs my hand. "I want you, Joy. More than I expected."

Tears stream on my cheeks and I'm so shaky. I told him he should go. *Why did I tell him to go?*

I pull away from him. "This is too much."

I get up. He doesn't stop me, though I can tell he's holding back again. I grab my crutches and turn away. It's too hard to watch him.

"Joy, please," he begs, his voice wobbling. "I want this to work. So much."

I whip around before I've taken a step. "But you're *leaving*, Jin!" My voice catches. It doesn't matter how strong I thought I was or how desperate I am for him.

He stares at me, lost for what to say.

"And you should go," I say. "But you should know that you're the brightest spot I've ever had in my life." Another fresh tear rolls to my chin.

I leave the rest unsaid. There are too many conditions to follow "but" and too many ways to say "goodbye" and too many well wishes I don't really want to give.

I turn my back to him.

"So are you, Joy."

I shiver as I press the heel of my hand to my eyes. I can't respond. So I focus on getting back inside the cabin. I shut the sliding door, sealing him off from me.

Precariously balanced on my crutches, I heave a sigh.

"What was that about?" Lena's sitting in the armchair, facing away. She looks over her shoulder.

I reveal my sore eyes to her and she gets stiff.

"Are you crying?" She rises and gets a closer look.

"I don't want to talk to you, Lena." My voice is low and cruel and I don't care how it makes her feel. It couldn't possibly be worse than me.

Her eyes grow wide. "What did I do?"

"Nothing. It's not even about you." I hobble past her. "Believe it or not."

I don't get far when she says, "I warned you, didn't I?"

I pause, gripping the handles of my crutches with white knuckles. Moments like these give me sympathy for Carson's outbursts. Hurling objects at walls, shoving things off of tables, screaming everything that I know would hurt her.

But I'm not Carson, and honestly, she's right.

She warned me that I'd get hurt. And I did.

Damn. I couldn't get the dirt stain out after all. It's just a pale grey splotch, judging me for bringing it along to the secret pond and dropping it carelessly on the dirty rocks.

The sun is some kind of uncomfortable devil today. It glares at us in a makes-you-wish-you-lived-in-the-Alaskan-tundra type of way. Thank goodness I brought my Mariners cap because I could see nothing without it blocking the bright beams. It's Carson's first day back on the field. This stain is foreboding, though.

I didn't think I was superstitious, but my fortune hasn't been great lately.

After Jin and I had our... I don't know what to call it. After that, my mom found me crying into the Cowboys blanket, alone in the basement. She asked what was wrong. I didn't know what to tell her, honestly. I said the "fight" was with Lena (because it kind of was). She asked if it was about Jin, and so I said, "Sort of." Then she actually switched likable-mom mode on and asked if I wanted to go home.

So that night, we left. And for the whole car ride, she didn't press it. She asked if I wanted to talk a couple times, but I just redirected the conversation to Carson. He healed up nicely, thanks to the specialized doctors at the resort rehab center. Apparently Victoria Lake is known for its muscular rehab program. Good news for Carson.

Anyway, Mom was apologetic for failing to mention the practice game. And forgetting to mention that I was the only family member who'd be able to make it.

Now I'm here. I have three unread texts from Jin burning a hole in my shorts pocket. But it's so hot out, I wouldn't notice anything burning a hole in anything.

"They actually sell Cracker Jacks! Like you got no idea how excited I am that they're a real thing!" Cale scoots past the other onlookers on his way back to our blistering plastic seats.

God, I'm glad he's here with me today.

"Why wouldn't they be real?" I laugh. Then I gasp. "Is that a slushie?!"

Cale hands it to me, candy red and glorious. "Figured you could find a use for it," he says.

"Today I could pour it in my shirt."

Cale laughs, but it drowns in the crowd's cheering when the ballgame song hits the speakers. I stand straight up and join the choir. My ankle isn't even sore today. The doctor yesterday said I can use it if I'm comfortable, finally. A week of crutches is long enough.

Cale screams the part about Cracker Jacks, wildly waving his box in the air.

"Play ball!" everyone shouts in unison.

I suck down the slushie and it cools my insides. I'm glad I didn't actually pour it down my shirt.

I really needed a day where not thinking about Jin was actually filled with something fun. Where I don't see his face whenever I blink or stare off.

I mean, I guess it's not really that day yet. I can't stop thinking about the first text he sent to me. I did read that one.

I still mean it.

Four loaded words.

I started a thousand messages, but never sent anything back. After that, he sent the same four words, once a day.

I still mean it.

Even though I read it in the notification, I let the number in the red circle grow. He hasn't sent one today. I'm kind of scared he won't.

The truth is, giving myself over to Jin means a ton of bitter confrontations and one really painful goodbye. I dread standing on the other side of airport security and watching him leave. And then the flood of all the smiles and touches and the things he said in his smooth voice just overwhelms me with desire. Straight desire. I want him.

Jin pegged me pretty well, too. If it had been flipped, I probably would have approached with equal caution. I would have done anything to make him feel safe before dragging us through the mud. But I darted for the exit anyway. He still pursued me. And not in a way that was disrespectful or selfish.

It takes a lot of energy to not grab my phone. My fingers itch. I've been doing a terrible job trying to get over him.

CARSON BECKER flashes on the screen with my brother's baseball portrait. It's time for the Gophers to take the field. The crowd goes crazy because his followers finally feel heard. This is their comeback as much as his, even if it is just a practice game.

"Woo!" Cale hollers, up on his feet and pumping his fist. "BECKER! BECKER! BECKER!"

I yank his arm. "Cale! Would you calm down?"

He plants himself hard in the chair. "When has asking me to calm down EVER worked?"

"Never," I admit. "But he's not a pro, so cool it!"

He snatches my slushie. "Yeah yeah, whatever you say." He slurps while eyeing me, and I ignore him by watching my brother step on the mound.

Carson spots me. He nods once from the down there. I nod once from the bleachers. And I grin. It's the first time in a while that "the nod" made me feel special.

I can practically see his muscles flex as he grips the ball. He eyes the umpire, winds up and hurls the ball. *Strike!*

That's my brother.

"That's her brother! WOOOO!" Cale wails, and I have to shush him again. He's twelve times louder than anyone else.

While sweat drips down my back, Carson gets the first two batters out. This next one is a strike away. They haven't gotten any runs yet. They're about to go to the second inning in under 10 minutes, which I rarely see.

"He's on fire!!" Cale says. He pops a Cracker Jack in his mouth. "You think he'll make it big?"

"I think he could. I'm biased, though."

"Speaking of big breaks, you ever email that guy? The band manager?" Cale asks me, his eyes on the game.

Crack! It's a hit. The opposing player jogs to first base. So much for a no-hitter comeback.

I turn my attention to Cale's question. "Nah. I'm too nervous to find out what they want."

He nudges me. "You gotta shoot your shot, Becker!" He's smiling big, but then he turns his head and bites his lower lip.

He turns back to me. "There's something I gotta tell you, actually."

Shoot your shot. My pulse races. I'm almost certain I know what he'll say.

For a split second, he looks down. Smiles. Flips his brown eyes up again.

"My feelings aren't fake," he says. "I really like you. Like for real."

He blows air out of round lips, like he just released a weight. Then he smiles with uncertainty.

We're doing this now. "I guess I kinda figured that out," I say, wagering a little smile. But that weight has been transferred over to me. It feels like I'm balancing Cale's heart on my head, but I'm the same old, clumsy Joy.

I don't know what to say.

Cale squeezes his eyes shut and, like it's all one word, says, "Actually, I kinda liked you this whole time. I was never into Lena."

My brow tenses. "Wait... the *whole* time?"

I stare off at nothing in particular. The whole time?!

His knee bobs up and down. "Yep. That crazy ploy was actually meant for you."

How did I miss it?

Thinking back, it's obvious. Always covered by a joke or song and dance routine. A diverted text chain. Nervous fake-fake affection.

Girl like I don't love spending time with my FGF!

You were beautiful and amazing today.

It's hard to get the girl you like to notice you.

The opposing team scores a run and a small section of onlookers cheer, while jeers moan everywhere else. Point for the away team. Meanwhile, I'm running backwards to process the fact that Cale has had real feelings for me for months.

Not like a week and a half. *Months.*

I punch his arm. "Why didn't you ask me straight, *Thomas*?"

"Ouch!" He rubs his arm, then meets my semi-annoyed gaze. "Would that have worked? Better than a convoluted master plan to convince you secretly?"

"Yes, you doofus!" Until I say it, I didn't know it was true. The scary part about jumping in is not knowing if the other person will go with you, but I think offering your hand is sometimes enough. Just knowing he felt that way might have made my feelings bloom.

"So you're saying I could've tried the traditional route?" he says.

I throw my hands up. "You mean the *normal* route!"

He folds his arms to mock me. "Well, I guess that depends on how you feel, Almond Joy!" He unfolds his arms. "Sorry. I'm really bad at 'serious.'"

"I know." My eyes fall on Carson, focused on his pitch. Before he throws the ball, there's suspension. People are antsy to know the outcome, even though it's a couple seconds away.

Just like Cale is, waiting for me.

"I know I've been kind of a wimp around him," he says, and I find him looking at Carson too.

I shake my head. "That's not the problem."

Serious doesn't seem to be an issue for Cale right now. "So it's me, then?"

"It's Jin."

His brow twitches in confusion. "Oh." It takes a second to settle, but it does. "Of course it's Jin."

I sigh. "But that doesn't even matter because he's going to Korea next week, so."

The heat bears into my flesh. I feel sour like forgotten fruit.

But Cale... laughs. Like, a lot. He slaps his thigh.

"Why are you laughing?" I ask him.

He nods once. "Wow, my plan backfired big time." He gives a post-laugh sigh. "I knew I shoulda been jealous of that guy! Man."

"He should be jealous of you, too!" I glance at him. "It's not like I felt nothing."

Cale looks at me, his eyebrows up. "Really?"

My heart thumps. He's hopeful.

In a split second, I imagine what it would be like with Cale. Easy. Fun. Lots of sing-offs and stolen bites of food. Everything I love about being friends would still be great as a couple. And I could kiss him.

But I'd rather kiss Jin. I don't know if I'll always feel that way, but right now, I do.

Cale scratches his head. The game's been at a bit of a standstill with foul balls. It's hard to pay attention.

Cale leans over toward me and his forehead almost bumps against the bill of my cap. His shoulder touches mine.

"Joy, I'll stick around for you. As a friend or... as whatever you want."

Cale doesn't give himself enough credit. He is really, really good at serious.

His hand reaches up to my hat, lifting it off my head so there's only humid air between us.

"All *I* want," he says, "is a shot." He looks at my lips.

I can't decide which side of this war should win. Jin, who'll be gone. Or Cale, who's staying here. Both of them lied. Both of them had good intentions.

Right now, I can figure out which one holds up.

I give Cale the shot. I kiss him, lingering on his full, salty lips. He's a good kisser. Soft and considerate.

I want to want it. But it's not enough. I never thought of Cale when I was with Jin. And now... I can't escape Jin. This feels wrong.

My chest twists and I break it. I take a deep breath in. Why did I do that?

My phone buzzes. I yank it out of my shorts.

JP: I still mean it.

Me too.

"I'm sorry, Cale." I look up at him, but his eyes are on my phone.

"It wasn't one-sided, was it?" he asks. I give him a bare shake of my head.

The crowd bursts into cheers. Carson struck the hitter out, just before another run. My eyes land on the mound. On Carson. He's looking right at me.

A gripping glare.

Oh God. He saw me kiss Cale.

And now he thinks I lied.

Track 24 - Heartless

The strings of our friendship are frayed. Not broken, but weaker. Our "deal" wasn't exactly broken; it was never really a "deal" to start with. But there was still the matter of the car.

Cale and I didn't talk much the next eight innings. The Gophers won, in no small part due to Carson's rage, which was obvious to me. One game, it gives them a ten run lead. Another he injures his shoulder. Unpredictable.

People shuffle out of their seats, most of them pleased with Carson's comeback win. I grab Cale's sweaty forearm and pull him aside, into the shade.

"I'll pay you for the car."

"Don't! Don't do that," Cale says, physically waving the notion away. "The Beater is yours, no strings."

I shake my head. "I'd feel better if I paid you, though."

"And I'd feel *worse* if you did." He rubs the back of his long neck. "I'd kinda like to not feel any worse."

I'm so sorry. I want to say it, but I just nod.

Cale stretches his arms, I imagine more to cut the awkwardness than because he's sore. "Okay, well, I'm gonna go back to my car and blast that AC."

"See you soon?" There's a lilt of hope in my voice.

He wants to smile but he winces. "Maybe... later."

The distance in his words hurts, but I can't blame him.

"Okay," I say. Then I watch as he escapes through the gates to the grassy parking area.

I want to cry. But I'm also somewhat relieved. But it also sucks to be relieved when you know you just crushed your friend's heart.

I *thought* I was helping him out, even though I wasn't thrilled about fake dating. Now, I'm not sure. If I'd just told him I didn't want to do it, maybe things would've been better. Maybe I should just stop being so compliant.

I'm not eager to go to my car. The AC is still out. Shade is better than a mobile sauna. I wish Mom and Dad had taken the day off work and driven me in one of their present-century vehicles, but they never do that for practice games.

I lean against the hot brick wall. I'm not sure what I should do right now. Usually I wait for Carson to get out of the lockers post-game, but I don't want to stick around today. Nothing good could come from it.

"Hey, are you Joy?" It's a blonde member of the Gophers team, can't remember his name. He doesn't wait for my response before he says, "Your brother's looking for you."

"Of course he is," I mumble. I peel myself from the wall. "Thanks. Tell him I'm coming."

So much for avoiding him.

The guy started jogging back before I finished thanking him. I take a slower pace to the lockers.

Here's to untangling whatever Carson has in his head.

I only wait outside the locker room exit for like thirty seconds before he comes out, freshly showered and changed. I can smell the musty sweat coming off his duffle bag but I ignore it.

"Come with me. I got a surprise," he says walking past me. No greeting. No amusement.

No anger, which is honestly the most terrifying part.

I follow him toward the parking lot. "What do you mean you have a 'surprise'?"

"I just got a surprise." This serious tone forms a pit in my stomach.

"Can I just explain what happened?" I start, though I immediately regret it.

He spins around. "Explain what? Why you were kissing your *boyfriend?*" His flash of anger dissipates and he starts walking again. "You don't have to explain, Joy. I don't give a shit."

My heart stops. It's obvious that he means the opposite of what he said.

I grab Carson's arm. "What's going on with you?"

He yanks his arm away and keeps walking. We reach his truck and he opens the passenger door, tossing his duffle bag in.

"Carson!" Why is he ignoring me?

The door slams.

"I said I got a surprise for you! Just hold your goddamn horses, Joy!"

I meet his angry eyes and recognize this state. There's no talking to him now. If I try, he'll fly off the handle. I don't want to give in, and I definitely don't want to know what his "surprise" is, but I'm certain it'll be worse if I argue.

"Now," he says, rounding the front of his truck, "You gotta just sit in here for a minute. I'm gonna be over there."

He points to the chain link fence twenty feet away. "You'll know it when you see it, little sister."

"Why can't you just talk to me like a normal person?"

"I didn't get this far by being normal."

You'd have gotten farther if you could reign it in sometimes. I keep the thought to myself. It's not worth it.

I do what he asks and sit in the driver's seat with the window down. At least this side of the lot is shaded by the stadium. Carson leans against the fence, checking his phone. I put my elbow on the open window and rest my head on my hand. This is so dumb.

Over the next few minutes, more people leave the stadium grounds. There's hardly any stragglers. This side of the lot must be where the teams park because there are still cars but hardly anyone is out here.

What is he trying to show me? That he can manipulate me into sitting in a hot car for no reason?

"It would have been less weird if you just invited me to watch you play."

Dread fills me. I know that voice.

Anyone but her.

"I thought you hated sports," Carson says, as she walks right in front of his truck, with her silky hair over a flowery crop top and distressed shorts.

Lena.

"Are you kidding? I don't hate watching sexy guys throw a ball around!" she argues, and then she throws her arms around his neck. He grins at her.

And they kiss. Lena's making out with my brother.

WHAT?!

I slam the door. I don't even remember getting out of the car. I barely register my ankle soreness as I pound my feet toward them.

"WHAT THE HELL!" I hear myself say. Lena whips around with eyes wide as baseballs.

"Shit!" she says involuntarily. "Joy! Oh my God!"

Carson's angry eyes meet mine. What nerve he has to be smug right now.

Lena's head bobs between us like a ping pong ball.

"Really? *Her?*" I say to him. I'm furious with her, too, but Carson is the one I truly don't understand. He's my *brother.*

"Joy, please don't freak out!" Lena says with her hands up.

I glare at her. "Freak out? Why the hell should I freak out when my brother is making out with my best friend *behind my back?*"

"Please listen! This is nothing. It's a fling!" she stammers. "It's nothing."

"It's not nothing!" I scream, sounding more shrill than I'd hoped.

She folds her hands and pleads. "Please don't say anything to Jin. Please, Joy."

Ugh. I want to vomit, I'm so disgusted with her.

Carson laughs. "Wow, girls are scary. Always lying to each other."

Lena shoots a glare at him. "You're an asshole, Carson!"

She thinks he's talking about her, but his eyes are locked on me.

"Me? You sure about that, Lena?" says Carson, not looking away.

Tears well up in my eyes. Inevitably, he would do this. I knew it would happen.

"I'm *not* lying, Carson."

"So you told her, then?"

My lips tremble, shut tight. He nods, knowing the answer.

"What the actual hell is going on here?" Lena says, catching on.

His eyes flick to her and he reaches into his back pocket. "You shouldn't be so worried about Jin, Lena. He knows what he wants."

I'm frozen in this god-awful heat. I can only watch him deliver more hurt.

He hands his cracked phone to her.

Damn it.

"What is this?" she says so muted that I'm not sure it's her voice. "You *kissed* him?"

I frown at her. "Are you serious, Lena?"

She rubs her temples, like she has a right to be frustrated with me. "I was extremely freaking clear, Joy."

"Who were you kissing just now? A ghost?"

She points at me, her brow tense. "You *never* said your brother was off-limits!"

"Did you say Jin was?" I square my jaw. "You didn't think you had to, right?"

She scoffs. "Well, why the hell would he go for you when you have a boyfriend, huh?"

"Cale was *never* my boyfriend! None of it was even real!"

Lena folds her arms. "Is that what you told Jin? Please tell me he bought it."

The humid air piles onto me as I try to figure out what's behind Lena's annoyed tone. "Did you know?"

"How can you keep this up, Joy?" Carson says. "You were making out with Cale like three hours ago."

"Wow, really?" Lena says, shocked and nearly amused. "So Jin was just a fling to you?"

"No! That's… ugh!" Are they both insane?

Lena rolls her eyes. "You know what? I'm over *both* of you."

"Fine with me," Carson says, not even looking up from his phone.

Lena takes off the direction she came. I chase after her.

"Carson doesn't know what he—"

She turns on a dime, every muscle committed to the action.

"Are you really stringing Jin *and* Cale along? *And* lying to me about it?"

"So you did know," I gather. "About the deal."

"Yeah," she says and off-sets her jaw. "The *deal* was my idea. Didn't expect you to go behind my back."

We're in a draw of betrayal. She knows she's a hypocrite. I know I'm a hypocrite. I could explain my side, and she could still come back with her side. Nothing will get solved.

But I've got enough fire left for one last round.

"You *forced* me to lie to you, but I told Jin the truth. Is it really surprising he picked me?"

Lena's face is tense with hurt and restrained anger. She tuts. "So then why kiss Cale?"

I sigh. "Because I was trying to give up on Jin."

Her jaw drops just enough that I know she wasn't expecting me to say that.

A pair of truth-wrought tears fall along my cheeks. I walk away.

And then I run to my car because I can run now.

I reach my blistering hot metal beast. My chest heaves. How did I not know they were meeting up? How dense am I?

My key makes it into the door, but I leave it there and drop to the grass.

I was trying to let Jin Park go.

But I can't. *I still mean it.*

Track 25 - Bluffin'

When we were kids, Carson used to cheat at hide-and-seek. He used to pretend he wasn't there when I found him. Most kids would grab the hider and shake them or something but we had a bogus rule that I always followed. Our rule was that the seeker would lose if they touched the hider at all. I tried everything to get him to acknowledge, but no matter what I did, it would result in me losing to him. I tried using the same tactic on him, but he'd pretend he'd gotten bored of looking for me and leave me in my hiding spot for however long I'd stay there.

The thrill of playing with my big brother strung me along for a while, but I gave up eventually. Then I refused to play it with other kids. Better to be out of the game than to lose when cheating is so easy.

I really didn't think that a brother could cheat on you, but that's what it felt like to see him kissing Lena. I was just starting to trust him. When he said I should try to make things work with Jin, I wonder if he was just interested in Lena. If it was really all about him, like it always is.

He cheats to win. With me, anyway.

It's a broiler inside my car. I slam my fists on the steering wheel, practically burning the skin on my hands.

"Please! Please," I cry, tears nearly dry from overflowing for so long. I take off my hat and violently toss it into the passenger seat.

I turn the key again and it sputters, but nothing happens. Then I hand roll the window up, ready to abandon the damn thing in the parking lot.

It's poetic justice. I broke Cale's heart, and his car is loyally screwing me over.

Just call him. You know you want to.

I click the lock down and slam the door. I slide my phone out of my back pocket. To hell with it.

I call Jin.

Ring. Ring.

He's not gonna answer. That would be so appropriate right now. I'd walk home before asking Carson or Lena for a damn ride.

"Joy?"

My throat catches. "Hey."

"Hey." I can hear a smile in his voice.

I swallow. "I still mean it, too."

"I hoped so," he says. I smile. He's perfect.

"Are you busy?" I ask.

"Not anymore." So perfect.

"Good because my car won't start."

"Where are you?"

"It's too hot for a bike."

He laughs. I missed his laugh. "Car it is."

I spot a mirrored '50s diner across the street, like a beacon. "Meet me at Glen's Diner. It's off of Highway 90."

"Glen's Diner, I know that place. I can be there in twenty minutes."

"Twenty minutes," I echo, no doubt in my mind that it's as fast as he can get here.

"Cool," he says. I can hear jingling keys like distant twinkling stars, growing my hope. "See you soon."

"See you soon, Jin."

"Hey, Joy…"

The streaks of tears tighten my skin as they dry on my face. "Yeah?"

"It's really good to hear your voice again."

I grin. I can't help it. "Yours, too."

"Bye." *Beep.*

I look at my phone in a daze. I fell hard. I'm almost glad my car is a beat up hunk of useless metal.

♫

Within exactly eighteen minutes, I jay-walked across the street, used the bathroom, praised God that I found a five dollar bill in my pocket so I could buy something, slid into a sparkly teal vinyl booth and ordered a strawberry milkshake. The sugar doesn't really help the nerves, but it cools me off.

Nineteen minutes. My milkshake is halfway gone as I avoid staring out the window.

The old-school bell twinkles when Jin opens the door to the empty diner. There is no better situation to describe "a sight for sore eyes." None.

His hopeful, relieved smile. That same white t-shirt on his skinny shoulders and blue jeans a tiny bit too loose. I'm glad I abandoned my hat in my car, because I would hate for anything to obstruct this view.

"Sorry about your car," he says first thing. The waitress brings him a laminated menu and walks away without so much as a "hello." It seems rude, but it occurs to me that she might've ignored him because he won't take his eyes off me.

"It's okay. I'm used to it."

"Need me to take you somewhere?" His genuine concern melts me. That he offered to play chauffeur so easily makes me smile.

"No," I tell him, still soaking him in.

"Do you *want* me to?"

The mysterious depth under his words squeeze my heart.

"Yes." It's instinctual. He starts to get up and hesitation floods in. "But can we talk first?"

He sits back down. "Of course. Anything you want."

His attention is latched onto me, which pulls me deeper into my affection for him. If this time apart has done anything good, it's strengthened my feelings.

"I broke off the deal with Cale today." Jin nods and I continue. "Apparently it was never fake for him, so..."

"I'm not really surprised. How'd that go?"

"He took it well. For getting his heart broken."

He leaves the talking space for me to fill, yet he's not forcing my hand. I can tell him anything. Everything. But I'm afraid to admit that I was trying to let him go.

Looking at him, though... my fear seems so unfounded.

"I'm sorry. I thought I was over you but..."

"I couldn't stop thinking about you either, Joy." A grin flickers on his gorgeous lips.

I play with the straw in my milkshake. Jin is so easy to adore. "I'm sorry I didn't text you back." The regret hurts. I was fooling myself by trying to stay away.

He grabs my hand. "No, no, no. I messed up. I should have told you about my dad when I figured it out."

"But you were right." I squeeze his hand. "I would've gotten scared."

"You still didn't deserve to hear it from Angela Garcia of all people."

I love him.

Jin leans over on the table and lowers his voice. "So, no pressure, but… can we get out of here now?"

I smile and nod. I'm out of the booth before he says another word, abandoning my shake even though it's half full and strawberry's my favorite.

I push the door open, breaking into the heat to the sound of a tinkerbell. I feel Jin's hand on my shoulder and I turn around.

I'm swung into his embrace in a moment. He kisses me.

Jin wraps his strong arms around the nape of my neck and small of my back. Surprise and bliss cascade down my body like honey. There is nothing else but me and him.

Goodness, Jin Park. If everything had to fall apart, I'm glad it was for you.

I don't know why I thought I could convince myself to let him go. I'm elated, pulling away from this kiss, looking into his glimmering eyes again.

Funny how quickly happiness can fly away.

"Joy! What the hell are you doing?"

Carson.

He found me. It takes everything in me not to pretend I'm invisible.

Jin runs his hand down my arm and squeezes my hand. He's in this fight with me.

"Why can't you leave me alone?" I say, trying not to raise my voice.

He rushes us, no care for making a scene out in public. "You still need to explain what the hell that was about."

The light beaming off the mirrored diner feels more intense than the sun itself.

I wipe sweat off my forehead. "Why don't you just ask Lena? Apparently you two are very intimate."

Jin's arm straightens and he shoots me a brief look of confusion.

Carson waves that off. "Bullshit, that was just kissing."

"Oh, so it's fine when you do it behind my back, but not when I do?"

"I'm not the one who's cheating!" His eyes flit over to Jin, making sure he heard. The cars driving by sound like slow bullets. I look up at Jin, stoic in the face of my erratic brother. I can't tell if he's disregarding everything Carson says… or if he's wondering if he's right.

"Is it really worth it, Joy?" Carson gets up close to Jin, looking him in the eye, but keeps his words and venomous tone for me. "Mom told me your little boy toy here is going to Korea next week. Apparently his mom is super proud. So what's the point in cheating with him?"

Jin cracks. "She's not cheating."

Carson laughs like it's a bad joke. Every nerve I have is anticipating more, but Carson doesn't tense up like he's ready to throw a punch.

He takes a step closer.

I pull my hand out from Jin's and point at my brother. "You're just scared because his dad is Tyler's lawyer, and you think all that stuff is gonna come back to us. It won't. It's over."

He looks at me, verging on hurt. "Really? You think it can be over after I lost everything?"

I stiffen. It's almost hard to breathe when it's this hot. These late July days are never usually this brutal.

I've been filled with so much regret ever since OSU called the meeting and pulled Carson's scholarship. I always felt like it was my fault. Repeated to myself that it wasn't. That it was over.

But it was never really over for him.

"I'll be happy when he's on the other side of the world," Carson says.

Jin rests his hand on my shoulder. "I'm not going anywhere."

I whip around. "What? But your internsh—"

"I'm gonna drop it." His eyes go soft on mine. "I told you I would fight for this. And I still mean it. If that means staying here, so be it."

I study his resolve. I know he means it, and I want him to. But the regret over Carson's lost future still yanks on my gut. In my mind, Jin staying was never an option. The Korea internship was his future, because it's what's best for him.

"You can't do that, Jin," I say. I've already ruined too many futures.

Carson scoffs. "You'd really give up your fancy internship for a girl who cheats?"

I look over my shoulder. "I told you, Cale was never my boyfriend."

Carson tugs on his shirt to air it out. "Yeah yeah, keep it up." He looks at Jin. There are flares in each of their eyes. "You believed that shit? Even though she kissed him today?"

My gut sinks like it's full of lead. Jin cracks a little more, a line in between his eyebrows forming. He brushed Carson off before, but now he's not sure what to make of it. He's looking at me with uncertainty.

"Did you?" he asks.

I raise my hands defensively. "Let me explain that."

His eyes widen. "You did?"

"Jin, it's not like that," I say, but this is like that scene in every movie where someone gets caught in their deception. And it does quick work of making things worse.

The subtle expression of hurt on his brow, the slow shaking of his head. He's wondering about it all. Rifling through every memory for some inconsistency to the theory that I lied about my relationship with Cale.

"You kissed him, and then you called me?"

I try to regroup. "Okay. I thought it would make me stop thinking about you." *Damn it!* I sound even worse. Textbook example of being caught in a lie.

He steps back. "You wanted to stop thinking about me? Why? Did you feel guilty?"

No no no no! Why can't I say anything right?

"Finally, he figures it out," Carson chides.

Jin's dark eyes linger on me, searching for a way to reconcile this chasm my brother ripped open so carelessly. "I believed you," he says to me, like he's upset with himself. "Maybe I shouldn't have."

I shudder. I can't watch this. I cover my face, blocking out the sun, Jin's hurt, my brother's smugness. I cry into my already damp palms.

I don't know how to fix this. I really don't.

I look at him, the rims of my eyes certainly red. "I'm so sorry, Jin."

He frowns, hearing my apology as confirmation. He breathes out like he's in physical pain. "Me too."

My breath hitches as he walks away. I can't bring myself to stop him. This was inevitable, wasn't it? All the reasons we couldn't work fill in the widening space between us.

An ignorant couple opens the door, the bell ringing amidst the carnage of this fallout. Jin gets into his car and I cast my gaze to the gray sidewalk under my feet. His car starts up.

And then he drives away.

I lift my head, hoping that Carson isn't still populated in front of me. But he is.

"Are you happy now?" I ask, muted and angry.

His beastly shoulders stiffen as his fuzzy hair dances in the hot, shifty air. "You shouldn't have lied."

"I never did, Carson. You're just so used to doing it yourself all the time, you can't believe that I might've had an honest reason for all of this."

He crosses his muscly arms. "What the hell would that be?"

I step closer to him, biding my angry hurt so I can speak clearly. "That even though I fell in love with him, I was already trying to let go. For you. For Lena. For Cale. Even for him." I don't know if Carson gets it, but I don't care. "So there you go, Racecar. It's just you and me again. You win."

"Joy, I wasn't trying to beat you or something," he says, with an oddly calm inflection. "You're just not who you were."

I shake my head, tapping into anger. "Did it ever occur to you that being this way is suffocating?"

The answer is all over his silent, slack-jawed face. It never did.

Track 26 - This Is On You

... auditioning as our lead vocalist... it's your call... crossing our fingers...

I've reread the email probably twenty times. I look at the date again.

August 2nd, 4 pm. Yep, that's troubling.

Choppy warm air from a dusty fan travels over my heat-lazed body. The three o'clock sun hits my bedroom window with ferocity. Apparently it's a heatwave this week.

It must be to melt my icy heart.

Might be working. It's kinda racing when I read the email again.

It's from Robbie Gonzalez, The Crux Constellation's band manager. Turns out he decided to stop waiting for me to reach out and grabbed my email from an unused Facebook profile. Apparently, they don't want to disband just because January, their lead singer, is headed off to London for grad school. I haven't responded because... well, I'm too much of a mess to write an email.

They want me to audition during a surprise pop-up concert, but there are two problems: the location and the date.

The concert's in Seattle, which is a four-hour drive. And that's the day of FredU's final mandatory orientation. The one I have to show up to if I want to attend classes.

It's also the same day Jin flies out from Seattle.

So obviously I'm desperately avoiding that geographic location during that specific span of time. It would hurt too much to be that close to him as he flies off into a better life without me.

Good thing I have the solid excuse of college dreams. If only they felt like *my* dreams.

I press my phone to my chest. I should just write the email.

There's a knock at my door.

"Joy Bear?" Carson says through the seam. I say nothing. I just stare at the nick in my door, willing him to go away.

"I want to make it up to you. Please come out." His voice is small, and it's not just because it's muffled by the door.

He's never said the words "I want to make it up to you."

"Why?" I say. The door cracks but not enough for me to see him.

"Lena's ghosting me, so I messaged Cale. He said you never lied about anything."

I throw my phone onto my down blanket.

The air shifts when I yank open my door. "Oh, so you believe me now?"

He jolts, like he's a little kid afraid of a disciplinary smack. "Will you come to the backyard?"

I stare up at him.

"Please?"

I follow him down the hall. I've been forced to pass that wall of pictures these past few days and my stomach lurches every time. Those happy kids feel so far away and fake, it hurts. I've mentally practiced a thousand conversations with my brother, but none of them went well.

Carson always wins. Even in my dumb mind.

He stops us in the kitchen. "I bought like four watermelons. Picked the best looking ones and knocked on them and everything. And I got you an iced coffee." He holds out a sweating plastic cup. It's black coffee.

At least he remembered that I liked watermelons.

"I always get a headache if I skip coffee," he says, daring a smile.

He's right that I've got a massive headache. "Well, I can't sleep if I drink caffeine after three pm," I say, "And I never drink it black."

His smile falls and he puts it back on the counter. "Oh."

I feel bad for a split second. Then I remember what he did and I have no sympathy anymore.

"Well, I cut some watermelon up. It's in the backyard." He tries to sound light, but it fails.

I go with him through the back door anyway.

It's fatally hot out again, like the sun decided it likes physically assaulting the skin. I thought the AC inside was broken, but I was wrong. Dad must've just turned temp up to give the poor unit a break from working so hard.

Mom's frosted glass tray sits on the patio table, under the umbrella's shade. It's filled with watermelon triangles. There are three other whole watermelons on the table too, like Carson said.

Carson squares himself to me, making direct eye contact. "I'm sorry I didn't believe you."

I snag a triangle and bite the sharp tip. The flesh is already warmer than it should be, but it's sweet and juicy. I squint at my brother. Should I even consider forgiving him? Since he hasn't apologized about shacking up with Lena, I'm undecided.

"That's it?" I finally say because my patience is hanging on a frayed thread.

He swallows. "Uh, no."

I won't lie, his struggle is gratifying. He's so full of himself all the time that genuine apologies are like speaking a foreign language.

I take another bite and raise my brows at him.

"I'm sorry for yelling at, um, Jin. And making out with Lena." He sounds like he's admitting he stole a cookie.

I'm chewing watermelon in my mouth when I add, "Behind my back."

"Yeah," he says, dejected. "That. I'm sorry, Joy. Um… can you forgive me?"

Now that he's done it, I've decided. I savor this watermelon a bit before answering.

Yum. "No."

"Okay…" Definitely not what he was expecting.

I scrape my bottom teeth against the pink part that's left, sucking on the juices. And maybe I'm a terrible person, but I enjoy watching him finally lose at something.

"What else should I do?" he asks. At least it's a genuine question.

I flick the rind onto the deck. "Nothing," I say, and I pluck another watermelon slice off the tray. I expect him to get mad. To flip the table or tell me that I'm a bitch or smash a window. And I promise myself I won't react. I won't give in this time.

But Carson doesn't get angry. He takes a sizable breath, and definitely concentrates on something inside his head for a minute.

I keep eating. It really is a good watermelon.

"Why?" he finally asks. "Why can't I make it better?"

"Good question," I say, and I have this little idea. "Let me show you."

I take the biggest watermelon in both hands and carry it over to the grass, setting it on the ground. Then I turn around and walk back to the deck, while Carson watches me utterly confused.

I snatch the baseball bat that's leaning against the house next to the door. Maybe he'll get it if he sees it in a familiar context.

So I stand over the watermelon and point at it with the bat. "This represents my heart, okay? Here's what happened when you showed me your little *surprise.*"

I swing the bat down onto the watermelon with all my strength. The thunk leaves a sizable crack, most of the inner flesh visible, but it's still held together. I look at Carson's upturned brow. Good. At least some regret shows through.

But there's more.

"And here's how I feel now that I have no remaining friends, mostly because of *you.*" I throw another swing onto it, which splits it in two mangled chunks.

Juice drips down the wooden bat. I sigh from the effort.

"But you didn't stop there, did you? You *could have* stopped, but you never do."

Carson's mouth tenses downward.

I smash the watermelon remains again. And again.

"I've only ever fallen for *one* guy, Carson! But you showed up and told him I lied when I *didn't!*" I slug the poor fruit one last time, but I'm shaky and out of breath. I stare down at the pile of pink pulp and green shards.

My voice lowers. "And I let it happen. Because Jin deserves better than what you made me." I toss the bat into the grass. "So what do you think? Do I have the heart to forgive you?"

Carson's eyes travel the span of our backyard where I murdered the watermelon. And there's a glimmer of regret on the rim of his eye. I've seen him cry before, even as a grown man. He's not void of emotion. The world has been cruel to him before.

But this is different. He looks at me and breaks. *For* me. He hurts *with* me right now. And he can clearly see that the cruelty was his.

He falls to his knees, witnessing the carnage. "I am so sorry."

Even though it's the most genuine sentence I think he's ever said, I'm not giving another inch. Not today. "I know you are."

I walk past him to go inside.

"Joy, please," he begs.

I pretend I haven't heard him and walk through the door. He deserves to face this alone.

When I'm inside, I find Dad in the kitchen, still dressed in his navy work suit. I pull the door a little too hard when I close it. Between the sharp sound of it shutting and Carson crumpled to his knees on the other side of the glass panes, Dad knows something's up.

He grabs an apple and takes a bite. "Your brother okay?" he asks. Fewest words possible, as usual.

I adopt his method. "No."

He stops chewing, uncertain how to proceed. "What happened?"

"Today, he didn't win." I weave past him and head for my room.

But Dad speaks again, "Was there a game?"

I halt. He's already talking more than I expected him to.

"Not anymore," I say.

"Joy." I meet my Dad's eyes through his coke bottle glasses. "What happened?"

"He always just has to win, you know?" I say, my throat catching. I clear it.

My dad blinks. "That's not true."

I slam my hand on the counter. "It is! He's a bad sport."

"Not true, Joy."

"Don't defend him! You're the one who's supposed to take my side."

"I don't pick sides."

We stare each other down. He's met his daily conversation quota, so I'm hoping he already exhausted himself and stops expecting me to elaborate.

He doesn't. Carson doesn't get his stubbornness from Mom.

"Carson loses to himself all the time," he says. "Most of the time, *you* pick up the pieces."

"What if I don't want to do that anymore? Why can't he handle life without me?"

"He's trying." Dad's so sure of it, I know there's something in what's unsaid.

"Really? How?"

"Therapy. Last couple months."

I'm a bit in shock. "No one told me that."

"Carson didn't want us to."

I can gather what's unsaid now. Carson wants me to be proud of him. Needing therapy bruised his ego. And he's enough of an idiot to think I'd consider him weak for going.

Was that what that was? Him *trying*?

Even though he sucks for hooking up with Lena, and he sucks for charging at me and Jin the way did, and he really sucks for thinking it could all be forgiven with some cut up fruit...

I don't hate him as much as I did a second ago.

Track 27 - Make It Without You

August 2nd

I stare at my outfit in the mirror as if I'm waiting for some revelation of what's missing. I can't put my finger on what's wrong. This cream Peter Pan collar top with the pearl detail is nice. The pleated A-line skirt is a flattering coral color. I even pulled a braid strand back, so I'd feel more... me, I guess.

I fight the urge to text Lena a picture and ask her advice.

Even if we'd forgive each other this second, the reunion would be a small reward in a pit of grief. Jin's leaving today, and neither of us get to have him. It's kinda funny. Lena and I would probably bond over the shared trauma if it wasn't the very thing that tore our friendship to pieces.

Good riddance, cruel summer of minor injuries. At least you were stupidly short.

I still have a couple weeks before classes begin, but attending Orientation today feels like it's the death of the summer in between high school me and college me. That's kind of why I picked the last possible slot to attend.

"You can do this," I whisper. I'm not entirely sure why I need to hear it. This is exactly the plan I started with. I took a detour but I'm still taking the original path I had planned.

I pick up my phone on instinct. There are three contacts my thumb avoids like they're upturned thumbtacks.

Cale. Because I broke his heart.

Lena. Because she broke mine and I broke hers, too.

And Jin. Do I even need to say it?

But my thumb kinda wants to be pricked for Jin. To set things straight. To tell him I still mean it, even though I disengaged completely. But there's a reason I haven't.

I want him to be free.

Knock knock. It's Mom's knuckle.

"Come in," I say, smoothing my skirt.

She presses the door open with more caution than necessary. "Hey, sweetie." There's a pity smile on her face. "I talked to Jan-di. I'm sorry, honey. I wish I'd known—"

"It's okay. I'll be fine." Even if I'm still sucking up something whenever he's tangentially mentioned.

"Your brother is very remorseful."

"Okay, Mom."

Her lips twitch, as if she's not sure about what to say. Or she doesn't know if she should say it. The crows feet around her eyes reveal the latter.

"If you hadn't been so secretive—"

"Okay! I get it." My heart twists.

"Joy, I don't mean to blame you."

I nod. "Okay." That word makes up half my verbal utterances lately.

She mercifully decides not to say more and puts her hands on my shoulders. Her eyes meet mine. And then she pulls me into her arms.

I don't want to at first, but I bury my face into her shoulder. She squeezes tighter.

"Are you really okay?" she asks.

My eyes tingle. "I will be."

"Joy," she says, pulling away to face me. "I always say Carson and you are my pride and my joy, but…" She brushes my cheek with her thumb. "I am so proud of you. No matter what you do, I'm proud to have you as my daughter."

I've never actually heard her say it so clearly. I mean, I guess she didn't have to. I feel now that it was always true, but hearing it gives my heart a glimmer of happiness.

"Hey."

Mom and I look back at my door. It's Carson. He slaps my door frame. "I'll be in the truck." Then he's off.

Mom rubs both my arms at once and sighs. "Time for you to live your own life."

I stare at her for a second. It feels weird to hear her say that, too. "Okay," I say, but… I might mean it.

She smiles at me as I move past her to leave, but I turn around.

"Mom?" I say. She waits for me to say more. "Um… it wasn't Carson who destroyed the watermelon the other day. It was me."

Her eyebrows go up.

"I just… I didn't want you to think he snapped or something. Actually, I think the therapy's working."

Mom nods, and I can see she's fighting tears. "Okay, sweetie. Now go. It's mandatory." Her smile has gained a few wrinkles since I started high school, but it's the same one she had before I went off to my previous freshman year.

I head out of the house and land in Carson's truck. I agreed to ride with him because I know he's trying. Once Dad told me about the therapy, I softened up.

I will always love him. Not because I owe it to him, or because he needs me to, but because I need to love him. And from now on, I'm doing it my way.

Today, that means letting him drive me to orientation. We get on the road, less than twenty minutes until I officially declare an end to my summer.

"So, I had this thing planned," Carson says. He doesn't take his eyes off the road. "I don't want to call it a 'surprise.'" He laughs like there's a bad aftertaste with the word.

"Probably better not to," I say.

"I'm, uh, supposed to give a speech at your orientation. They picked a couple student representatives or whatever, and I chose your orientation day. So, I'm gonna go up on stage."

"Oh." My eyes trail away from his cautious smile. I almost feel bad for having such a flat reaction. I pick at the peeling pleather on the car's bench seat.

"I just wanted to be there for you, too," he says. His curls droop around a semi-sad expression. There's something different about him. Like he's practiced calming himself for long enough that he doesn't have to try so hard anymore.

"I'm looking forward to it, Racecar." I hazard a small smile. He joins me.

When we get to the overfull parking lot, I survey my surroundings. Campus is... fine. Landscaped with a few flowering bushes, trimmed grass on small hills, and mature trees to shade the concrete walkways. There's a large angular fountain in the middle of the rows of buildings, mismatched by the decades they were built in. Some little kids play in it, waddling and squealing as the fountain shoots sparkling streams into the air, soaking up their last bits of summer.

The time when the toddler walked up to me at Victoria Lake tickles my memory. I'm kind of jealous of those carefree kids.

The Student Union building is utilitarian in essence, working overtime to represent literally every side of identity with multicolored flyers in the windows. Carson and I split before I head into the ballroom and find the alphabetical line A-J.

For a brief second, I remember Mr. Allen Jr. and his sarcastic passes with Cale during glee practice.

I miss Cale.

I figured the best course of action was to let him have space until he made the first contact. It's been brutal going to bed at night knowing it's still not "later" enough. I know I'll see him once classes start. We're in the same FreshQ, which is the nauseating term for the "freshman qualifying course" that all students must endure. Cale will make it bearable. If he'll talk to me.

My arms are overflowing with school merch that I know I'll never use. I pass by the booths. Study Abroad. School of Business. Beekeeping Club. Dentistry.

Right. Because free toothbrushes will sell me on a lifetime of dentistry.

"WILL NEW STUDENTS PLEASE TAKE THEIR SEATS!" blares through the speakers a little too loudly, in some man's monotone voice.

I plant myself in a cushioned chair, facing the stage draped with lackluster navy curtains. The man speaking into the mic has the energy of a bored cat. He introduces a video: *The History of Frederick University.* I zone out halfway through the title. Spoiler: it's remarkably boring.

"Wasn't that soooo great?" says a chipper blonde woman into the mic once the video's over. It's like FredU can't decide the energy they're going for here. Reminiscent of the singing contest at Americanafest.

"Up next, our resident *baseball* star, Carson Becker!" she says, and my heart skips. I don't know why I'm nervous

251

for him. Entering the stage wearing a baseball cap, he salutes charmingly and wins hearts in three seconds flat. When he hits center stage, mic taps echo from the tip of his finger.

"Hey everyone! F-U!" he chants, and there are laughs, a cheer or two and a whole lot of eye-rolls. I'm in the eye-roll camp.

"I'm a pitcher for the Gophers," he says, his dimples are visible even from way in the back. "I really found my center in baseball. As a kid, I liked trying to see how far I could hit or how fast I could pitch. But I learned something real fast. No matter what your gameplan is and no matter how hard you train, there's nothing like the pressure of the game. I also learned that I'm not a great hitter. I strike out a lot."

Carson pauses. His eyes flutter to the ground and he measures a breath. The audience grows silent.

"But I keep playing. In baseball, striking out is basically inevitable. You have to deal with it. Now, here's something that I did not learn so fast. In life, the same thing is true. You're gonna strike out. Even if you trained hard, or planned it all to a T, or you're left counting on your lucky charm." His eyes pick me out of the crowd. "You'll fail your team."

My pulse latches onto his words. He goes on, "In my life, I kept trying to force wins where I should've accepted defeat. It doesn't matter if you win or lose. There's always another game coming. Another ball hurtling toward you. What matters is that you play."

Everyone else may think this speech was meant for them, but I see it in his eyes.

It's for me. Just me.

Suddenly, everything else fades away, we're standing on the field.

"Even if it means you lose, show up and play your game." His voice is like an echo.

I'm holding my breath like I'm on home plate and he's on the mound readying a pitch.

"If you don't play, you don't win."

It hits me. Carson doesn't always win... *I never play.*

I'm still in the bleachers of my own life.

Carson must've thanked the audience, because everyone applauds.

I can't be here. This isn't my game.

I stand up. Sporadically the crowd joins me. And amid the cheers, I leave the ballroom because Frederick University is Carson's game, not mine. It's time for me to leave his field and go figure out where mine is.

Because like Carson said, I'll never win if I don't play.

When I'm in the hall, the crowd's cheers fizzle out and someone mumbles into the mic what's next in the mandatory orientation session. It no longer applies to me.

My heart races. I see his contact, push my finger on his number. Hard.

Still August 2nd

He didn't pick up. It kind of feels like karma.

"Joy, wait up!" Carson jogs down the maroon carpet toward me. When he gets close, I realize he's farther from me than he's ever been. My big brother doesn't need me to hold him together anymore.

"I have to go," I tell him.

He reaches deep into his jeans pocket and keys jingle when he lifts them out.

Then he gives them to me.

"I know, Joy Bear." And there's a Carson smile that's meant just for me. Adoring, protective, and now, crooked and bittersweet.

My fingers wrap around the truck keys. "Thanks, Racecar."

We both jump into an embrace without warning, like we read the other's minds. His tight bear hug squeezes the air out of me, but I wheeze it out willingly.

Then I ask, "Wait, what about you? How will you get home?"

He grins. "I'll find my own way."

♫

I'm finally in the driver's seat of Carson's truck. It's awkward and roomy. I dreamed of driving his truck, but I never expected him to hand me the keys. He dangled them above my head often enough. I don't hate the memories now, though.

My ringtone sounds. *He called back.*

"Cale!" I answer, nearly squealing.

"Hey, Almond Joy! What's up? How you been?" He sounds like his normal self, which is a relief.

"I'm okay," I say. And I'm not lying. I lay my forehead on the steering wheel. "I wanted to apologize."

"But you already did, and you didn't even need to. I shoulda… I don't know. I should have done this whole thing different." His laugh is light, but nervous.

I chew on my lip. "There's stuff you should know, Cale. I mean, I don't know what you figured out, but you should know the truth."

There's a beat of silence. But then he sighs. "You don't gotta do that. But I'll listen."

Before I manage to start off on my speech, I pause. It feels wrong to tell him like this. I look down at the keys in my hand.

Cale breaks the silence. "Wait, aren't you supposed to be at orientation right now?"

"Yeah. But I'm, um…" Where was I going, anyway? Where's *my* game?

"Hey," I say with new inflection, "Are you up for a day trip? Because there's somewhere I really want to be and I could use the moral support."

"You know, Almond Joy," he says, his voice low enough to fill me with anticipation, "I can make that happen."

♫

"What, the beater wasn't up to the escapade?" Cale asks as he plops into the passenger side of Carson's truck.

My heart's a rush just seeing him. I don't address his question.

"It's good to see you, Cale."

His face softens and he smiles on one side. "You, too." He slaps the dash. "So! Where we headed?"

I twist my grip on the steering wheel. "Don't worry too much about the destination, Cale Salad. The journey might be all you can handle."

"Whoa." He puts his hand on his chest like an offended old lady. "Was that vaguely threatening or is it just me?"

I laugh and pull out of the parking lot of Cale's apartment complex. "I don't think it was a threat."

"You don't *think* it was?" He flashes me an expression of increased worry.

I missed having him around.

GPS is unnecessary for now. I just have to head north for a few hours. I'm guessing there will be signs to warn me when I get close. But as I enter the freeway, my main concern is clearing the air with Cale.

I'm still struggling with how to start the whole story.

"So... you gonna explain what happened with orientation today?" he asks before we've even gone a mile from his house.

"Yeah. But it's a long story so sit tight."

"I ain't perfected my duck and roll out the car move yet. You're good."

"Everything has to do with the reason we left Salem more than a year ago." And from there, I tell him about it. About Tyler Fuller and the police and Carson. He gets real quiet and I leave the cab empty of noise for a little while. He stares out the window as we leave town, but it doesn't seem like he's struggling with what to say. I think he's just sitting with it.

It's not uncomfortable, being silent with him. I'm not sure how long we're there. Sitting in a length of utter quiet without any awkwardness is a good marker of friendship. We let each other think our own thoughts.

"That never shoulda happened," he finally says, his voice muted and contemplative.

"If it never happened, I wouldn't be here with you. I'd be living a fake life, still trying to please everyone but myself. Honestly, I think that's what I was doing until I left FredU today."

I explain how things changed after graduation. How I developed feelings for Jin, despite trying not to. Then I'm regaling what really happened when I twisted my ankle, or rather right *before* I twisted my ankle.

"So you literally fell for him?" Cale says. I'm glad his humor has remained intact.

"More like I crashed and burned for him. Against my own will. But… even though we both wanted it, it's impossible."

And I explain why. Jin's dad. My loyalty to Lena. Him moving to Korea. And the whole blow-up after Carson's return game.

It's the first time I verbalize the truth even to myself. I let Jin believe that the fake dating thing was a lie because I didn't want him to give up his internship for me.

I believed you… Jin's regret stung. Like he was shocked at himself for being so reckless.

By the time I've finished the entire story, my throat is dry from talking so much. We're nearly to Seattle.

Actually, it wasn't the whole story. I guess there's time to address the part I left out.

"About the game... or, the part where we kissed," I start, pursing my lips with hesitation. "It wasn't out of pity. I do like you, Cale."

"Wait, really?" His surprise is evident in the high pitch of his voice.

"Yeah," I sigh. "You're the obvious choice. I'm happy whenever you're around. You bring light everywhere you go, and more importantly, you're here." I glance at him. I want to want Cale. I want water games and clever puns and interlaced, two-toned fingers. I really like being with him.

But... I *love* Jin. And I won't run from that.

The exit for the SeaTac airport warns us a quarter mile ahead.

"Girl, you're gonna miss the airport exit if you don't get over."

I refuse to move.

"You think I didn't figure it out? Jin's leaving today. We're heading to Seattle. Simple math."

I shake my head. "But I can't make it right anymore."

"Like hell, Becker! I see it all over your cute little face, you are still hung up on that Korean Prince Charming. Get your BUTT into that lane!"

I hold my breath. We pass the SeaTac exit.

"You missed it!" he shrieks.

"Jin's plane left this morning," I say with a large portion of sour regret. "My mom talked to Jan-di right after. He's already gone."

I linger on Cale's shock for a second longer than I should, then look back on the grey stretch of freeway.

"Do me a favor, Cale Salad?"

His mouth hangs open before he answers. "Are you serious? I thought we were gonna dash through TSA in a grand romantic gesture this whole damn time! You swindled me! I want drama, Joy!"

I hand him my phone. "You'll get drama. Route me to Alki Beach."

"Fine," he says with mostly false resistance as he plucks my phone from my hand.

The road noise and artificial clacking of my phone's keyboard are all I hear for a minute. Google's pleasant female voice starts us off.

"I hope this mystery trip makes it up to me," Cale says, settling my phone into the mount.

My lungs fill with nervous air. "Forgive me?" I keep my eyes on the sun-baked road. "For still choosing him, even though he's gone."

"Kid, there's nothing to forgive."

♫

I didn't expect my summer beach trip would involve Cale, my brother's truck, or a beach so small it should really be called a "sliver of sand." But here we are.

Cale snagged the pin of the exact location from Robbie's email. He also confirmed from various social media platforms that The Crux Constellation is indeed setting up a surprise concert and fans are freaking out.

"What song are you gonna sing?" Cale pesters.

I bite my lip. "I didn't exactly pick one."

"Well, they know you're coming, right?"

I avoid eye contact.

"GIRL."

"I'm taking a chance here, Cale. If it's meant to be, then it'll work out. Right?"

"You really got no plan?" His high voice judges me.

The exit becomes visible. HARBOR AVE SW.

"My *plan* was to call you. And somehow I convinced you to jump into the car and we ended up at the top of the state. I achieved my goal. We're good again, that's all I wanted."

"Hey, my grand master plan to win your heart may have backfired, but we were always good, Joy." His seriousness on the latter part cuts straight to my soul. I take in how he looks, as Cale as ever, but I find something deeper now.

"I don't deserve you."

"No one does, Almond Joy." He folds his hands behind his head. "I am a generous gift."

I laugh. "I'm glad you recognize it."

The sun beats in through the gradient tint on the windshield as we spend the next few minutes slowing down on the residential streets. Modern beach houses and aged brick apartment complexes confuse the horizon before the water comes into view against coin-colored sand. My heart rate picks up the closer we get to the plaza.

I once told my primary school friends I'd seen the Statue of Liberty because I'd witnessed the miniature version of her at Alki Beach. Calling this place "the beach" feels as lackluster as calling that tiny hunk of bronze "the Statue of Liberty." I'd envisioned lying back on the massive, breezy oceanside of the Oregon Coast. But here, the wind comes off the water and people walk around in shorts and sunglasses, so it does the trick.

I parallel park next to a seafood restaurant that advertises too many types of cuisines. When I cut the engine, it's real. A few blocks up, I see bulky guys carrying speakers to the makeshift platform at the plaza.

"You ready?" Cale asks. I don't move, so he elbows me. "You ready? YOU READYYY?"

I giggle, but I'm still terrified. "I don't know," I sigh.

"Hey," he says, "There's not really such a thing as 'ready.'"

I meet the gleam in his brown eyes. It isn't until this moment that I realize how bad it hurt not to have him around. I'd been uncertain of our friendship, but he never was. There may not be such a thing as "ready," but there is definitely comfort in being supported.

Cale pumps his fist. "Let's do this, Becker!"

A gust of violent wind whips my hair across my face when I get out of the car. I don't know how I'm gonna keep it cool when I get on stage.

If I get on stage. I have no idea how forgiving "Robbie Gonzalez the band manager" is.

The Statue of Liberty Plaza is paved with rectangular stone and people are already seated on the grass and benches, even the stairs. The statue obstructs where people will crowd, but their fan base is loyal enough not to care.

Cale flashes his white teeth at me as we walk. My gut does flips the closer we get. I recognize the band and their respectively distinct hairstyles. Krista with the magenta bob, Fiona with the emerald side-buzz, Geo with stick-straight blonde hair down to his hips, January with the bleached pixie cut, and Javed with absolutely normal, shaggy black hair.

Even if I didn't plan to come, I did my research.

Robbie Gonzalez is the one guy I have not seen a picture of, but there's a stocky man covered in tattoos who looks like the name might belong to him. The sides of his head are shaved with a dark plume of gel-covered hair on the top. Also a full beard. The hair might mean he belongs with the band. My hasty plan is to ask him if he knows who Robbie is, but he spots me and his eyes light up.

"Joy Becker?" he almost yells.

I step closer and raise my hand sheepishly. "That's me. Sorry I never emailed back."

"And you brought your partner in crime, I see!" Robbie slaps Cale on the back and they both laugh, but Cale rolls his shoulder when Robbie isn't looking.

"I'm stoked you're here! I just wish we'd set up for you. It's been crazy all around today." He has a genuine, friendly laugh that puts me at ease. "What do you say if we have to take 'Back To You' after our first fiver?"

"Fiver?" I wish I knew the lingo and didn't sound like a little kid.

"Oh, yeah, it's a five-minute break. Like forty-five minutes into the show the band will cool off."

Back To You. I know it. I've played it five hundred times.

And specifically avoided it for the last week.

"I can't," I say.

Robbie's positive energy dissipates. "Oh. Wow. I'm sorry, I thought you came because you were still interested. I should've asked." He rubs the back of his neck. "I can hardly think straight today!"

"No, I want to sing! I just... I don't know if I can do that song. It's too..."

Robbie's brow goes up waiting for me to finish. But it's hard to say it.

"Raw," Cale finishes. He points to me and frowns. "Lost love. Too raw."

At least Cale's bluntness has benefits.

Robbie perks up the way someone does when they're excited, but also feel they shouldn't be. "Well, what song do you want to do? I can tell you if it's in our set and send you on up. Just gotta warn the band."

"How about *Cosmos*?" I say. One of my favorites. Upbeat and well-practiced in the shower.

"Yeah yeah yeah! I'll let January know you're taking that one over." Robbie grins and shakes his head in disbelief. "This is gonna be good."

I hope he's right.

"He's right," Cale says like he's reading my mind. "You're gonna kill it!" He whips out his phone and taps the back of it. "And I'm gonna document."

"Okay, so I just have to enjoy the music and keep my nerves from causing me to implode."

Cale lands his wide palm on my shoulder and squeezes. "You got this!"

Despite his encouragement, performance anxiety scratches at the edges of my soul and begs me to run.

But I'm not a runner. Not anymore. I found the game I'm meant to play. If only I'd realized it sooner.

An airplane cuts the sky overhead, a whooshing noise trailing behind it.

Jin's voice echoes in my mind. *I really want to hear you sing again.*

As thrilled as I am to be on the ground, right where I am, I kinda wish I was singing up in the sky, somewhere over the Pacific Ocean. I wish I was with him.

But I'm not.

The true farewell show of The Crux Constellation is void of dancing lights or quality speakers. It's no more than a fiery set of humans who meld with the energy inside each of their songs. January exudes sex appeal I'll never match. She's way more rough-edged than I am, too. But I'm not deaf; I know our voices are crazy close. Raspy in all the ways that count, powerhouse on cue, feminine and light when it works.

I don't know what Robbie sees in me. I'm nothing like their current frontwoman, but maybe that's the point. My voice does justice to the songs and I'm still me. The girl at Americanafest wasn't trying to be January Evans.

Their heavy drums and stretched-out synths carry listeners to worlds where robots fall in love and waves crash against bleeding hearts. The drummer can also play the fiddle and the basswoman gets lost in her chords like she's unafraid of drowning in the song.

The people around me eat it all up. Cale has become a total fangirl, "woos" and all.

Meanwhile my stomach turns into foam each time they end a song. The buzz of anticipation is like a drug that heals you and makes you sick. My limbs feel like they've fallen asleep.

I sober up when Robbie shoves me toward the stage and says, "Okay, kid! Your time to shine!"

My heels skid on the paved plaza ground. *Deep breath. You can do this. You'll never be ready.*

Like singing for Jin. I look at the water, imagining the sparkling waterfall. Remembering how the water reflected sunlight against his face.

I slam my foot onto the platform and force myself up there.

January talks into the mic, "Hey, we got a friend here today to sing for you CruxConvicts! She's little, but she's got one hell of a voice on her! Give it up for Joy!"

Everyone cheers louder than they should for me. She pulls the mic from the stand and hands it over, mouthing "good luck."

I grab it, feeling like I'm suddenly drunk on something strong. The crowd's bigger than I expected. Or the nerves are, I can't tell.

Cale lifts his phone up, undoubtedly recording.

I lift the mic up, ready to say whatever I planned about the song *Cosmos* and what it means to me and that I sang it into a hairbrush like a proper dork.

But I freeze. It's not right.

The last time I sang, Jin kissed me. I haven't piped out a single note since then.

I blink like mad, willing long-built tears to stay back.

"Um," I say into the mic, my breath reverberating in the speakers. "I can't sing the song I came up here to sing. I'm kinda stuck on something else."

People grow quiet and I feel my honest self reaching through the cracks of what's broken in me. I don't care if it's awkward. It's real.

I'm stuck on you, Joy.

I meet eyes with January, and some of the people in the crowd. There's a lot of raw expectation, but some of them have honest, supportive expressions. They don't even know me.

Well, one of them does. I'm glad he's here.

I step to the precise center of the platform. "I'm gonna sing a song you might know. Maybe it means something to you like it does to me. But it's the only thing on my heart right now, so it's all I have to give."

In my mind, instruments swell, but everyone else is baited on the silence before my voice flows into the mic. I close my eyes.

And sing *Rainbow Connection*.

I pay no mind to how I sound or how people react. I'm sitting on the rocky floor next to a pond, the hum of my voice floating into the sky with ethereal song. The lyrics mean something different now. They don't tell of an unattainable dream swirling out of reach like a balloon.

The Rainbow Connection is our journey to seeing true beauty. Or, that's what it means to me.

By the second verse, the pianist lifts notes into the song, the guitar strums beachy chords and the bassist carries depth under it. The song takes on new life and the crowd travels to another plane of appreciation. Songs are that way. Like a vehicle for your soul, taking you off the grid of reality for however long they last.

I sing the bridge, reaching the moment where Jin stopped me. I let the word carry out too long, and the silence after, too. With my eyes closed, I can see his face like a vivid picture. The moment replays in my head.

How did I get so entwined with Jin so quickly? How can my heart be threaded to him, stretched out over time and space and this moment of a song?

I sing the words of the next verse, like I'm gently plucking flowers from the ground for a bouquet. And this is far more beautiful than the last time I sang it.

Before, I couldn't finish. I wasn't finished. Jin interrupted my life and brought a halt to my heartache, like the apex of a hill, before rolling quickly down and crashing at the bottom. But I've completed the journey now. I climbed the mountain, and now I live at the end of the rainbow.

I finish the song, with some Kermit fans who happened to join me, and something clicks.

I am my fairytale dreams, my tumultuous past, and my uncertain future. My essence is a spectrum. Both real and ethereal, like a song can be.

I'm beaming when I notice the cheers. But even bigger than that is my own sense of wholeness. The crazy part of finally feeling whole is that you don't feel unbroken. You're different, a new thing altogether. Changing back isn't the right path to normal. It's not even an option. Accepting is.

I have no idea if I belong on this stage, but I know I belong somewhere. And I don't have to try fitting into someone else's life. I will find my game and I'll play hard when I do.

Cale whoops in decibels high above the rest of the crowd, bringing me somewhat to reality.

Oh, God. I just threw professional musicians off their own concert to sing a kids song about rainbows.

I shove the microphone back into January's hand, garnering feedback on the speakers. At least she's smiling at me right before she takes over again.

Cale's right at my side to help me off stage. "Joy Becker, you tantalizing muppet-lover!"

I laugh at him but something catches my eye. Someone standing on the sand, not far off, staring me down.

I meet a set of familiar, pear-colored eyes.

Lena.

Track 29 - Homecoming Queen

That's Lena.

When she won the title of Homecoming Queen, Cale told me all about the girl with the shiny hair and big reputation. She was so glamorous and sparkly, I thought I could never make friends with a girl like that. Not again.

Molly Hannigan was Junior Homecoming Queen at West Salem High. A partier, charismatic debate team president, the girl with a boyfriend in college, one of my friends. I figured Lena wouldn't be any different. In some ways, I was right. They both did a pretty good job betraying my trust.

But Molly never came back.

"That's Lena," I say, staring at the girl on the beach. Strands of her silky black hair dance across her face and collar bone. "What's she doing here?" My question comes out like a breath.

"Okay, so, don't freak out but I texted her," Cale says, stringing the words together rapidly. "She came up today for U-Dub orientation. She… feels bad about everything. That's what she told me, anyway."

She watches me, fiddling with her sweater, gazing off into the water for a few seconds before landing her eyes back on me.

When I left Salem, I had no one. Every person I counted on turned out to be a fairweather friend. They chose Tyler's side, believed lies about my family, ignored me crying in the bathroom stalls. I felt like I was floating above myself, forced to watch a tragic film that never relented. Molly, Amber, Gavin, Thea. Names I used to say daily. Faces that greeted me warmly in the morning. They became sideways glances and whispering heads.

All I wanted was for one of them to talk to me. I thought at least Molly would.

I learned a long time ago that loneliness isn't worth protecting. Carson did that, with rage-covered shame. I resolved never to be the kind of person who made reconciliation impossible.

None of my friends ever tried.

Not until right now.

"Joy? Are you mad?" Cale asks.

I look up at him and shake my head. "No, I'm not mad at all."

And then I run to her.

It takes me five seconds and I hear her start an apology, "I'm sorry about me and Car—"

I crash into her and wrap my arms around her waist before she can finish.

A second later, she hugs me back, laying her head on the top of mine.

"I really suck," she says. I distance myself and notice she's crying.

"No, you don't suck. You did a sucky thing, but you don't suck, Lena."

"God, Joy, do you have to be such a mom?" She taps the edge of her eye with her fingertip.

Cale walks up to us and points at Lena. "Stop! Just stop! I'm a sympathetic crier!" I can't tell if his throaty voice is real or genuine, but it's welcome regardless.

I turn back to Lena and she heaves a sigh. "I am sorry, Joy. I got jealous and tried to strangle control out of something I had no control over. Like my mom. Shit." I note a few freckles on Lena's glistening cheekbones. "I should've never met up with your brother. Or tried to keep Jin to myself. I knew he liked you and I just..." She sniffles.

"You knew?"

She nods hard. "Oh yeah. He had the hots for you, like, the first day you met."

I blush, recalling the on-the-floor moment we first saw each other. "Really? How do you know?"

"He *told* me!" She laughs with a twinge of bitterness. "Jin's basically halfway between a friend and a brother. He's not shy with me."

"But you're still in love with him."

"Yeah, well..." Lena looks off, her vision landing on the hazy blue hills in the distance. "I don't know if those were *my* feelings or my mom's visions of a perfect future projected onto me. She was the one always telling me my boyfriends were wrong for me, no matter what. She was right sometimes, but not always."

The air is fresh but heavy with humidity. The crowd cheers behind us, but it's out of place with Lena's turmoil. She's felt a lot more loss than I ever realized.

"The point is," she says, "Regardless of how I feel, I know he's *not* in love with me. He didn't even tell me he was leaving until yesterday." Her lip trembles.

"I'm so sorry, Lena," I whisper. I don't know what else I should say.

The wind picks up and she tightens her cardigan around her shoulders. "I was at the airport this morning before he left and I told him the truth. He deserved to hear it." "What did he say?" I ask. What I really want to know is what he did, but I'm afraid to ask that.

"He thought about it for a sec. Then he said, 'If she wanted to clear it up, she would have.' And then he hugged his mom and left."

I feel a shudder in my heart.

Lena's judgemental tone kicks in. "Why didn't you set things straight, Joy?"

I stare at her, my brow knit together as I try to form an answer.

She folds her arms. "He would've heard you out! He *wanted* to hear you out."

I still can't answer. I avert my eyes to the nearby fish and chips place, the bike going by, the driftwood lying on the sand.

"Why'd you let him go?" She's near yelling.

I pinch my mouth closed, fighting tears. Why is it so hard to say?

"Isn't it obvious, Lena?" Cale says, breaking his uncommon silence with uncommon gravity. "She'd rather suffer than ask Jin to jeopardize his future. That's who she is."

My wide eyes meet his. Since I told him my past, he sees the patterns of my choices. If it saves someone, I pour myself out. Even when I shouldn't.

"What if Jin *wanted* his future to be here?" Lena bites back, even though this fight isn't with Cale. She shakes her head and lands her pretty eyes on me. "Maybe we should just let these stupid boys make their own choices."

Her eyes flit to Cale when she says "stupid boys" and, to my surprise, he nods in agreement.

I look up at the clear, blue sky. "He already did."

"Guess so," Lena sighs.

Cale clutches me and Lena each on the shoulder, giving us each a start. "Are you both legit crazy right now?" We gape at him, since he's clearly the crazy one.

He continues, "Just cuz he's flying over the ocean don't mean it's over! Take it from a dude: he wants c-lar-i-ty." Cale enunciates each syllable on "clarity."

"What am I supposed to do now?" I ask Cale, as if he's the keeper of such knowledge.

"Call him. Leave a message." He drops his hand and gestures a check mark in the air. "Simple!"

My lungs fill with uneasy breath. It's almost too simple. *Call him.*

I can do that.

I yank my phone from my skirt pocket and find his contact. His silly winking face is his contact picture. My heart pounds as my finger hovers over the number.

Tap.

Straight to voicemail, as expected. *You've reached Jin Park, leave a message and I'll call you back when I can.*

I hope that's true. Wow, I desperately hope it's true.

Beep.

"Hey. It's Joy. Um…" *Deep breath, Joy.* Each word comes out separated from the others. "I just wanted to say that, um—" I swallow. I know this isn't right. "I hope you'll be happy in Korea. And I'll miss you."

I hang up in a rush.

"Joy! What the hell was that?" Lena shrieks.

Air shudders out from my lungs as I look between her and Cale, both surprised.

"You don't get it!" I say, the entrails of desperation escaping into my voice. Halfway through the voicemail, it hit me. "I can't make it harder for him. I don't want him to regret leaving."

They're both frowning at me, trying to make sense of my tangle of emotions. If I can't, I doubt they will.

"I don't want him to regret anything," I say. It's not really to Lena or Cale, though. I know I have to make a plan and reconcile, like my old friends never did.

I stand up taller. "I'll make it right. Later, I promise."

"You better," Lena says, but the snare in her words is a farce. She cares about me.

"I will personally hack your phone to keep you honest, Becker."

My eyes rim with tears as I look at them both. "I don't deserve to have you as friends."

"Oh, come on," Cale says, throwing his head back dramatically, snapping it back to me. "We all know who the real MVP of our friendship is, Joy."

Lena nods. Both of their eyes are on me.

I gape at them. Words don't exist, just disbelief. And honor.

There's a tap on my shoulder and I whip around. It's Robbie the band manager.

"Hey!" he says with a beaming smile, "Thanks for coming out. They're about to wrap up. You should stay and hang out."

I suck in a breath and try to level my emotion, with minimal success. "Sure! Yeah," I say. He's about to leave but I catch his attention. "Hey! I'm sorry for changing things up. Something came over me, I guess."

He shakes his head. "It's cool! I don't speak for everyone, but I like a little unpredictability in a show." He winks and laughs, simultaneously young and grown-up. Then he points his thumb back to the stage where January screams into the mic. "See you over there!"

Robbie walks off, weaving into the crowd and patting shoulders like he knows everyone.

"He's cute," Lena says, her chin slightly up as she checks him out.

That's Lena.

And I, for one, am glad she came back.

Track 30 - Handmade Heaven

The memories of this summer flip through my mind like fanning the pages of a book. The challenges, the rewards, the strikeouts. My future is uncertain now, but I also kind of needed that. It's bitter and sour like a grapefruit, but refreshing like watermelon. Now that I think about it, the memories themselves are like that, too.

I don't regret that it all happened, because in the end, I stepped up to the plate and swung. It sucks that I missed. But I don't regret playing.

My headphones are crackling a little, which means I've loved them well. A dreamy summer song helps me relish a stillness so rare in my life so far. The song is interrupted by the chime of my text tone.

> *LG: Meet me at the fallen tree in 30 minutes*
> *LG: Don't be late*

Wow, two seconds into making up and Lena's returned to her old, demanding ways.

I missed her.

I finish out my heavy rotation and head for the front door. It's finally not oven-weather today, but I can't walk the field in sandals, so I opt for Converse. I tuck my newly acquired Crux Constellation t-shirt into my acid-wash jean shorts and pull my hair half-up into a bun. Then I stare at my reflection in the entry hall mirror, freckled and sun kissed. This girl looks different than the one who's faced this mirror time and again. I'm not the pushover, can't-miss-a-game-or-get-a-B kid anymore.

I'm the college-dropout who never went to college. The singer who flubbed the biggest opportunity of her life. The magnet for minor injuries and Korean lawyers.

The girl who somehow charmed Jin Park into falling for her, then convinced him to fly to the other side of the world.

I wonder if he checked his messages. He never called back. It's 6 AM there. Not that it matters with jet lag.

Am I giving up again? I don't know. If I could, I'd get on a plane and find him, just to tell him face to face. But I didn't make *that* much money this summer. Maybe I'll ask Lena what she thinks I should do.

Still staring at my own gold-flecked hazel eyes, I remember how it felt to kiss him. It's like it ended two seconds ago. Potent memories always sting, because if they're bad, they still hurt. And if they're good, they're already gone.

"Where you headed?" Carson asks, shoveling midday cereal into his mouth.

I'm out of my trance. "Meeting Lena."

He blushes. "Oh. Hey, can you, um…"

I adjust my bun, my eyebrows lifted at him.

"Can you tell her I'm sorry for being an asshole?" he says.

I smirk. "Sure thing, bro."

"Joy. I know Mom was kinda annoyed about what you did yesterday, but you're gonna do great, no matter what you do." His dimple appears beside a really great brother smile. He'll be cheering me on from bleachers this time.

I smile back. "Thanks, Racecar. Go put on a shirt."

I walk out into the bright, breezy summer day, stuffing my phone into my back pocket.

"Joey!"

Immediately to my left Jan-di Park is leaning against her slick white Mercedes parked by the sidewalk. It looks like she was talking to my mom.

I can't help but smile seeing her. "Jan-di! How are you?"

She grins, her eyes creasing. "I'm doing so good."

"You going somewhere, sweetheart?" Mom asks me in that light tone of voice she uses when she's talking to me in front of another adult.

"Yeah, meeting Lena." I look back at Jan-di. "How's Jin doing? I bet you miss him."

Her smile doesn't fade, but her eyebrows go up. "Oh, yes! Every mom miss baby, Joey. But he so good."

Jan-di sure is good at keeping a smile on. Then again, I guess I am, too.

"Tell Lena I said 'hello,'" Mom says, in that gentle way of urging a child away from the adult conversation.

"I will. Bye, Jan-di." I wave goodbye to the pair of oddly pleasant moms. Moms are so good at keeping a cool head around each other, especially when their children make drastic life decisions they don't approve of.

I'm not sure how Jan-di felt about Jin's decision, but I know Mom wasn't too happy with mine. I'm not going back to Frederick University. The fallout wasn't as awful as I expected, though. Less a shrill "the world is ending" and more a reluctant "back to the drawing board."

Walking along the sidewalk, I note the hum of a lawn-mower and smell some faint smoke from a barbecue. It's a remarkable summer day. I wonder if the secluded fallen tree will feel like it did before. Chatting Lena up about future plans and Puerto Rican culture, promising to bake cookies next time I go to her house. I guess I don't have to convince her to watch *Greatest Showman* anymore. And she doesn't have to ask if I'm eyeing anyone.

Before I leave my neighborhood, I stare out at the field on the other side of the street. The golden swath of grass, lined by rows of tall trees that sway and rustle. I can't see the fallen tree from here, but I know right where it is. Into the middle of the woods, just beyond the line.

That dead, scraggly log has the tendency to inject life and brightness into my friendship with Lena. We crafted an emotional oasis out of nothing but air, tree bark, and solitude.

I cross the street and jog into the field. The dry grass tickles my legs all the way up. I brush my hands across the tops of the tan strands. After traversing the uncut field, I pass under the sporadic shade of the trees, birds singing in pure confidence. The rustling leaves hush every other sound. It's been a while since I soaked up an atmosphere like this.

The trees peter out and I walk into the hidden clearing. My eyes fall on the centerpiece: the fallen tree. In a stream of amber sunlight, perched on top of it... isn't Lena.

It's Jin. Looking up into the sky like a contemplative work of art.

Am I dreaming?

He turns his head, slowly. A current of wind strikes us both.

I study him. His neutral expression, the lines of his bony shoulders, that same white t-shirt. The sun rays cast him in harsh yet angelic light.

I slowly walk toward him. I'm not sure if the ground will give way. He leaps from the felled tree. When his feet hit the ground, my heart pounds and I stop. He really is here.

"I thought you were in Korea," I say.

He takes a second to answer. "I'm not."

"Clearly." I sound annoyed even though I'm not. I adore the way shadows hug his cheeks and lips and long neck. I can't believe I'm looking at him.

I don't know why it's taken me until this moment to realize that Lena's text and Jan-di's diversion were a set up. They both knew I'd meet Jin here.

Confusion and happiness swirl together in my heart. I'm happy he's here, but I can't read him. I don't want to screw up again.

Deep breath.

"Do you not want me here?" he asks.

His question surprises me. "I just thought you were gone, that's all."

"That's not why I'm asking, Joy." There's heaviness in his serious eyes.

The bewildered part of me grows. What does he mean then?

I scan the parched ground to keep composure, but I can't keep myself from catching the way he's cloaked in the glow of the afternoon. I feel like I'm not ready for this. *There's not really such a thing as "ready."*

"I'm really sorry for everything, Jin. I am."

His brows pinch together, like he's pained. "Everything?"

"Yes! I hate that I hurt you. I didn't mean to. I just... I thought if you were unattached, it would be easier for you to go."

"You thought breaking my heart would make it easier?" There's a thread of irritation in his expression. He angles away from me, and he's right to.

My jaw trembles. I was so stupid to think it was better that way, but I was convinced.

"I couldn't let you give up your future for me." My eyes sting with tears and my voice fills with emotion. "I didn't want that to happen again."

I bury my face in my hands, sobbing into the darkness of my palms. Carson lost everything because of me. Jin was about to do the same thing. I didn't want to hurt him, but I couldn't let him do that for me.

But… Jin's the one who showed me that I can't bear the responsibility of other people's choices.

Jin clears his throat. I lift my wet face out of my hands and my nose tingles. I'm sure it's red. I'm a splotchy mess and he's painted porcelain.

"I'm not your brother," Jin says. "I wasn't giving up anything I didn't already want to give up."

I narrow my eyes. "But you went to the airport. Lena said you went through security."

Jin nods. "Yeah. I got on the plane. Because I was hurt. It's not like you just ended it, Joy. You let me think every amazing thing we had was…" He holds his breath before blurting, "Fake. Like you were never all in."

His hurt flickers when he sets his jaw and fear constricts me. It's like a neon "Open" sign has shut off and I missed my chance to walk in. He won't look at me.

He walks toward the tree, facing away. He hunches over with his palm on the bark.

"Nothing was fake, Jin," I insist.

He glances over his shoulder. "That's what Lena said."

Jin suddenly walks up to me. "I have to tell you something, Joy."

My stomach flips. I nod, bracing for whatever it is.
What is it?

His dark brown eyes study my face, like he's not sure how to say it.

"When I sat down on the plane, I couldn't fasten the seatbelt. I didn't know why. But I couldn't stop thinking about you. Wondering why you'd let me think you lied." He steps closer and my heart races. "Then I thought about who you are. How you've given up so much just to benefit other people. The deal with Cale. Running off to spare Lena's feelings. What you did for your brother. You always sacrifice your own feelings for other people. That's why you let me go. It was for me."

His voice is so dreamlike. *Am I dreaming?*

Jin reaches out to brush a golden string of hair behind my ear and his finger brushes my cheek and, boy, I am definitely not dreaming.

"Jin—"

"I'm not done," he says like a command. "Tyler Fuller wasn't worth your mercy, Joy. Maybe your brother was. Knowing what Tyler did, I definitely understand Carson better. That made me realize I'm not meant for translating business law. Not when people like you are standing up without someone behind them. Protecting those people… *that's* what I want to do. *That* is a rare kind of wonderful." He looks down, almost embarrassed. "I want to be worthy of that."

"You are, Jin." I'm flush and so, so certain. "You are."

I can't describe the light that turns on in him. It's not just an "Open" sign. It's like an entire skyscraper lights up.

"I don't deserve that," he says. "Not from you. You're far more wonderful than I am."

His sudden, unrestrained adoration pummels me.

Jin draws closer. The scent of jasmine dances with the breeze that whispers into the inch of space between us.

I'm breathless. No one has looked at me this way. Even my parents were always bent on shielding me. They didn't look at me like this. With...

Admiration.

I can't move. This moment is so big. I can already hear the swell of an invisible orchestra, building to what he's raring to say next.

In sunbeams, Jin's eyes gleam. His breath goes shaky.

"I'm all the way in love with you."

Just like that, I am fearlessly deeper in love with Jin Park.

"Me too," I whisper, just before impulse takes over. I reach up and grasp the back of his neck, standing on my tiptoes, catching his brief look of surprise before I pull him into a kiss. His arms find me, tighten around me and lift me off the ground until I'm above him.

This love doesn't feel like falling. It feels like flying.

Jin was hidden in my life long ago, tucked away in the background when I thought I would never see light again. But here, I'm bathing in light, inside and out.

All we have is a melody of birds, the beat of rustling leaves, and each other. It's the sweetest song I've ever heard.

Track 31 - Out Of The Woods

Color me surprised. This is not how I thought this day would go.

Jin and I are stealing time at the fallen tree, talking between dreamy make-out sessions that leave me giggling every time. I don't know how I moved into this sheer bliss, but with the falling sun and cooling air, it gets easier to want Jin's arms around me. It's like a drug, the coupling of our lips touching and my heart bursting. Every part where he touches me, my hands, my back, my hips, my jawline… it tingles.

The sun has turned into a rainbow and lights up everything like neon. The colors of my life.

We sit on top of the log facing each other. Jin confirms what Lena told me. He was into me from the first moment we met.

"That was the most embarrassing introduction I've ever had," I laugh.

"It didn't seem like it. You brushed it off. And you were super cute, too, so I took notice."

I avert my eyes, blushing. "Yeah, I took notice, too."

I take an eyeful of him, his one leg dangling off the side of the tree. I press both my hands on the scratchy bark, leaning into them so I can get closer.

He meets me in the middle, with exactly the kiss I wanted. One we each take a full breath through.

"So what did you think when you thought I was taken?" I ask when we've parted.

"That I had to back off."

"Of course you did." I should've known. "You're an actual gentleman."

"Yeah, well, I'm also naïve. My mom told me not to believe you, but I did because I wanted to. I'm too honest. Might make me a terrible lawyer."

I palm his cheek. "Or one of the best."

He smirks. "You don't have to say that just because you're my girlfriend."

Girlfriend? I gape at him, pulling my hand back because I'm caught off-guard.

"Oh." He reacts to my abrupt shift at his word choice. "I never asked, did I? I—will—"

"Yes!" I say, unable to contain my smile. "Absolutely yes."

I don't know why the thought of Jin being my honest-to-goodness boyfriend gives me a fresh wave of butterflies, but it does.

His fingers graze mine one by one. "So why *did* you kiss Cale that day?"

There's a flicker of insecurity in him. He looks down and continues tracing my fingers.

"Cale said he wanted to shoot his shot, so I let him," I say, my tone somewhat somber. "But it was all wrong. You texted me right then and... I knew it was you."

We make eye contact and my heart's ticking resounds deep in my chest. The corner of his mouth curls up.

284

"But Carson saw it," I add, hating to ruin that smile. I explain what happened from that side. Carson didn't believe me, then he did, then he didn't again. Now that I know Carson has been talking to a therapist, it makes sense to think he just struck out that day. But the fact that he can pull himself back together now makes a huge difference.

"So how will your brother react to me being your boyfriend?" Jin asks, just a little smug.

"He'll survive," I jest. The truth is, Carson might feel mixed up, but it won't matter. I'll fight for what I have with Jin. I hope I don't have to, but I will.

"One last question," he says, scooting toward me. "Why were you in Seattle yesterday?"

"Lena didn't tell you?" I'm kind of surprised.

"Nope. She just said you drove all the way up there for me. But, the timing was off, so I'm missing something."

"I didn't actually go up there for you. I knew you were gone. Or, I thought you were."

"So why were you there?"

I put my finger up and reach for my phone with my other hand. When I pull it out, I find Cale's TikTok, where he posted the video of me singing for The Crux Constellation.

Ten thousand views. And counting.

"Oh my god!" I say, laughing in shock. "I'm viral!"

I give my phone to Jin, leaning in close so we can watch it together. The emotion is clear. It's weird to view it from this side. Singing that song was healing and ethereal in the moment. Now I see a girl with a broken heart, letting her voice carry her through something no one else can really see but they can somehow relate to.

"I was supposed to audition for the band, but I couldn't do it. After the show, even though they said I sounded good, they didn't say they'd contact me. I'm pretty sure I missed my chance." I say all this right before the part when I stop singing because Jin had kissed me there before. The video captures my hesitation, but only me and Jin can tell what's there.

"I was thinking about—"

"I know." Jin gently puts his hand behind my head and draws me in.

Here he is again, kissing me, interrupting the song. Is it always going to be like this?

God, I hope so.

♫

August 4th, 2:08 AM

Jin and his mom stayed for dinner. And after dinner. And then Jin and I took to the den ourselves for an episode of *The Walking Dead*.

We didn't really watch much of it, if I'm honest. Too busy kissing.

I cover my face with my blankets. Am I really blushing alone in my dark bedroom where literally no one will see me? My cheeks are sore from grinning so much. I'd rather smile than sleep anyway.

This yearning aches. Like when we said goodbye. Jin kept his eyes on me as long as possible, before my front door closed. I slid down the door and dropped to the floor. Maybe I was hoping he'd come back if I laid in the entryway.

Separation from him feels so wrong. Like someone so in love shouldn't feel heartbroken, but I do. The reality is a thrill, though. He's mine. I'm his. Bless this summer, injuries and all.

All I can think about is when I'll see him next, which is serious cardio for my brimming heart. It keeps me awake, but my eyes are starting to droop.

Buzz.

My hands are faster on my phone's notifications than they've ever been.

> *JP*: *I'm still thinking about you*

I type very, very quickly. My cheeks hurt again.

> *JB*: *Me too*
> *JB*: *It's hard to sleep*

> *JP*: *Agreed*
> *JP*: *I'm kind of in awe that today even happened*

> *JB*: *How do you think I feel?? I didn't even plan to see you this year!*

> *JP*: *Haha I guess that's true*
> *JP*: *I'm sorry I didn't just call you. I wasn't sure you still felt the same.*
> *JP*: *Lena only said we needed to talk. And your voicemail was discouraging. I thought you'd moved on already.*

I audibly whimper when I read that. It didn't occur to me that keeping my true feelings to myself had hurt him. Not until now.

> *JP*: *I'm really really glad I was wrong :)*

I can hear it in my head, the text in his voice. Emphasis on the second "really." An actual smile at the end. I wish he was here, saying it in person.

JB: I love you so much, Jin. I mean it.

JP: I still mean it too.

JP: You should get some sleep.

JB: I'll call you before you drive back to Seattle

JP: Can't wait to hear your voice Joy. Goodnight.

JB: Goodnight <3

Grief is the other emotion keeping me up right now. Jin has to go back up to UW to talk to his academic advisor. Apparently his sudden forfeit of the Seoul internship involves signing some paperwork, plus meeting professors to get in classes he needs. He'll be there for a few days with Jan-di, and it is definitely going to kill me. I'm grateful we live in a time where cell phones exist, but they're not much when the real thing is so, so good.

I'm not excited about potentially having a longish-distance relationship. It's not South Korea, but it's a long drive my car won't survive after a few round trips. And it's not like I can just move there. I might have rich friends, but even if they offered to help me get there, I couldn't take it.

I'm playing this game. Me. I'll do this my way.

Since I can't sleep, I think I'll look at Seattle job listings. I reach for my phone and check the time. It's already 2:20 AM. I set it down. I should *try* to sleep.

Buzz.

I snatch it and see it's not Jin. It's an email. I'm about to ignore it, but it's from Robbie Gonzalez. Robbie Gonzalez *the band manager,* Robbie Gonzalez.

"So about that audition..." the email subject line reads.

Holy crap. I fight tremors in my hands and my over-worked racing heart to open the email.

I read it.

They want me.

HOLY CRAP. The Crux Constellation wants to give me a shot at being their lead singer!

Nope. Not sleeping. Not even trying.

I waste no time calling Jin. Of course he picks up right away. I don't keep my voice down just because the world is sleeping. I'm squealing. I don't care if Carson brings his fuzzy head here to complain.

Nothing stops me from sharing in this life-altering news with the boy I'm in love with. He couldn't be happier for me.

Or for himself. Since it probably means his girlfriend has to move up to Seattle.

September 7th

Finally I can move my weights out of the garage and blare my music." I'm standing in my mostly bare room and Carson's taking up my doorway. It suddenly occurs to me that this frequent sight is one thing I'm leaving behind.

Mom already told him there's no way he's taking over my room. She refuses to do one thing that might deter her baby girl from visiting home, her words. It makes me feel pretty special, actually.

I ignore his comment. "You're gonna come up for some shows, right?"

Carson grins. Then he nods once. And I nod back.

I can hardly wait to see him do it from an audience. I think I get why he wanted me at every game now.

Robbie's email said the band wanted to feel out having me up front, so I drove up that same week and practiced. I also got to see Jin sooner than I expected, which motivated the beater. Dad also fixed her up a bit, thank goodness.

Anyway, they GAVE ME A CONTRACT. After making the drive a few times and practicing more than I thought I could, they wanted me.

I guess going viral has perks. I still have to find a part-time job to make ends meet, but thanks to my Dad's scary good job-searching skills, I've already got a couple interviews lined up. I still have time to apply for part-time school at community college. I'm not mad at that prospect.

"Are you gonna be okay, Joy Bear?" It's hard to ignore that my big brother is actually worried about me.

I walk up to him and rub his face on both sides, making his curls bounce. "Yes, Racecar. I'll be fine."

I wouldn't be so certain, except that Jin will be there. And Lena. Part of it is my faith in them, and part of it is their faith in me. I might be young, and small, but I've tackled bigger arenas than the ones ahead of me.

Knock knock. Lena pokes her head into view.

"Hey, Lena," Carson says. He moves aside for her, a charming cadence covering him instantly. As if I'm not standing right here. "You look nice today."

"Whatever, Carson. You still haven't invited me to a game." His smile falls off his face.

Okay, I still love how she reams him.

"Uh, yeah, well, I thought…" he stammers. "There's one today. If you wanna make it."

Wow. He's trying the coy approach. Haven't seen that one. It's clumsy.

Lena sizes him up. "A solid B for effort. But no. Can I have Joy now?"

"You're just delaying the inevitable, Lena," he says with a sly smile on his face as he walks by her.

"Dream on, Carson," she says, rolling her eyes. Even so, I give her a look that says "is he on to something??"

She frowns like I don't even know who I'm talking to. "Please, that's *way* over," she affirms, running her hand through her long hair. "It's weird that you're moving there before me."

"I know! I'm excited for when you get there, though. My apartment's not far from campus," I say, though I can hardly believe I just said "my apartment."

"Do you have anything else that needs to go?"

I scan my room. "I don't think so."

"Actually, there is one thing. Shouldn't be too hard to move, though." Lena pulls something out of her pocket. It's a silver necklace with a triangle watermelon charm on the end of it. The seeds look like tiny, sparkly black gems.

When I look up, I notice she's wearing an identical one. "You got this for me?"

"Yeah. After asking around for what you might like. And, well, I hate the ones where, like, you have to put them together to make a whole piece and say something dumb like 'BFFs FOREVER' which is stupidly redundant, so I got matching ones."

I pluck it from her hand and it sways beneath my fingers. "I love it. A lot."

"Good," she says with a huge smile.

I pull my hair to one side so I can clasp it behind my neck. It drops just below the neckline of my pineapple tee, the coral pink popping against the yellow and green like a vibrant fruit salad.

"You ready to go?" Lena asks.

"Yep," I sigh. It's weird, leaving the bedroom that cradled me through the most intense time of my life, but I am ready.

Lena and I walk out to where *the boys* are still loading boxes in my car.

This summer started with a ridiculous deal for this very car. This beat-up, ugly beige, 90s sedan, that practically begged me to call Jin to my rescue on multiple occasions. I couldn't leave her behind.

Cale rubs her roof in nostalgia.

"Be good to her," he says with his eyes closed.

"She's been good to me so far," I assure him.

"I was actually talking to you, Almond Joy. This is my baby."

"It's a big, metal object, Cale," says Lena. "It's so weird when guys talk about cars like they're people."

Cale clings to the side of the car. "Don't listen to her, my precious, beat-up beauty!"

"Thanks for the help, Cale," I say, getting a little choked up. "I'm gonna miss you like crazy."

"No, no, no, no! Stop that! I told you, I'm a sympathetic crier!"

But I don't comply. I snatch Cale into a hug and a tear escapes the corner of my eye. He squeezes me back.

"I'm about to object to the length of that hug," says Jin. The tone of his voice tells me Jin definitely isn't worried about the hug, but Cale's arms fling away from me anyway.

Turns out, Jin makes him nervous. But Jin still makes me nervous, too. In a different, much better way.

I kiss Jin's cheek after he's loaded my last box.

"That everything?" he asks. And honestly, I've already forgotten what he's asking about. I can't believe he's here, about to drive us up to Seattle, to a tiny apartment I'll share with *my* bandmates Krista and Fiona, in close proximity to where Jin will be studying law.

I've been ready for days.

"Just one thing," I say, and I jog back inside my suburban home, straight to my brother's room.

"I'm leaving," I say as I hang on to his door frame.

He bolts off of his bed and envelopes me in a bear hug. I'm proud of him. So proud. Even though he's sad that I'll be gone, he can fight his own battles. I grip him with all the strength I have in these bony arms.

I feel in his muscles all the sport and rage. He squeezes me until near death, and then he relaxes, letting me linger. This is the last time I'll hold my brother up.

"I love you, Carson," I say into the shirt he's thankfully wearing.

"I love you, too." They say your heart can be on your sleeve, but Carson's is in his voice.

He decides to step outside so he can wave at me as I drive off with Jin. I see Dad is wiping down the beater's windows, doing his best to leave the beast squeaky clean, which is better than "I love you" coming from him. Mom races out of the house with ziplock bags full of snacks for the road. She hands them to Jin and pats him on the arm.

I think she's still a little in awe that I snagged him. In a good way. Like me.

She turns to me, laying claim on the final farewell hug. She kisses my forehead and then stares back at me with the hazel eyes I inherited, stroking my head a few times. Fighting tears.

"I'm so proud of you. I'll see you at your first show," she says tenderly.

"Okay. I love you, Mom. You too, Dad."

"Same," Dad says, and that's more than I expected. It makes me laugh.

Or maybe I'm just giddy.

I look up at the clear blue sky, entirely empty of clouds. This is the sky that watched my summer live out, in all it's scandal and glory. I never thought it would end up like this.

Deep breath.

It's a pretty magnificent sky.

Jin takes the driver's seat and I take the passenger seat. Piled in with all my things, including, of course, my wonderful and embarrassing Lisa Frank pillow and Barbie blanket.

"Soooo," Jin says, a mere thirty seconds into our journey, "You said you have some music for the trip."

I plug my phone into the auxiliary port, old school. "It's kinda dumb, actually. I made a summer playlist and added songs as things happened. It's like a record of our summer."

"A musical commemoration of our love story?" he says with a silly grin.

"I know it's like melodramatic middle school vibes," I laugh. "I can pick something else."

"Play it," he insists.

I flip through the list of playlists I've gathered. *Joy's Summer Playlist.* "Are you sure?"

Jin takes his eyes off the road for long enough that I worry his adoration will cause an accident. "Absolutely. Make this summer last as long as possible."

Joy's Summer Playlist

1. Can't Blame A Girl For Trying - *Sabrina Carpenter*
2. The Middle - *Zedd, Maren Morris, Grey*
3. Starving - *Hailee Steinfeld, Grey, Zedd*
4. One Call Away - *Charlie Puth*
5. Never Been In Love - *Will Jay*
6. Hold My Hand - *Jess Glynne*
7. Just A Friend To You - *Meghan Trainor*
8. Better Now - *Post Malone*
9. Woke Up Late - *Drax Project, Hailee Steinfeld*
10. Take on Me - *Weezer*
11. Catching Feelings - *Drax Project, SIX60*
12. Space Age Love Song - *A Flock of Seagulls*
13. Style - *Taylor Swift*
14. Bad Liar - *Imagine Dragons*
15. Forever Young - *UNDRESSD*
16. Rainbow Connection - *Gwen Stefani*
17. I'M DOWN - *Meghan Trainor*
18. Sucker - *Jonas Brothers*
19. Rewrite the Stars - *Zac Efron, Zendaya*
20. Feel It Twice - *Camila Cabello*
21. Somebody That I Used To Know - *Gotye*
22. Say Something - *A Great Big World*
23. Grip - *Seeb, Bastille*

24. Heartless - *Diplo, Julia Michaels, Morgan Wallen*
25. Bluffin'- *Khalid*
26. This Is On You - *Maisie Peters*
27. Make It Without You - *Andrew Belle*
28. Clearly - *Grace VanderWaal*
29. homecoming queen? - *Kelsea Ballerini*
30. Handmade Heaven - *MARINA*
30. Out of the Wood - *Taylor Swift*
31. Young and In Love - *Ingrid Michaelson*

BONUS SONGS

Love - *Lana Del Rey*
Deep End - *Daughtry*
Unconditionally - *Katy Perry*
Chapter - *Christian Paul*
Young & Alive - *Bazzi*
All In - *Bearson, Georgia Ku, JRM*
Crashing - *Illenium, Bahari*
Adore You - *Harry Styles*
Dream of You - *Camila Cabello*
Want to Want Me - *Jason Derulo*
Put It Out - *Hellogoodbye*
Someday - *Michael Buble, Meghan Trainor*
King of My Heart - *Taylor Swift*
Anything Could Happen - *Ellie Goulding*

Sing It With Me - *JP Cooper, Astrid S*

GIRL - *Maren Morris*

Crush - *Avril Lavigne*

Acknowledgements

We're doing this Award Show style. Let's get right to it, shall we?

I thank the Lord God Almighty, Jesus Christ, for his love and sacrifice every day of my life. Victory goes to God, always and forever, and this sweet book is His domain. He used it to carry me through the massively difficult season of Coronavirus and inspired me to finish despite all the madness. So, He's MVP, and that's that.

The award for **Most Supportive and All-Around Good Guy** goes to my husband, Jimmy. You powered through this with unprecedented enthusiasm for someone who never reads young adult romance books. I know that it was all because you love me.

The triple-threat award for **Bubbliest Humans and Most Efficient Havoc-Wreakers** go to my three children. EV, Sammy, and Gideon, you are and always will be the reason I was brave enough to do anything. Also, the reasons I am certain of how much the world needs buckets of hope and cuteness.

The award for **Biggest Jan-di Park Fan** goes to Alicia Groff. You get bonus stars for being so cute and arting really well all the time. If not for you, we wouldn't have the adorablest member of the JSLP cast, who is clearly Jan-di.

The award for **Earliest Member of Team Cale** goes to Givens Lam. You also get bonus stars for being so cute and arting really well all the time. Your Jin-chokes-on-a-donut sketch will warm my heart forever. Also, to Givens and Alicia: my love life is a lot like Cale... ;)

The award for **Most Helpful and Gushiest Reactions** goes to Cait Elise Vandiver. I seriously don't know how I snagged you as a beta reader AND friend, but just know, I cannot function without you now. I feel like that should read as a warning.

The award for **Best Eyeballs and Softest Heart** goes to my editor, Elsie Bryan. I am so abundantly blessed to have you on my team, and to know you, and to be in awe of your creations that are separate from this project but not from my heart. You're wonderful.

The award for Most Precious Cheerleader goes to Zar Foster. Your praise was wildly undeserved and eternally appreciated. You are a beautiful soul, and I'm the luckiest person alive to have you as my partner-in-crime. (Bonus stars for arting greatly to you as well.)

The award for **Absolute Most Fantabulous Cover Designer** goes to Amelia Buff, who made the cover of this book. You were FAR, FAR more incredible to work with than I dared hoped for, and the results are excessively amazing! I'll be real, I constantly STARE.

And the award for **Best Listener and Beautifullest Sister** goes to my sister, Sophie Aston. Your insight and love and friendship gave me lots of energy and hope while I was worrying about the aspects of this project and life in general. There is no one more perfect I could wake up and call every morning. No one can replace you.

Now, I'd love to give awards to everyone, but there are only so many (read: I've reached my capacity to come up with clever award titles). **Honorable Mentions** go to my mom, Tanja Newby and my dad, Jeff Lemire, for being supportive MY WHOLE LIFE and loving me the way I needed. To my brothers, Lucas Lemire and Travis Lemire, for giving me lots of sibling material, showing me how beautiful sacrifices can be, and filling my heart and soul with familial love. To Noliecha Reid, for loving my kids while I developed my writing skills and attempted to learn Japanese. To my Grammie, Susan Dorr, for faithfully liking, commenting, and following my author journey posts, and also faithfully liking and loving me my whole life. To all my other family members, all of whom are genuinely wonderful, unique, and precious to me. To my friends Haley Sharp and Michelle Mertes for supplying me with the most incredible friendships of my youth. Without you two, this book would never have existed. And finally, to all of the inspiring individuals on the Instagram writing community I somehow stumbled upon. Seriously, you all leave me in constant awe.

Wow, I didn't think my acknowledgments section would be so big, but I owe this debut novel of mine to a lot of people. More than I've named. Thank you, everyone.

About the Author

Piper Bee was born and raised in the Pacific Northwest. For three years, she also lived in Charleston, South Carolina, where her love of air conditioning and fried food fully blossomed. She was married as a teenager and now has three kids who are pretty good at Japanese. She loves singing, learning about other cultures, watching cheesy romantic and/or undeniably epic TV shows, and eating just, like, in general. Currently, she has a princess fantasy series and a co-authored science fiction project in the works.

You can contact her at **piper@piperbeeauthor.com** and follow her on:

Instagram: @piper.bee

Twitter: @piperbee_author

Facebook: facebook.com/piperbeeauthor/

Blog: www.piperbeeauthor.com

Did this story give you any FEELS?

Are you #teamcale or #teamjin?

Did a song play in your head while you were reading?

Piper Bee would love to know (for science) the answers to these questions on whatever platforms you use: Instagram, Facebook, Goodreads, Twitter, etc.

Leave a review on Amazon, Goodreads, or any other book-related website!

Don't forget to snag a JSLP bookmark, available at piperbeeauthor.com

Made in the USA
Las Vegas, NV
02 March 2021

18910314R00184